A Mighty Love

A Mighty Love

ANITA DOREEN DIGGS

KENSINGTON PUBLISHING CORP.
http://www.kensingtonbooks.com

For my brother Brevard Diggs.
Thanks for always having my back from day one.
I love you.

DAFINA BOOKS are published by

Kensington Publishing Corp.
850 Third Avenue
New York, NY 10022

All Kensington titles, imprints and distributed lines are available at special quantity discounts for bulk purchases for sales promotion, premiums, fund-raising, educational or institutional use.

Special book excerpts or customized printings can also be created to fit specific needs. For details, write or phone the office of the Kensington Special Sales Manager: Kensington Publishing Corp., 850 Third Avenue, New York NY 10022, Attn. Special Sales Department. Phone: 1-800-221-2647.

Dafina Books and the Dafina logo Reg. U.S. Pat. & TM Off.

Library of Congress Card Catalogue Number: 2002106111
ISBN 0-7582-0231-8

First Printing: February 2003
10 9 8 7 6 5 4 3 2 1

Printed in the United States of America

ACKNOWLEDGMENTS

My heartfelt thanks to:

My mother, Gladys Haigler Smith, for cheering me on when I got tired.

My daughter and best friend, Tayannah L. McQuillar, for her unconditional love and support.

My editor, Karen R. Thomas, for "feeling" Mel, helping me breathe life into Adrienne, and making one of my childhood dreams come true.

Tanya McKinnon for a superb job of agenting. Thanks for hanging in there when the going got rough.

Leslie Meredith for her excellent suggestions that improved this story tremendously.

Fred L. Johnson for his hard work, patience, encouragement, kindness, and for being a great listener during my sad times.

Earl Cox for reading the manuscript and for Lloyd's smooth inscrutability.

Sheree R. Thomas for her insight, terrific advice, and patience.

God Bless you all!

PROLOGUE

M elvin Jordan was driving the M15 bus, which was headed east
on 125th Street. An attractive brown-skinned woman dressed
in a skin-fitting black halter top and matching pants got on at
Lenox Avenue. As soon as their eyes met, he knew what was coming. She rooted through her purse, pretending that she could not
find her Metro Card.

"I know that card is in here somewhere," she said, smiling se-
ductively.

Mel had Adrienne and Delilah at home waiting for him. He was
happier now than he'd ever been in his life and wasn't about to
jeopardize his marriage for a fling with this woman or any of the
other pretty women who were constantly throwing themselves at
him. He just wanted her to get out of his space and find a seat
somewhere way in the back of the bus. "You can't stand here, miss.
Don't worry about the card. You can ride for free this time." He
turned his head away and checked his rearview mirror. When he
turned back, the woman was still standing there smiling at him.
Stupid bitch, he thought.

"Are you always this kind to the ladies?" She asked.

Mel kept his eyes on the road. "No. I'm usually only kind to my
wife." When he looked again, she had slipped away.

Mel had not started out as a bus driver. His first job out of high school was with the telephone company. For five years he'd worked as an installer without any trouble; then his womanizing caught up with him. Mel had been fucking his supervisor as well as several different telephone operators. At one point, he'd seriously considered asking the landlord of his bachelor pad to install a revolving door so that he wouldn't have to get out of bed to let in and out each woman who came to see him. Some of them fell in love and wanted to become Mrs. Jordan; others were already married and just liked going to bed with him; a few were good-time girls who simply enjoyed the party.

When his supervisor started demanding a ring, he dumped her. Then his life at the phone company became a living hell. She talked to every female operator who would listen. They all became vengeful, and one day a little voice told him that if he showed up for work again, he would never get out of there alive. So he applied for a transfer and took a leave of absence until it went through. The transfer took him out of Harlem and into Greenwich Village, where his first assignment was to install a separate telephone line in an apartment that already had service. It was a common request, and Mel didn't think much about it until the customer, Adrienne Montgomery, answered the door. Mel knew that she was someone special. She looked like a woman in her early thirties, yet she seemed younger and very naive in a way that made him feel protective toward her.

After that first meeting, he could not keep his mind off her. Every woman who came to see him afterward seemed like a slut in comparison.

He took her to the movies on their first date, and it wasn't long before they were finding time to see each other every day of the week. Adrienne introduced Mel to the jazz clubs and the experimental theater groups that were so numerous in Greenwich Village. He taught her how to play cards: bid whist, spades, and poker. He enjoyed Sunday dinner at the Montgomery home and marveled at the fact that her parents had been married for thirty years, kissed frequently, and never raised their voices at each other. It took Mel a few weeks to overcome his shame and admit that his family consisted of only two people: the aunt who had raised him and now lived in the Bronx, where she wanted to be left alone, and his sister, Debra.

Before taking Adrienne to meet Debra, he held her tightly in his arms. He spoke plainly, "My sister isn't going to like you, but that doesn't matter to me at all." When a surprised Adrienne asked why, he said, "She wanted me to marry this girl named Rose that I was going with for a long time. We broke up a few months ago, but she keeps hoping we'll make up."

Mel never saw Rose again. And since he was determined to make a clean break with his past, he left the phone company, too, and signed on with the New York City Transit Authority. He wasn't sure if he wanted to drive buses forever, but right now life was good.

* * *

Motherhood was turning out to be much more work than she'd bargained for. Adrienne Jordan was awakened at 6:00 A.M. Her six-month-old daughter, Delilah, was crying loudly. For food, cuddling, a human voice? It didn't matter. Adrienne had to climb out of bed for the umpteenth time and soothe her only child. The two of them had been doing the same dance all night. Her husband, Mel, was working the midnight to 8 A.M. shift, and it would take him another hour to get home. They lived in a two-bedroom apartment and they had worked hard to decorate it. By the time they'd finished, it had wall-to-wall carpeting, a five-piece bedroom set with curtains that matched the spread, pictures on the walls, and walk-in closets that were bursting with clothes. He had once surprised Adrienne with a state-of-the-art stereo system and a matching sofa and love seat for the living room. The kitchen was furnished in what Adrienne called "a country motif," and the separate dining room had a full-length table, eight chairs, and a beautiful chandelier that they had found together on Jamaica Avenue.

Adrienne gazed down into the crib, and Delilah's screams immediately subsided to a series of whimpers. Adrienne smiled and lifted her, cooing softly, "Is mama's baby wet?" She kissed the little brown forehead and hugged the infant against her chest. Delilah uttered a little mew of contentment and grew quiet. Adrienne changed her diaper and heated a bottle of milk. It took some feeding and rocking, but soon Delilah was once again back in her crib, sound asleep.

Adrienne lay back down across her bed, feeling resentful. She hadn't had any time to herself in almost a month and was feeling dog tired. *I'm going to Harlem today and get my hair done*, she thought, *and after that I'm going to stop by Dan and Charlene's house. They're always good for a few laughs.* Satisfied, she drifted back to sleep. A kiss on the cheek woke her up. Mel, still dressed in his bus driver's uniform, smiled down at her. She saw smooth, deep dark chocolate brown skin and perfectly straight teeth. As he lowered his head to kiss her lips, she took note of his medium-length 1970s-style Afro. Mel was slender, and although he was only five-feet-ten, most people believed he was at least six feet. It was probably the Afro, which made him seem taller.

"Tough night?" he asked.

Adrienne stretched and groaned. "Delilah didn't sleep four straight hours the whole time. I don't know a lot about infants, but shouldn't she be past this stage by now?"

Mel started to undress. "I don't know, baby. I just need a shower and some sleep. I'm exhausted."

Adrienne sympathized with him, but as much as she adored her husband, she needed to get away from Delilah for a while. She chose her words carefully. "Mel, I'm going to get my hair done today."

He had stripped down to his T-shirt and shorts. "Take lil' darlin' with you. I can't baby-sit."

Adrienne sat up. "I won't take her to the beauty parlor; she doesn't need exposure to all those chemicals and that dust and noise."

"I'm tired, Adrienne. Do it tomorrow."

"Tomorrow is Sunday. The shop I go to will be closed."

He sighed heavily. "Okay, baby."

Adrienne got up and put her arms around his waist. He was so good to her. "Go on to bed, Mel. I'll clean the house, cook some food, prepare the formula for the baby, and stay home until one. Everything will be fine, okay?"

Mel pulled her close. "What else will you do for me?"

Adrienne laughed and pulled away. "I thought you were so doggone tired."

Mel didn't answer. He took her hand and slowly eased her onto the bed, then flung aside the bedcovers. Adrienne wriggled out of her gown.

A low groan came from her throat as she easily placed her long, slender legs on his powerful shoulders with her toes pointing skyward. "Oh, Mel!" she moaned, with her strong hips moving up to meet his downward thrusts.

"Oh, baby!" Mel caressed her shoulders and gripped her back. They lay nude, their bodies intertwined, slick with sweat. Mel kissed her face and ran his hands up and down her bare back. Adrienne could feel the warmth spread down her spine.

Their cries of ecstasy had awakened Delilah, who started to whimper.

Mel untangled himself from Adrienne's arms, slipped out of their four-poster bed, pulled on his robe, and walked across the cold parquet floor to soothe the baby. Delilah was his pride and joy. He would spend hours just gazing at her through the bars of her crib. The child looked just like him, too. Same dark skin, round eyes fringed with long lashes, dimpled cheeks, and wide smile.

Adrienne observed the tender scene from her spot on the bed. Tears came to her eyes as she thought of how much she loved her husband and child. She slipped her gown back on and joined Mel at the crib. Mel suddenly turned to her and said, "Every child should have two parents in the house." At that moment, Adrienne wished that she could go back in time to Mel's childhood and give him all the love that had been missing in his drab home. Adrienne knew that part of Mel's attraction to her was the fact that she had grown up in a two-parent home, with a mother and father who provided the necessary material things and didn't fight each other all the time.

By 1:00 P.M., Adrienne was on the road. She popped a Bessie

Smith CD into the player and sang along as she drove. Bessie was crooning something about yella women having all the luck. Adrienne chuckled. She was light-skinned, slender, with high cheekbones. Her eyes had an oriental slant to them like Nia Long's, and her lips were full and pink-tinged. Adrienne didn't know about the women of Bessie Smith's day, but it took more than light skin and a beautiful face to make it now.

Adrienne had once tried to make it as a singer. In fact, she had dropped out of college to join an all-girl group. They were getting regular bookings and, at one point, were close to signing a record deal. Then one girl ran off with a drummer from another band. The remaining girl and Adrienne became enemies soon after, their friendship ripped apart over a man. Once the group disbanded, Adrienne spent years chasing one deal or group after another, supplementing her income by working temporary secretarial jobs. Then she built a solo act and set out on her own. It was a disaster.

Back then, her love life fared no better. There had been Oswald, a bass guitarist who didn't believe in monogamy. Jerome, a photographer whom her brother Dan had introduced her to, had been a nice guy but cheap as hell. He never wanted to go anyplace nice when they went out. She dumped him after three months.

Warren had lasted the longest. They met when she was working as a temp for an insurance company. He was a salesman. Smart, funny, and caring, but he'd been taken to the cleaners by his ex-wife. "I like you, Adrienne. We can date forever, but I'll never get married again." He was dead serious, and when the temp assignment ended, so did their relationship. Adrienne didn't see anyone else until Mel came along two years later.

Sometimes she regretted giving up her dream of a career in entertainment, but it was too late to turn back now.

Traffic was light from Rosedale to Harlem, and it took Adrienne only forty-five minutes to reach Sharon's House of Beauty on 125th Street. She had always loved the hustle and bustle of 125th Street. It was the commercial and cultural center of Harlem. She parked the car in a lot around the corner and headed for the shop. Sharon's House of Beauty was nestled between a 99-

cent store and a wig shop, which also sold loose hair for braiding. Older men in *kofis* sold incense and black soap on small card tables that were set up on the sidewalk. Other vendors hawked books by African-American authors at well below retail prices. Adrienne pushed the door open and was grateful for the blast of air-conditioning that greeted her. Her eyes met a row of booths filled with curling irons, straightening combs, and other hair utensils. The wall across the room was lined with hair dryers, and on one end was a desk where the manicurist plied her trade. Sharon kept the salon neat and clean.

The ladies who frequented Sharon's House of Beauty rarely saw eye to eye on anything. They came to Sharon's seeking braids, weaves, perms, twists, or a press 'n' curl. Sharon and the stylists who worked for her provided exquisite hairdos along with the latest magazines and light refreshments. The ladies themselves furnished the heated debates, which usually started about men, wandered into politics, sashayed into the latest music and fashion, drifted into their personal lives, and ended up back on the subject of men.

When Adrienne arrived, Sharon was braiding another woman's hair. "Hey, girl," she called out cheerfully. She motioned Adrienne toward a chair. "I just got the latest *Essence* this morning. By the time you finish reading it, I'll be almost ready for you."

Adrienne waved hello to the few women she knew. "What do you mean, 'almost'?" she asked, smiling.

Sharon pointed toward a middle-aged woman who was using the phone and threw Adrienne an apologetic glance. "I had to cancel on Emily last week, so I have to take her next," she explained.

Adrienne couldn't complain. The shop was crowded since it was already midafternoon, and she didn't even have an appointment. She flipped open the magazine and started reading about a new singer who had just reached number one on the R & B charts with her first album. Adrienne felt a twinge of bitterness as she remembered the day a club owner told her more cruelly than necessary that there wasn't enough "suffering" in her voice to make it as a blues vocalist. Adrienne couldn't remember the woman's name anymore, but she recalled limping out of the audition and sobbing all the way back to her Greenwich Village apartment. After ten years of struggling to make it in the music industry, Adrienne had decided that she didn't have enough talent to become a star.

Mel had come into her life a few days later. When her bell rang and Adrienne had opened the door, she was surprised to see Mel standing there. He didn't look like any phone man she had ever seen. He wore his tool belt hanging loosely off his hips, Timberlands, and a neat navy blue shirt that set off his smooth, dark-brown skin. He peered at her under the brim of a blue Yankees hat and smiled, putting her immediately at ease. She'd shown him the hall closet, where he found the network interface, and he'd kept her laughing, joking and telling her stories about some of his other customers. When he'd finally finished running the wire for the new jack, she didn't want him to leave. Although he was a street guy, there was something about the way Mel looked up to her that soothed her broken spirit, and so she gave up chasing her dream. They married after a yearlong courtship and moved to Queens.

Mel had given up his rough, hard-drinking, trash-talking, card-playing, street-running ways for a life that he had never known. Though he was not a professional man, he worked hard. Most important, he was kind. His idea of a good time was spending the evening at home talking to his wife. They had been married for three years and still acted like newlyweds. It had hurt at first, letting go of a dream that had been so much a part of her, but she was happy with Mel—and he still made her smile. She rarely looked back at the years when she was singing solo in third-rate clubs and sending out demo tapes to recording executives who returned the packages unopened.

Adrienne spent another two hours in the shop, but the results were lovely. Sharon had washed, conditioned, clipped, dried, and styled Adrienne's shoulder-length chestnut-colored hair into a sleek pageboy that framed her honey brown face perfectly.

As Adrienne left the salon, she wondered how long her hair would hold up in the stifling weather. It was hot—the type of hot that was oppressively humid, a distinct feature of New York City in

July. She started the car and hesitated for a moment, knowing she should go straight home. It was 4:30 P.M. now, and Mel had to leave for work by ten. Adrienne shrugged. *I'll be up all night with Delilah*, she thought, *I'm entitled to a little fun. I won't stay at Dan's house long.*

Dan was Adrienne's little brother, but people couldn't tell by looking at him. He was over six feet tall and stocky. His beard, sideburns, and mustache also made him look older than his thirty years. He was a photographer who specialized in weddings and sweet-sixteen parties. Adrienne loved him and her sister-in-law, Charlene. The couple lived in a one-bedroom apartment on West Fifty-second Street.

As usual, he was delighted to see her. "Come on in," he said grinning as he stepped aside to let her pass.

Adrienne gave him a peck on the cheek. "Hi, yourself. Is Charlene here?"

"No, she's up in Connecticut, visiting her parents."

Adrienne sniffed the air and smiled at her brother. "I don't smell anything cooking and I'm real hungry."

Dan headed for the kitchen. "I was going to make some salmon cakes later, but I don't mind doing it now."

Adrienne pushed him aside on their way to the kitchen. "Man, go away. I can do a better job."

Dan laughed and sat down.

Adrienne took an onion and a green pepper out of the refrigerator. A can of salmon sat on the counter nearby. She opened the can of salmon, chopped the contents into a bowl, and cut pieces of onion and green pepper into it. A small amount of flour quickly followed. Adrienne cracked open an egg and floured her hands before starting to mix the concoction. When all the ingredients were blended, she washed her hands, poured a small amount of oil into a frying pan, and turned on the flame.

Dan watched her movements closely, just as he had done when he was a little boy. Adrienne noticed the hungry look on his face and laughed. "They'll be done in a minute. Do you want eggs or grits?"

"Grits. How is married life and my beautiful niece?"

"My marriage is wonderful. I just wish we could get Delilah to sleep more at night."

"Sleepless nights go with the territory, Sis. Just be grateful that everything else is going well. When are you going back to work?"

"In two weeks."

"Who is going to watch Delilah?"

"Mel will stay on the night shift so we don't have to pay a baby-sitter."

"That's great."

She nodded in agreement and continued to cook.

"Have you heard from the folks?"

"Yeah, Mama called yesterday," Adrienne said dryly. "I didn't give her a chance to start grilling me about my mothering skills. Delilah was fussing, so that gave me an excuse to get off the phone real quick."

"Well, if you hadn't hung up so fast, you would know that she and Dad are coming to New York for a visit."

Adrienne sighed. "Why?"

"I didn't ask but they probably just want to see Delilah. Besides, it's boring as hell in Dietsville."

Adrienne laughed. Her parents had retired and gone to Alabama two years before. They had come back once when Delilah was born and had stayed at her house for a week. "Is Mama still insisting that Delilah looks like her?"

"No. She finally gave in and admitted that her only grandchild is the spitting image of Mel."

"How is Dad?"

"All right. Says he's doing a lot of fishing."

"Good," Adrienne said. "What's new with you?"

"I had two wacko customers at the studio yesterday."

Adrienne stirred the grits. "What happened?"

"This guy comes in with his woman, and they start looking at my portfolio and wall samples. She wants them to have a formal engagement photo. I could tell he wasn't feelin' it, but it was her show. Anyway, I started to help some other customers and then I heard shouting. Well, I couldn't have them disturbing the peace, so I politely went over and asked them to quiet down."

"What were they arguing about?"

Dan chuckled. "Her engagement ring. She said he had to go out and buy a bigger one or she would hide her left hand in the photo. That pissed the brother off, and I couldn't blame him."

Adrienne laughed heartily. "That union is off to a great start."

"She decided to sit on both her hands while I took the picture!"

The two of them laughed some more.

"If it were me, I'd call the whole thing off," Dan ended.

Adrienne set two steaming plates of food on the table as her brother gathered the utensils, napkins, and soft drinks. When they sat down to eat, Adrienne said, "This place is so quiet when Charlene isn't here."

Dan nodded. "That's because my wife likes noise. The TV or radio always has to be on. She doesn't value solitude at all."

"Leave my girl alone," Adrienne chided him.

"I think you sometimes forget who your sibling is," Dan teased. "Every time I turn around, she's on the phone with you. What do you find to talk about all the time?"

"Charlene is my friend, and we talk about woman stuff. Do you want to hear some of it?"

Dan held up a hand as though he were warding off an evil spirit. "No way."

Adrienne chuckled, and the two chatted easily until their stomachs were full.

* * *

Delilah was sleeping soundly when Adrienne left. Mel took a shower, slipped his pajamas on, and crawled wearily into bed. He awakened hours later to Delilah's furious screams. Cursing, he got up. She must have been crying for a long time, because her face was contorted, her body was rigid, and the baby pillow was wet from her tears. Mel lifted her out of the crib and held her close until she stopped crying. "What do you want?" he asked her in frustration. "Daddy needs some sleep so he can go back to work."

Once calm was restored, he laid her back in the crib. As soon as his hands were removed from her body, the little face scrunched up and she began to wail again.

"So that's it," Mel chuckled softly. "You don't wanna sleep in this cage. Come on. You can lay down in the bed with me." He placed the baby on the bed beside him. She closed her eyes, and Mel sighed in relief. All he needed was a cigarette, and then he could settle down again, too. Mel hoped that Delilah would sleep until Adrienne returned from the hairdresser. His face sagged with weariness, his eyes heavy with fatigue. He reached over and grabbed a cigarette from the pack on the nightstand, then fumbled around on the crowded surface until he found a book of matches to light it.

The cigarette was still lit when he dozed off. It fell out of his hand, igniting the sheets and acrylic blanket that covered him and his daughter.

Delilah's cries woke him a few minutes later. *Shit!* he thought, *the bed is on fire.* He dashed to the bathroom, ran some water into a pail, and careened back into the bedroom just as a *whoosh,* followed by brilliant, soaring flames that danced rapidly, almost daintily from his side of the bed to the other.

Mel charged into the glow, trying desperately to reach Delilah.

* * *

By the time they finished eating, it was nearly dark outside. Adrienne glanced at her watch. "Goodness, it's eight o'clock!" she said, grabbing her purse. "I've got to get going."

"Why don't you stay for dessert? Charlene baked a chocolate cake last night."

"No. Mel has to leave for work at ten. Maybe he can catch a few winks before then." Adrienne paused with her hand on the doorknob. "I'll call you tomorrow." She blew her brother a kiss and was gone.

Adrienne took the midtown tunnel onto the Belt Parkway east and reached Rosedale in a half hour.

When she turned the car onto 147th Avenue, a smile flitted across her beautiful face as she thought of her husband, and she speeded up slightly. She hated it when Mel worked the night shift. Lying in bed alone, she longed for his gaze, his touch, his scent. Adrienne grabbed a tube of matte red lipstick out of the glove compartment and glided on a fresh coat. Mel loved that color on her because it accented the small round mole near her mouth. Smoothing back her hair, she stole another glance in the rearview mirror. She couldn't wait for Mel to see how beautiful she looked.

Since the car windows were up, Adrienne didn't smell the smoke, but two fire trucks and an ambulance whizzing by forced her to pull over. The lights flashed and the alarms screamed their purpose as Adrienne covered one ear in a futile attempt to block out the noise. It wasn't until she made a right turn onto 149th that she realized that the fire was on her street. Even then, it didn't occur to her that the angry flames shooting into the night sky were coming from the peach-tinted two-family house on the corner. A fireman approached the car and motioned her to open the window.

"You'll have to turn back, ma'am. No one is allowed past this point."

Adrienne peered anxiously over his shoulder, and panic seized her. The fire trucks, police cars, and ambulance were all double-parked right in front of the house in which she and Mel rented a two-bedroom apartment from an Indian couple.

"I live on the top floor of that last house on the end. Is that where the fire is? Please, I have to make sure my husband and daughter are all right." Adrienne's heart beat furiously and her mind raced. Suppose Mel and Delilah were lying on the lawn suffering from smoke inhalation, or worse, had broken bones and internal injuries from leaping out the window?

The expression on the man's soot-covered face changed from annoyance to sympathy. Adrienne opened the car door and stumbled out. Before he could say another word, she ducked under his arm and charged forward. Her arms and legs pumped furiously as she ran. She felt like a character in a silent movie. There was a lot of action and noise surrounding her, but she couldn't see or hear it.

The neighbors lined both sides of the street, held back by police officers and blue wooden barricades. Some of them cried softly; others screamed Adrienne's name. Consumed with terror, Adrienne was only dimly aware of them. The Indian landlord and his family stood by helplessly. His facial expression was one of shock. Adrienne couldn't even remember his name as she looked up at the house. Flames and smoke poured from the top-floor windows of her apartment. A fireman caught her as she reached the house. Adrienne struggled in his arms, trying to get free. "My husband and baby are in there!"

"Miss, we got them out," the fireman told her.

Adrienne's body relaxed. "Oh, thank God!" She breathed. "Where are they?"

Mel was unconscious, lying in the back of the ambulance with an oxygen mask pressed over his face and white bandages wrapped around both hands and arms up to his elbows. The only indication that he was still alive was the slow rise and fall of his chest. Two of the paramedics worked feverishly on him. A third paramedic patted her shoulder, saying, "He has some shards of glass in his arms. My partners are more worried about smoke inhalation than anything else right now."

Adrienne shouted to Mel over the noise, "Mel, I'm here. What happened? Where is Delilah?"

The paramedic rubbed her back. "Ma'am, he is in shock right now and probably doesn't remember what happened. We're taking him to the hospital." He took her elbow. "Have a seat. You can ride along right beside him."

Adrienne kissed Mel's forehead and then looked frantically from one face to the other. "Where's my baby?" she pleaded. The paramedics looked away, but not before their eyes told her what their lips could not.

Adrienne jumped from the ambulance, and a black female police officer rushed over to guide her.

What remained of Delilah was zipped up in a body bag and already placed in the coroner's wagon. "Ooooooh," a cry of pain escaped from Adrienne, and the agony ripped through her body with the force of a thousand knives.

Adrienne knew she had to be sleeping, that the horrific scene in front of her was a bad dream. She would go mad if it were real. Black tears from her mascaraed eyes streamed down her face, and her perfectly manicured nails began to break as she clawed at the doors of the vehicle that held her baby girl. Strong arms grabbed her from behind. It was the female officer, and she was crying, too, as she clutched Adrienne to her bosom.

PART ONE

A BLAST FROM THE PAST

CHAPTER ONE

"Wake up, fool." Debra Jordan shook her brother's shoulder. "Your wife is on the phone."

Melvin groaned and pushed his head deeper into the pillows. *What the hell did Adrienne want now?*

"Tell her I'm just walkin' out the door," he said.

Debra shook harder. "What you talkin' about? She say you was supposed to meet her this afternoon. Now git up and talk to her. I got company."

Six months after the fire, Mel lay on a thin mattress on a single bed that was much too short for his lanky frame. He had never bothered to decorate these sleeping quarters, so his back room in Debra's thirteenth-floor housing-project apartment was practically bare. One scarred bureau held a broken mirror, a rickety lamp, and a cheap clock that didn't work most of the time.

Mel sat up and shook his head in confusion. "I just laid down for a minute. What time is it?"

Debra sucked her teeth on her way out the door. "Nighttime, fool. It's just after eight."

Mel groaned. He had been supposed to meet his wife at 1:00 P.M. to see an apartment. "Damn! Adrienne must be boilin' mad."

The sounds of the Mississippi Mass Choir were blaring. Debra played gospel music every Sunday. She also held a card game in her apartment every Sunday night to pick up extra spending money for the coming week. It didn't matter which players won or lost, because the house got five dollars per game. Debra was a big woman with a toothy grin and dyed red hair, which at this moment was standing straight up on her head, her black roots showing.

It sounded as if there were a hundred people in Debra's living room, but Mel knew that it was the same half dozen who played blackjack and bid whist and drank rum there every Sunday night. He pushed himself up off the bed and went out into the noisy, smoke-filled living room.

There was a new face at the card table. A woman who looked to be in her late thirties, with caramel skin, full hot pink lips, and wearing a low-cut hot-pink dress to match. Her dark-brown hair was all twirled up in a fancy style. The thin gold bangles that decorated both her arms jingled as she played the cards. Mel had not planned to join the game, but the beautiful unknown female in the living room changed his mind. He knew he'd be playing his last five dollars as soon as Adrienne finished telling him off.

It didn't bother him that Adrienne was annoyed. Sooner or later, she was going to have to face the truth, and then she would dump him anyway. When he and Adrienne first separated because she blamed him for the tragedy, he had prayed for God to take him to his mother so that he wouldn't have to think about his lost wife and daughter.

With nowhere else to go, he had arrived on Debra's doorstep, mired in grief and anger. For the first few weeks he didn't sleep for more than three hours a night. The bus company had forced him to take a three-week leave of absence after a cop found him sobbing at the wheel with a load of irate passengers and other drivers honking their horns and shouting obscenities in the traffic around him.

The truth was that her husband was a street guy who had turned his life around, only to find out that God was determined to return him to the gutter where he belonged. God had killed his baby, driven his wife almost insane, and returned him to his sister's house, where nothing mattered but the next card game. Mel no longer believed he could have the American dream, but he would not risk Adrienne's mental health by telling her that. Sooner or later she would realize it herself. Until then, he'd just go along with the charade.

He winked at Hot Pink, who was sitting between Ann and Ann's mother, Belle, Debra's coworkers. From Tuesday through Saturday, Debra worked in Harlem as a barmaid for an illegal dive that couldn't be seen from the street. The owner paid the cops off every week to keep them from shutting the place down. Everyone prospered except the semiliterate women who worked there. Most of them were middle-aged high school dropouts, who worked for the less than minimum wage plus tips because they couldn't get a job anywhere else.

Big Boy, a three-hundred-pound fool with only five teeth left in his mouth, took up the whole sofa, which had been pulled up next to Belle. He was an asthmatic who chain-smoked cigarettes. He had also started more than one feud in the projects, yet always emerged with his few remaining teeth intact. Mel didn't understand why no one had killed his ass yet. Big Boy slapped an ace down on the table and noticed Mel at the same time. "If I was as ugly as you and somethin' that pretty was on the phone for me, I'da been outa that bed long before now."

Everybody thought this was real funny. Mel ignored the laughter while he shuffled through the room and picked up the receiver, which was lying facedown on a washing machine that hadn't worked in more than twenty years. Debra refused to get rid of it, because, aside from some old pictures, it was all they had to remind them of their mother.

"Hey, Adrienne, what's up?"

"What do you mean, what's up? I waited at the token booth for over an hour."

Normally, Adrienne's voice was low and husky, but right now it had a shrill quality to it.

"I'm sorry, baby. I laid down and fell back to sleep. Debra just woke me up."

"Are you lying to me?"

"Naw, baby."

"Look, Mel, if you're not going to meet me halfway, then this is not going to work," Adrienne said angrily.

"Come on, Adrienne. I'm sorry. Don't be like that."

"Dan and Charlene haven't said anything, but I know they must be tired of me pulling out their sofa bed to sleep on every night. I've been here for six months and it's time to move."

Mel knew that Dan's living room was crammed with Adrienne's clothes, books, and toiletries. Everything was stuffed into supermarket crates because there was no extra closet to hold them.

"Yeah, yeah. I know. Do you have any more appointments set up?"

It was amazing how quickly time had passed. Two weeks after Delilah's funeral, Adrienne had sunk into a severe depression. Her grief and anger had been almost palpable, and she had had trouble eating and sleeping. It was three months before she could bring herself to talk to anyone, especially Mel.

"Yes, there's a two-bedroom apartment available on West Thirty-ninth Street. The rent is only fifteen hundred a month."

Mel understood why Adrienne wanted to stay in Manhattan, far away from the tragedy, but now they would be paying twice as much as they had in the old apartment. New York City was becoming more expensive each year. Neither one of them would be able to pay $1,500 alone since neither made more than $30,000 per year. Mel sighed. What if one of them got laid off? Surely Adrienne could find less room for less money.

A lump formed in Mel's throat. "Why do we need two bedrooms?"

"I thought maybe . . ." she hesitated.

"Thought what?" he asked gruffly.

"Nothing," she said quickly.

Mel switched the phone to his other ear. If Adrienne was going to look at two-bedroom apartments, it meant she was thinking about getting pregnant. That scared him.

"Are you working tomorrow?" Adrienne asked.

"No. Why?"

"I'm looking at the apartment on my lunch hour. Meet me outside my job at twelve."

"Okay. I love you."

"I love you, too, Mel."

He hung up and turned around. Everybody was looking at him. Debra had a grin on her face. She started clapping.

"My brother, the actor."

Everybody in the circle laughed and clapped along with her. Mel couldn't help grinning. Debra and her friends always acted so stupid. He dragged one of the kitchen chairs over to the circle.

"I'm playin'."

Big Boy poured half a glass of straight rum and took a gulp. "Let's see your money, muthafucka."

Mel took out his last five dollars and threw it on the pile on the coffee table.

"Adrienne think she so cute," Debra started. "Just cuz she light-skinned. Hell, she tall, skinny, and got a flat ass like a white girl." She shook her head from side to side, then gave her brother a teasing smile. "And Melvin ain't no bargain in the looks department either!"

"Sheeeit, I'm the finest brother out here." He punched her playfully on the arm.

"That's a damn lie," Debra chuckled.

"Debra, if I wasn't your brother, you'd be callin' me all the time, too. In fact, you woulda just hung up and jumped on in a cab to come see me."

Debra was shaking with laughter along with everyone else.

"I doan know your sister-in-law," said Ann.

"That's cuz she never visits me," Debra said tartly.

"Isn't she that yella girl that Mel left Rose for?" asked Belle.

"Yeah," said Debra, after taking a long pull from the beer bottle on the floor beside her. "That's Adrienne, all right."

Melvin stole a glance at Hot Pink. She was hanging on to his sister's every word.

"Debra, find somethin' else to talk about," he said tightly.

"Don't tell Debra what to talk about. This is her apartment," shouted Big Boy.

Debra slapped hands in agreement with the giant and continued.

"Adrienne's brother is even worse. Think he hot stuff cuz he live in Midtown instead of up here in Harlem. Hell, it's just a goddamned tenement."

Mel laughed this time also.

"He got a nice place?" asked Ann.

"I only bin there once for a birthday party before he got married. Dan had a nice dining room table, but he prob'ly got the rest of that shit from the Salvation Army. Plus, the living room window opens on a back alley full of stray cats. It stunk like hell in there when he opened the window. And those cats was makin' all kinds of noise. Screaming, mewing, fighting, screwing."

"Sounds like Big Boy's house!" shouted Hot Pink.

Everyone laughed until they cried, and Melvin was relieved to find that his wife and brother-in-law had been forgotten.

"Debra, you need to stop lying," Mel said while picking up his cards. He smiled across the table at Hot Pink. "My sister has left her manners in the kitchen tonight, pretty lady. I'm afraid I don't know your name."

"It's Lillian, you rogue."

Mel thought her laugh was pretty as she spoke.

"Tell me who brought you here tonight, Miss Lillian, so I can thank 'em properly."

Debra groaned and rolled her eyes toward the ceiling.

"I'm Big Boy's cousin."

Melvin was momentarily taken aback. Quickly regaining his composure, he showed Lillian his dimples before answering. "That's not possible. The man is not even human."

"Fuck you," said Big Boy.

Mel slapped an ace on the table.

"Twenty-one!" he shouted.

He ignored the grumblings of those who had lost their money, and scooped up his winnings. About thirty dollars. Just one more win and he'd be able to go out and get high enough to forget about sad wives, dead babies, and his own heavy heart for a little while.

He had been a fool to think he could leave this seamy world and find happiness with a good woman on a quiet suburban street. There was that thing called karma, which he had not factored into his plan. Mel had hurt a lot of women before meeting Adrienne. As payback, God had given him a brief taste of happiness, then snatched it back. Mel knew when he was beaten. The gutter was beckoning, and who was he to fight God's will?

Big Boy took out a cigarette and crumpled the empty pack in

his gigantic hand. He leered across the table at Debra and then focused on Mel. "So, when you goin' back with your wife, boy? When you movin' out?" Big Boy gave Debra another meaningful leer.

Melvin looked at his sister, who was staring fixedly at the cards in her hand. So, she was fucking Big Boy now. He gave Big Boy a warning glance. *Back off.* The huge man grunted and let it go. He had made his point to Debra.

Mel won the next two games. After slowly counting out a profit of sixty-five single dollar bills under Big Boy's malevolent stare, he rose and winked at Hot Pink. "I'll see you soon, Lillian."

* * *

In the 1980s Mel had sniffed coke just for fun, but then the drug scene started to bore him, and he gave it up for over a decade. In the dark days after Delilah's death, when his wife would not speak to him, Mel had gone searching for the white powder again. The drug scene had changed. There was nothing fun about it now. Teenage dealers had replaced grown men. They didn't chitchat while doing business, and most of them were tense and dangerous.

Mel grabbed his coat out of the hall closet, kissed Debra on the cheek, waved good-bye at the rest of the crowd, and left the apartment in a hurry.

There was a ten-minute wait for the only rattling, piss-stained elevator that was working, and Mel tapped his foot impatiently. As he rode down to the lobby, he felt a moment of panic. Suppose Little Jimmy had been arrested? Or worse, what if there had just been a whole sweep of the area, and there was nothing left to buy? Mel left the building and walked quickly through the cold winter night until he reached 106th and Amsterdam. He turned the last corner and breathed a sigh of relief.

Little Jimmy was in his usual spot. Mel's aunt had raised Mel and Debra in the same building where Little Jimmy's parents used to live. Mel easily remembered the day the boy was born.

Little Jimmy's father had just been arrested for armed robbery, and while his mother stood in front of the patrol car, begging the police to let her husband go, her water broke right there in the street. They placed Little Jimmy's mother on her back in the front seat of the car, and she lay there moaning and groaning until an ambulance arrived. Her husband went off in one direction and the ambulance in another.

Both Little Jimmy's parents were dead now, and he supported himself by selling drugs on the corner. The kid would have to be about eighteen years old, but Mel didn't know for sure. Little Jimmy didn't like to talk, and he never smiled. Mel pulled out fifty dollars of his winnings and palmed the bills into his fist.

"How many?" asked Little Jimmy.

"Half a gram."

The transaction was completed in seconds.

Mel had barely slipped the envelope in his pocket when a young woman who had been leaning against a parked car started toward him. She smiled hesitantly, but when Mel gave her an impatient jerk of the head, her walk turned into a semijog. Mel was relieved. Ducking alone in doorways to blow was no fun at all. There was nobody to talk to, and every footstep sounded like that of a cop.

"My name is Juana," she said.

Mel shrugged. "Where we goin'?"

"My girlfriend's house down the block."

"She home?" Mel asked.

The woman nodded. They passed under a streetlight, and Mel got a good look at her. Juana couldn't have been more than twenty. At one time she had probably been a good-looking Puerto Rican girl, but now she was just a burnt-out crack whore. Mel felt in his pocket. *Shit!* He didn't have any condoms. There was no way he was going to share his stuff without getting something in return. "We gotta stop and get some beer," Mel said.

They ducked into the nearest bodega, which was surprisingly crowded for a Sunday night. It was a tiny store with four aisles, crammed with dusty cans of food and cleaning products. The young man behind the counter was selling loose cigarettes to a line of teenage boys who were rapping, roughhousing, and trying everything else they could think of to impress the baby-faced girls who hung on their arms.

Juana stood with them, never taking her eyes off Mel as he sped down an aisle and picked out four quarts of cold malt liquor. The teenagers pushed and shoved one another out of the store as Mel reached the counter. The clerk rang up the beer.

"Let me get four rubbers," Mel said.

The man turned around and counted out the condoms from a huge box behind him. He threw the foil-wrapped packets on the counter and spoke rapid Spanish to Juana. Mel thought he heard the word *negro* but wasn't sure.

"Mind your business," Juana said to the counterman in English.

Juana's face was red as they left the store. Mel carried the bag, and she fished around in her pocketbook until they reached a dilapidated four-story building half a block away. She pulled out a key and turned to face him. "You got cigarettes?"

He nodded.

She opened the door and started running up the stairs. Mel closed the front door, waited for the lock to snap in place, and followed. Juana was unlocking the door to the second-floor rear apartment. When she put the key back in her pocketbook, Mel took out his knife and put a finger to his lips. Juana looked bored with the routine, but Mel didn't care. He had not forgotten the rules. This could be a setup. He pressed his ear against the wooden door but there was no noise inside.

"Where's your friend?" he asked.

Juana shrugged. "I guess she went out."

"Open the door . . . slowly."

Juana obeyed. He kept his knife out as they entered.

Mel found himself standing in a medium-size room with dirty white paint on the walls. A ragged red sofa stood against the left wall, and a TV with a hole in the screen was on the right. Juana locked the door and turned on a floor lamp. Mel sat down on the ragged sofa. There were used screens on the coffee table and a shattered stem on the floor. Juana had been smoking and had run out of crack. With no more money to be had, she must have thrown the pipe down and hit the streets. Now she knelt on the floor in front of him. Her mouth hung open and he saw that her two front teeth were missing. Mel felt disgusted and threw the condoms he'd purchased on the floor among some other garbage. There was no way he was having sex with this broad. He would just get high and get out. Her brown eyes begged him to hurry. Mel felt a flash of sympathy and pulled out the envelope. He folded a matchbook cover and used it to scoop up enough coke to give her a snort in each nostril. He smiled at her and then took two blows himself.

"Pour me some beer," he ordered.

By the time she got back, Mel had taken three more blows, and he was feeling real good.

CHAPTER TWO

It was Monday morning, and Adrienne sailed along Manhattan's crowded streets on her way to work. She was wearing a navy blue linen suit with a matching cape and pumps. Her hair was combed into a smooth French roll that accented her slim face and hazel-colored eyes. Her signature pageboy had disappeared. Charlene did her hair these days, and she didn't possess the skills to create any elaborate hairdos. Adrienne had tried to enter a beauty parlor once after the fire, and it had been a traumatic experience. Just standing in the doorway inhaling the intermingling scents and listening to the hum of several hair dryers had brought it all back. The hair salon had become a symbol of the selfishness that had cost her her baby. She had run from the doorway, hopped in a cab, and headed back to Dan's house and his sofa, which had become her home.

Although Adrienne looked as spectacular as she always did on her way to work, she was so busy watching the woman and child in front of her that she didn't even notice the appreciative stares of the men who passed. The little boy was about two years old, and the woman was walking too rapidly for him to keep up. Adrienne watched his stubby little legs moving as fast as they could to avoid being dragged by the woman who clutched his hand. *I would never have forced Delilah along the street like that*, Adrienne thought. *I'm going to tell that woman to slow down.* Just as she was about to move forward and say something to the woman, an inner voice stopped her cold. *Who are you to lecture anyone about mothering?*

*   *   *

After the coroner's wagon had pulled away, she and Mel had both been taken to Jamaica Hospital. Mel stayed a week being treated for smoke inhalation. Adrienne was there overnight, undergoing treatment for shock and hysteria.

A few days after the fire, she and Dan had returned to the scene to see if anything could be salvaged. Debris was all over the lawn. Delilah's charred stuffed animals, some clothing, and lots of papers and sheets. The pink floral sheets that had been on the bed had been a present to them from Debra when they got married. The piggy bank and everything else on the dresser was covered with soot from the smoke. If Adrienne touched anything, her fingertips came away black. The top of the television, which was sitting on the chest, had melted, giving it an unusually lopsided shape. A lump caught in her throat as she remembered lying in bed watching her favorite programs on that same TV set while snuggled in Mel's arms.

The kitchen had been the least destroyed, although everything in it was unusable because of the smoke and water damage.

Adrienne opened the refrigerator. The food was undisturbed; the violence had wreaked havoc only outside its frigid home.

The closet. Oh, heaven help her. All of her books were burned, wet, or covered with soot. Mel's two crates of albums from the seventies were soggy and stuck together. The door was open, and the volumes spilled out into the narrow hallway. The floors were covered with burned carpet and broken and burned items. Adrienne had to climb on and over everything in order to walk.

There were no living room windows, if "windows" meant panes of glass. The heat had blown them out and then the landlord had boarded them up. The sofa and love seat were burned down to the metal frames. The lamps were merely twisted wire without any fabric at all.

Adrienne had wept inconsolably until Dan insisted that they leave.

At the funeral, Mel had murmured, "It's all my fault," over and over while holding his head between his hands. Sitting beside him in stony silence, she had agreed with him as he repeated the phrase over and over again.

Afterward, she had taken refuge at Dan's apartment, unable to get out of her fetal position and off the sofa bed except to wash up. She'd also refused phone calls from concerned coworkers, and, most drastically, refused to see or talk to her husband. Once, Charlene patted her on the shoulder and said, "Come on, Adrienne. Please talk to Mel; he's going crazy because you've shut him out. The two of you should grieve together." Adrienne had just balled herself up tighter on the sofa bed.

Weeks later, she saw that the fault was not his. The blame lay with a woman who had decided to escape motherhood for a day. She could never tell anyone that she had left the house to get away from Delilah.

Adrienne had been overwhelmed with feelings of guilt and remorse. She had no home, no furniture, no clothes. Everything, including all of Delilah's pictures, had gone up in flames. That was the one loss that pained her more than any of the others. One day, when she could stand it, she would ask her family and Debra to let her see the photos they had taken of Delilah. Adrienne had sometimes felt that years had passed since she had driven her car down a pleasant Queens street and made that right turn into a scene from hell. Then time would suddenly shift, and it would seem as if the firemen had blocked off 147th Avenue only hours before. With her eyes closed tightly, Adrienne would replay the events of that dreadful day again and again. Each time, she wanted to die. Occasionally she felt the presence of her brother or Charlene. "I've made you a cup of tea," one of them would say. Or, "I'm going to work; do you need anything while I'm out?" Adrienne tried to pry her lips open to say "Thank you" or "I'm all right," but the words would form in her brain, travel down through her head, and get stuck somewhere in the back of her throat. It was the first time since she had decided to stop singing that Adrienne was glad she was voiceless. No matter how hard she tried, she just could not find the words. After a pause, she'd hear footsteps walking away. She lay in a long state of denial before she could accept the fact that Delilah was truly gone forever. Adrienne's world was dark and silent.

Adrienne had thought the grief and pain would never end. Mama and Daddy had come to New York in time for the funeral and stayed on for several weeks, but even their nurturing and praying had failed to get her off the sofa bed. It was only when Dan and Charlene threatened to start legal action to have her committed that she started thinking about the rest of her life.

Mel, his face ravaged from suffering alone and drinking too much, had cried when Dan finally let him in to see her. Adrienne could tell from the look in his eyes that she looked horrible, too. They held each other for a long time that first day. They agreed to stop talking about the past and to save for the day when they would resume their life together. That day was upon them.

Adrienne turned away from the woman and the little boy with the stubby legs and fled down another street. Her briefcase, which contained a copy of the *News*, a sandwich, and a plum, bumped against her right leg as she walked crosstown to Sixth Avenue. Mel accused her of trying to look like a big shot, because she carried the briefcase, but Adrienne felt that the whole world didn't have to know that she was just a secretary. After walking six blocks, she decided the briefcase was going to tear her pantyhose, so she tucked it under her arm.

She reached the thirty-story rose-colored office building on Forty-sixth Street at 8:45 A.M. She didn't see any of her coworkers on the way up to the twenty-fifth floor, and that was just as well. She wasn't in the mood for small talk. Adrienne got off the elevator and paused to hold her electronic pass card in front of the sensor. After the door clicked, she walked briskly through the corridors.

Parton, Webster & Elliott was an advertising agency. Though they paid well and offered good benefits, it was still corporate America, and Adrienne found the atmosphere stifling and repressive. The fact that she had ended up in such a dead-end career was her own fault. She had dropped out of college to chase a musical rainbow.

The secretarial bull pens were called units. Each unit was set up for four people, and no attempt was made to match them in terms of personality or temperament. New hires were just shown to the nearest empty seat. Adrienne shared unit 6 with a nosy gossip named Sherry Ingles, a Jewish woman from Long Island who had been married briefly to a Puerto Rican. Sherry had been quick to inform Adrienne that she was not Hispanic and that the only reason she hadn't changed her surname was because she had a four-year-old son who shared it.

Adrienne didn't care one way or the other. There were two empty seats in unit 6, and she sincerely hoped that the company would start a hiring freeze before the seats were filled. Sherry was enough to deal with.

It was only after Adrienne sat down and booted up her computer that she remembered the company was getting a new president today. She wondered idly what the new boss would be like, and she picked up last week's memo, which had an article from *Advertising Age* attached.

Parton, Webster & Elliott has completed a long overhaul of its management team with the appointment of 35-year-old Lloyd Cooper as president of a new division called PWE Multicultural.

Cooper, most recently V.P./Creative Director at the Chicago branch of Parton, Webster & Elliott, started his advertising career ten years ago as a summer intern with Lewis & Wyse in Chicago. "He has intellectual rigor as well as fresh energy, which is just what our new venture will need," said CEO John Elliott.

Other recent PWE promotions include Human Resources Director Warren Kellner and Media Planning Director Regina Belvedere.

The memo also stated that all staffers were expected in the boardroom on Monday morning at 9:00 A.M. sharp to welcome Lloyd Cooper.

Adrienne took out her compact to check her hair and lipstick.

She added a little blush and practiced a smile for the new president before putting the compact away. She wondered what PWE Multicultural meant.

Sherry Ingles breezed in. Her sleek black hair was pulled into a professional bun that rested on the nape of her neck. Her beige Ann Taylor dress fit perfectly. Her matching handbag and slip-on flats completed the ensemble.

"Good morning."

"Hi, Sherry. How was your weekend?"

Sherry sighed dramatically as she sat down and removed the protective cover from her keyboard. "Horrible. My ex-husband came to see Jason and we argued the whole time."

Sherry opened a paper bag and started munching on a roll. "What about you? Did you see Mel?"

Adrienne was tempted to tell Sherry that it was none of her business. Instead, she lied. "Yes."

Adrienne glanced at her watch, noticed some handwritten notes from her supervisor, and turned away from Sherry before she could ask any more personal questions.

Sherry was the company gossip, and Adrienne didn't want her business all over the office. She searched through her computer disks until she found a report she had started typing the week before. As Adrienne typed her supervisor's revisions, she realized that her forehead was creased with worry. She and Mel had decided to give their marriage another chance, but what if it didn't work out? What if she could not forgive him for falling asleep with a lit cigarette in his hand? What if he could not forgive her for going to the beauty salon? What if he never returned to the sweet, charming man she had once known?

Before the fire, he was kind, caring, and very romantic. He wrote love notes to her and came home with cards, stuffed animals, flowers, and candy for no reason at all. It wasn't possible that such a loving man could disappear forever. The real Mel must be hidden, simply tormented by what had happened to them.

She was only halfway through the report when Sherry tapped her on the shoulder. "It's time to go," she said. Adrienne stood up and stretched, hoping that the meeting wouldn't take too long. She sighed and followed Sherry out of the bull pen. Dozens of

people clogged the corridor, and the elevators were packed. She
and Sherry had to let several go by.

The boardroom table had been pushed into a corner, and rows
of folding chairs filled the room. There was a podium in front
and a microphone. The CEO, John Elliott, was just winding up
his introductory speech as Adrienne and Sherry slipped into two
seats in the front row.

"Let's welcome Lloyd Cooper!"

A black man! Adrienne was shocked. Parton and Webster had
only one African-American executive, and she worked in Human
Resources.

Adrienne studied her new boss carefully as he stepped up to
the podium. He was about six feet tall with close-cropped black
hair, velvety smooth dark-brown skin, broad shoulders, and a
neatly trimmed mustache. He used his hands a lot as he began a
well-crafted speech.

"Hello, everyone. I know it's early in the day, so I won't take up
too much of your time. Actually, *time* is what I'd like to talk about.
The time has come for Parton, Webster and Elliott to establish itself as a leader in the field of ethnic marketing. The African-
American population now totals 34.5 million and will reach 45.1
million in the next two decades. There are more than 7.6 million
Hispanic households in this country, and those numbers are in-
creasing five times faster than any other group. The 1990 census
counted 6,908,638 Asians, which is a 99-percent increase over the
1980 census count of 3,466,847."

Adrienne frowned.

There was something familiar about his voice and gestures. His
eyes swept the front row and landed on her. His eyes widened,
and he stammered briefly but quickly regained his composure.

Sherry whispered in Adrienne's ear, "Do you know him?"
Adrienne shook her head, puzzled. He moved away from center
stage and continued his speech, not looking in her direction
again.

"The combined buying power of all three groups currently ex-
ceeds 550 billion dollars per year, and that is a conservative esti-
mate." He paused for a moment to let the full impact of his words
sink in. "Of course, PWE has always serviced those clients who

wished to target one or more of these markets, but it is now *time* for us to take a giant leap forward. PWE Multicultural is that giant leap. It will be a full-service boutique designed to successfully influence consumer purchasing decisions in a highly innovative yet cost-effective manner." He took a deep breath and gave his audience a disarming grin. Adrienne noticed that his two front teeth had a gap between them. It was a feature that she had always found sexy on a man.

"If my history is any indication of what is to come, I guarantee you that there will be some mistakes before our new venture is running smoothly."

He gestured, and the lights went off. Someone started the video machine. Lloyd Cooper was funny and got quite a few laughs when he critiqued his own bad reel of TV commercials, which he had tried to get on the air early in his career. Adrienne could feel the goodwill swelling in the room. A man who started off by showing how many mistakes he'd made was a decent human being at heart.

The meeting ended with the staffers giving their new boss a heartfelt round of applause. He stepped down from the podium as the lights came back on, and their eyes met again. Adrienne felt a small charge under his gaze. He was the first to look away, a slight smile playing around his mouth. Again Sherry noticed his reaction to Adrienne.

The crowd surged toward the corridor. Adrienne allowed herself to get swept up with Sherry and a group of people from unit 10, who gossiped freely as they headed back to the elevators.

"He's cute," said a chirpy blonde.

"I think he's gay," said Sherry.

"What an awful thing to say," said Adrienne.

"Are you saying that being gay is awful?" asked Sherry.

Adrienne felt confused. "No. I just meant that we should give our new boss a chance and that malicious gossip is wrong."

The other women looked to Sherry for a response. "Sounds homophobic to me," Sherry stated.

As soon as they were seated back in unit 6, Sherry started, "What was that all about?"

"What do you mean?"

Sherry stared at her with open curiosity. "I saw what happened when he looked at you. Have you two met somewhere before?"

Adrienne bit her lip, trying to remember. "No."

"Maybe at another company?" Sherry pressed.

Adrienne thought hard for another minute, and then shook her head vigorously. "No."

Sherry arched her eyebrows in disbelief. "You must have just forgotten."

Adrienne turned around and went back to work without saying another word. She and Lloyd Cooper had obviously crossed paths before. But where? Before she could rack her brains, her supervisor called.

"Adrienne, could you come in, please? I have a couple of documents that need to be typed and some faxes that I need you to send right away."

"Sure."

Regina Belvedere was a statuesque redhead with green eyes and a warm smile. Her office was efficiently organized and decorated in an oatmeal tone. She looked up when Adrienne entered. "Guess what I'm doing next weekend?"

Adrienne smiled. "You're going camping with Al."

Regina sighed. "No. We broke up last week."

"I'm so sorry, Regina," Adrienne said sincerely.

"Thanks. I'm going to a dude ranch upstate with a singles group. According to the brochure, all the men are doctors and lawyers. How about that?"

The two women shared a laugh and then settled down to work.

When Adrienne returned to her desk almost an hour later, Sherry was hanging up her phone. "Lloyd Cooper wants to see you in his office, pronto!"

Adrienne's heart skipped a beat. Her eyes widened in panic. "What could he possibly want?"

Sherry's voice was a whisper. "I don't know, but you better get moving."

"Where is his office?"

Sherry gave her a room number that was on the other side of their floor. Adrienne ducked into the ladies' room first and gave herself a once-over in the full-length mirror.

A few minutes later, she knocked on the closed door. A female voice answered, "Come in."

Adrienne turned the knob and entered. "Mr. Cooper, my name is . . . "

Eight pairs of eyes around a long glass table looked up from paperwork and stared at her. A man's voice stopped coming out of the speakerphone on the table. Another man, who was taping the meeting on video, quickly paused the tape. Adrienne mumbled an apology and backed out. She leaned against the wall and concentrated on her breathing, which was now ragged and shallow. Sherry had been wrong. She had walked into a conference room. Locating an empty desk with a phone, she called the switchboard operator, who gave her a room number up on the thirty-fourth floor.

This time Lloyd Cooper's voice answered Adrienne's knock; she felt uneasy as he told her to come in. She walked past a large potted plant near the window, and a wall of framed diplomas and certificates. He was seated behind a huge mahogany-colored desk that seemed half a block away. Adrienne crossed the wide expanse of beige carpet and held out her hand.

"Hi, I'm Adrienne Jordan. Did you wish to see me?"

"Ah! So you've married and changed your last name." He stood up and came around to her side of the desk, extending his hand. "Hello, Mrs. Jordan. Have a seat."

Adrienne gulped and sat in the leather chair. She had talked to this man somewhere before. "Where do I know you from, sir?"

He chuckled mildly, but his dark-brown eyes never left hers. "Sir? Well, that's a switch!"

His stare was unnerving, and Adrienne was confused by his comment. "A switch?"

He laughed heartily.

Adrienne began to get annoyed. She had no time for whatever silly game her new boss was playing. She struggled to keep her voice polite. "Your voice is familiar, but I've never met anyone named Lloyd Cooper." Adrienne almost added the word "sir" again but caught herself in time. She didn't want him to start laughing at her again.

There was a knock at the door, and for a moment her comment hung in the air as Lloyd's secretary, Sally Gomez, poked her head in.

"Yes, Sally?"

"I'm sorry to interrupt, Mr. Cooper, but John Elliott needs to see you right away. He says it's urgent."

"I'll be in touch with you, Mrs. Jordan," Lloyd Cooper said formally. His eyes twinkled with mischief as he dismissed her.

Adrienne puzzled over the strange encounter on her way back downstairs and then decided to let it rest. Lloyd Cooper would tell her where they'd met before in his own time. She only hoped that his memories were good ones, since he was a new executive at the company.

When she got back to her desk, a new stack of handwritten notes from Regina awaited her. The report needed a lot more work. Adrienne rifled through the notes and sighed.

Sherry started chattering away, but Adrienne ignored her nosy questions about the new boss and kept typing. She couldn't afford to get stuck doing revisions through lunch. She was meeting Mel at noon to see an apartment. It was a two-bedroom, and the advertisement had described it as sunny and spacious. Best of all, it was in Manhattan, which meant she'd be living only minutes away from her job and Dan.

It was a busy morning. The phones rang incessantly, and Regina kept interrupting her to add more tasks to her long list of assignments. At 11:45, she was done. Adrienne stood up and stretched, hoping that Mel would be on time. If they were late, someone else was likely to snap up the apartment.

Regina was waiting anxiously when Adrienne walked into her office. She grabbed the report eagerly and opened a thick green folder that lay on her desk. "Thanks. It will take me about fifteen minutes to read through the report. I'll need you to start on final revisions as soon as I'm done."

Adrienne looked at her watch in consternation. Regina noticed her distress and frowned. "What's the matter?"

"Regina, can this wait an hour? I need to leave at noon to see an apartment. I'll run right back, and I won't eat lunch. Please?"

Regina sighed and rubbed her temples. "My meeting is at two."

"The report will be ready. I promise."

Regina ruffled the papers in front of her impatiently. "Okay, okay. But hurry up."

It was noon when Adrienne reached the street. Mel was leaning against the side of the building, smoking a cigarette and stamping his feet to keep warm. Adrienne wondered why he looked so drawn and tired.

"Hi," she said shyly.

He kissed her full on the lips. "Let's get the show on the road!"

They started walking. Adrienne wondered if Mel was as scared as she was. He took her hand, and they smiled at each other.

"It's going to be okay," he said.

"But not easy."

"No. We had a good thing going once. It won't be easy to get that back."

An image of Delilah lying in her crib flashed through Adrienne's mind. She closed her eyes for a second, swallowed hard, and willed her emotions away. She didn't want Mel to see her upset. She and Mel still had each other, and she intended to have another baby as soon as possible. To ease the tension, Adrienne told Mel about her encounter with Lloyd Cooper.

Mel seemed amused. "You worked in a lot of places before we got married, baby. I'll bet he was some manager at one of those temp jobs. He was just having some fun with you."

Adrienne shook her head. "I don't think so."

Mel squeezed her hand. "I think you're just feeling stressed out about our situation." He kissed her on the nose. "Don't worry about it, okay?"

Adrienne wasn't convinced, but she smiled up at her husband anyway.

Light snow flurries had started to fall by the time she and Mel reached Thirtieth Street and Ninth Avenue. They were pleased to see that the block was clean and the front door to the tenement was locked. The building faced Ninth Avenue above a video rental store and a Korean fruit-and-vegetable market. The doorbells were outside, and Adrienne rang the first one, labeled "Super." A raspy voice came through the intercom. "State your business."

Adrienne was cold and tired. Her own voice was impatient as she replied, "We're here to see the apartment."

There was no answer, but a minute later a short white man with a hairy potbelly that was bursting from a ragged T-shirt appeared in the vestibule. He had shaggy gray hair and a matching walrus mustache. A smelly cigar dangled from his lips, and a pair of bright-blue eyes stared at them suspiciously. Finally, he opened the glass door that separated them. Adrienne and Mel followed him inside. The hallway was clean, carpeted, and mercifully warm. The door to his apartment stood open. A TV game show was on, and Adrienne wondered if the man had a hearing problem, because the volume was up so high. He motioned toward his door, then pointed toward the back of the hallway.

"Two apartments on each floor. I got one and a cop lives in the back. If you smoke dope, he'll smell it."

"Why do white folks say *dope* when they mean *reefer*?" Mel whispered in her ear. "Sounds like he's talking about heroin or something."

Adrienne giggled and poked Mel in the ribs to shush him as they climbed the stairs behind the portly superintendent. The vacant apartment was on the second floor, right above the super. He pulled out a huge ring of keys and, after several tries, found the one that opened the door.

For Adrienne, it was love at first sight. The living room was huge, which made up for the two windows that faced the noisy front street. The master bedroom was spacious enough to hold a queen-size bed and a full set of furniture. Although the second room was tiny, it was big enough to hold a crib. The kitchen had a brand-new stove and refrigerator. The bathroom tiles were blue, her favorite color.

Adrienne took a deep breath and made a silent vow. She would put the past behind them and have a new baby as soon as possible.

CHAPTER THREE

Mel and Adrienne had been saving for a new apartment ever since they had returned to work. Each week, Mel had turned over a portion of his salary to Adrienne to hold for him. He had known that putting it in a bank account would be a mistake. They would give him an ATM card to access the money, and whenever he got high, he would pinch off the sum until it finally disappeared.

As Mel dealt the cards for a game of bid whist, he thought about how his easy life at Debra's house would soon be over. The lease had been signed, Adrienne was happy, and now Mel was beginning to panic. How could he erase Delilah's death from his mind when Adrienne's sad eyes were a constant reminder? How could he break Adrienne's heart by not going back to her? Would things be the way they had been before Delilah was born?

Mel was convinced that Adrienne would immediately start trying to get pregnant. To make matters worse, guilt ate at him so much that he was now popping antacid tablets, smoking two packs of cigarettes a day, and visiting Little Jimmy whenever he was the lucky winner in a card game. Even though Adrienne said she had forgiven him for causing the blaze, he had not forgiven himself. These and other thoughts swirled through Mel's mind until his hands began to shake.

"Come on, man, deal the damn cards! What's wrong with you?" Big Boy shouted.

Mel came out of his reverie with a start. Everyone except Lillian was staring at him impatiently.

"Are you all right?" she asked softly. "You're sweating." There was warmth and concern in her voice and eyes.

"I'm fine," Mel answered gruffly. He ignored Debra's questioning gaze, and she turned away. A minute later, Mel was forgotten amid the party atmosphere.

After the game, Mel walked Lillian downstairs to help her get a cab. By the time it pulled away from the curb, her phone number was in his wallet.

A week passed, and on the Friday evening before he and Adrienne were to resume their marriage, Mel called Lillian. He'd treat himself to one last fling before returning to the hard work of marriage. They arranged to meet for drinks at Beefsteak Charlie's on Fifty-second Street and Eighth Avenue.

When Mel got off the phone, he went to the bathroom to clean up. He looked in the mirror. He was forty years old and twenty-four hours away from a reconciliation, which frightened him. He shaved and then found some Visine in the medicine cabinet to clear his eyes. Then he showered, picked out his Afro, and greased his hands with Vaseline to pat it into a perfect ebony sphere.

Lillian has a soft voice and a dainty way about her, he thought to himself. *She knows I'm married, so I can relax and just have a good time.*

Lillian was inside the restaurant. She was wearing a sleeveless, low-cut, skin-tight royal blue satin dress. A fake fur coat was thrown over one arm. Her shoes were black stiletto heels. Mel hummed an old Teddy Pendergrass tune as he gave her a chaste little kiss on the cheek.

"Do you remember that?" he asked.

She nodded. "'Close the Door.' I used to love that song."

They smiled at each other, and Mel guided her to a table away from the window. He sat down beside her. Lillian's hair looked different, but she only smiled mysteriously when he asked why.

A waiter approached the table with a grin, gave them menus,

then left. Mel looked meaningfully at Lillian. "I already know what I want."

Lillian frowned, and Mel quickly turned to concentrate on the menu. Maybe he was moving too fast. They read silently for a moment, and then Mel turned to her.

"What you drinkin' tonight, baby?"

"Vodka. Straight up, no ice."

Hot damn, this is one tough woman! Mel thought. He signaled for the waiter. "Rum and coke for me. Straight vodka for the lady, and let me get the buffalo wings and potato skins."

The waiter scribbled furiously and then looked at Lillian. "Do you need more time, ma'am?"

Lillian closed her menu with a snap. "No. I want the same thing."

As the waiter turned to leave, Mel told him, "Keep the drinks coming until we finish eating." Lillian nodded her approval.

"So, Big Boy say you gonna be movin' soon."

In other words, was he going back to his wife? Damn, women thought they were so slick! "Yeah."

She played with the napkin on the side of her empty plate. "You goin' back to your wife?"

"I'm not sure yet," he lied. "But I owe my wife a lot. Maybe somehow I can make it up to her." He turned the conversation away from himself as the waiter returned with the food and drinks. "You ever been married?"

"No. Ain't never found nobody worth marryin'."

Mel threw back his head and laughed. "Is that right, Miz Lillian?"

"That's right. Most men nowadays expect the woman to take care of them. Not this lady!"

Mel took a drink. She had a pretty smile. "Sheee-it, I doan blame you, girl. Fact is, if I was a woman, I wouldn't work no place. I'd always have a man to take care o' me."

Lillian gazed at him thoughtfully. "In other words, you don't like workin'."

"Hell, no! Do you know anybody who does? I play the lottery every week. Soon as I hit, I'm gone!"

That response seemed to satisfy her. She shrugged and took a sip of her drink.

"Where do you work?" Mel asked.

"I only been in New York a month. One of Big Boy's friends got me a job down in the garment center. I sew ladies' blouses."

She barely made minimum wage. A man would have to help pay her bills and buy groceries, Mel thought.

"What about you? Big Boy say you a bus driver."

"Yeah. I work for the city."

"You got kids?"

"No. Adrienne wants one, though." Melvin felt a stab of pain in his chest when Lillian mentioned children, and he took a huge gulp of his drink to make it go away. It wasn't her fault that she'd hit a nerve. She was new in town. He was surprised that fat mouth Big Boy hadn't told her about the tragedy. But Mel knew that he would soon enough.

"Is Adrienne your wife?"

"Yeah."

"Debra tole Big Boy that your wife is stupid—says she always got her head in the clouds."

Mel didn't like that. Adrienne was smarter than any woman he'd ever met, and prettier, too. Adrienne's only problem was that she'd had the bad luck to marry a man who was destined for failure. "Debra should mind her own business."

Lillian realized that she had said the wrong thing, and moved quickly to restore Mel's good mood. "I got two sweet little girls, but they down South with my grandma."

Mel didn't want to hear about anybody else's kids. He started to eat and drink a little faster, and Lillian unconsciously followed his lead. They were both slightly drunk by the time the meal was over.

After the waiter removed their plates, Mel kissed her lightly on the lips. She didn't protest, so he got bolder. He slipped a hand underneath the table and between her heavy thighs. Lillian put her lips to his ear. "You got strong hands," she whispered. That was all Mel needed to hear. He winked at her. She smiled her assent and stood up. Mel threw two twenty-dollar bills on the table and watched Lillian's swishing blue satin ass as he helped her on with the fake fur coat. They left the warmth of the restaurant. After kissing and hugging under a streetlight, Mel hailed a cab to take them to the next step.

Lillian's studio apartment was located in a tenement only five blocks away from Debra's place. They climbed the four flights of stairs to her place without saying anything. When Lillian opened the door, Mel sniffed the air. It smelled nice, and he realized that the fragrance came from a bouquet of fresh flowers that was in a vase on the wall unit. As soon as he sat down on the sofa, Lillian's arms encircled his neck. "Are you seeing somebody besides that silly wife of yours?" Mel's arms slid around her waist, and he pulled her so close, their bodies were crushed together as he leaned down to whisper in her ear. "Yeah, Miz Lillian. I'm seeing you."

*   *   *

The next morning, Mel woke up and immediately felt alarmed. All of a sudden, his words from the night before descended on him and began to replay inside his head. *"I love you, Lillian. Will you be mine? Yes, I would definitely get married again!"* Christ! The night before, he had said everything that a woman liked to hear, because it always made the sex hotter. But now she was clinking dishes and silverware in the kitchen. Worse, the smells of bacon and French toast were wafting into his nostrils. Smells of home. She was cooking breakfast for him just like a married woman would!

Why the hell did single women start planning a wedding after one evening with a good-looking man? Some of them were smart, too. The most dangerous kind were like Lillian—women who pretended not to care about marriage. To make matters worse, they showed up on the afternoon talk shows complaining about men having all the power. Since when? Sheee-it, women were the most devious creatures on earth. All of them. It was the one thing black men had in common with white dudes. They were all at the mercy of these goddamned scheming women. Mel sniffed the air. Yeah, she was working hard in that kitchen.

He thought frantically. Maybe he could pretend to be unconscious so he wouldn't have to eat breakfast with her. No, that was ridiculous. She'd only call an ambulance, and the paramedics would know he was bullshitting. In the kitchen, Lillian started to sing a quiet, contented song.

He looked at the clock on the wall. It was 8:15, time to stop this nonsense before it got out of hand. He had to get the moving van and pick up Adrienne at nine.

He looked around the room for an escape route. There were two small windows that he would never fit through. The front door was too close to the kitchen, and to reach it he'd have to get off the sofa bed, get dressed, quietly ease the security chain off the door, and flee while Lillian was bustling about in plain view.

He sat straight up in the sofa bed, clutching the sheet to his chin with both hands. His knuckles were starting to hurt. Mel released the sheet and took a deep breath. He was beginning to panic, and if Lillian were to peek into the room, he would make a sorry sight. He quietly lay back down and shut his eyes. Pretending to be asleep was his best bet. That way he could figure out what lie to tell her without fear of interruption. A few minutes later, the plan was firm in his mind. He yawned loudly and called her name. She appeared instantly, wearing a black slip that he hadn't seen the night before. Her hair was neatly combed into place and there was bright red lipstick on her smiling mouth. Mel felt his own lips turn down at the corners. It was time to go.

"Breakfast is almost ready," she sang.

He tried to look surprised and regretful at the same time. "Aw, baby. I'm sorry. I have to take Adrienne to the dentist this morning."

Her lower lip poked out just a little, but then she shrugged. "Okay."

What the hell did she mean by okay? He didn't remember asking her permission to leave. Mel climbed out of the sofa bed and, without saying another word, reached for his clothes, which were lying in a heap on the floor. Then he headed for the shower. Adrienne's face flashed before him, and he hung his head in shame for a second. He'd had his last fling. There would be no more nights with other women. It was time for him to be a faithful husband once more.

CHAPTER FOUR

Adrienne stepped out of the shower and grabbed a fluffy white towel. As she dried off, she surveyed her body, trying to see it through Mel's eyes. In the past six months she'd lost about ten pounds, and it seemed as if her breasts were a little smaller because of it. *At least my thighs are still firm and my butt is nice and round,* she thought to herself. Adrienne lotioned her skin and dressed in underwear, a T-shirt, jeans, and sneakers. She pulled a brush through her brown hair and let it hang loose to her shoulders.

She stared at her reflection. Would Delilah still be alive if she had not gone to have her hair done that fateful day last July? It hadn't been absolutely necessary for her to leave the house that day. What if she hadn't prolonged her stay in the city by stopping by Dan's place? If she hadn't left her tired and sleepy husband alone in the apartment. A man so exhausted that he'd fallen asleep with a lit cigarette between his fingers.

Adrienne left the bathroom, breathing deeply to steady herself as she walked. Today was moving day and she was a bundle of nerves. Thinking about the past too long might push her back to that emotional space from right after the fire, when she was deep in depression and could not speak. She couldn't afford to return to that place.

Dan and Charlene were already dressed. Charlene was almost as tall as Dan. She wore her black hair in shoulder-length braids and usually wore a headband to keep them away from her face. Charlene never wore makeup and had little interest in the latest fashion. She practically lived in slacks, loafers, and oversized cotton shirts. Right now her plain face was scrunched up in concern. Her thin lips were in a straight line of disapproval—or wariness. Adrienne couldn't tell which it was. They looked up from the sofa when Adrienne walked into the living room. Dan's eyes were serious. "How are you feeling this morning?"

Adrienne sat down. "Wonderful," she lied. "Mel should be here any minute!"

"I just want you to know that I'm here if you ever need to talk."

"Dan, lighten up. Mel and I are putting the past behind us. Everything is going to be fine." Seeing Dan shrug, Adrienne continued, "We both know it isn't going to be easy."

"I just wish you guys had gone for some counseling, that's all," said Charlene.

"Maybe it would have made things worse. Mel says a lot of times marriages end in divorce after the couple starts therapy."

Charlene looked doubtful. "How has poor Mel coped with his sadness over the past six months?"

"What do you mean?"

"I mean just that. Mel may still be running away from his grief. The last time he was here, I could tell he'd been drinking."

Adrienne started to feel warm. Charlene was her girl, but she was also a social worker, and it seemed as if she was always analyzing everyone around her.

Adrienne jumped up from the love seat and walked across to the sofa, with her arms folded across her chest. "Drop it."

"Don't get mad at me, Adrienne," Charlene answered defensively. "Mel is carrying a heavy emotional burden, and he needs to get some help."

"Mel and I just need to be with each other. We've both agreed not to talk about what happened. Never again."

"I know, Adrienne, but I don't think it's a good idea for you and Mel to avoid the subject forever," Dan said mildly.

"Honey, Dan's right," Charlene interjected. "Not talking about it will tear the two of you apart."

Adrienne said nothing.

Dan threw up his hands. "Fine. Let's get to work and finish taping all these boxes."

Adrienne was still fuming. "Are you suggesting that Mel is an alcoholic?" she asked Charlene.

"That's not what I meant," Charlene protested wearily.

Dan stood up, lifted Adrienne's chin, and stared directly into her eyes. "I don't know whether Mel has a drinking problem or not, but I do know that you two need to talk about what happened. Adrienne, you can't shop your pain away."

Adrienne jerked her chin away. "I don't know what you're talking about," she said defiantly. Dan was starting to sound like Charlene. In another minute he would give her some dime-store psychoanalysis, that the purchases she made were little representations of Delilah, or some such nonsense.

Dan waved one arm around the living room in a sweeping gesture. "Look at this! Clothes with the tags still on. CDs that have never been played, dozens of makeup kits, books that you haven't read yet. Every week you find something else to buy."

Adrienne couldn't believe the callousness of Dan's statement. How would he feel if he woke up one morning and found that every single thing he'd ever owned had simply vanished? Wouldn't he feel compelled to replace all that he'd lost? Her weekly shopping trips took away the awful sense of powerlessness that gnawed at her insides. Once the new baby was born, she had no doubt that the pain, which ate away at her inside, would disappear entirely.

Adrienne stamped her foot. It was a childish gesture. She knew that, but she was too wound up with worry over what lay ahead for her and Mel, to contain herself any longer. "Have you forgotten that I arrived on your doorstep with just the clothes on my back?"

At that moment, the doorbell rang. Adrienne ran for the door as her brother and sister-in-law lapsed into a troubled silence.

CHAPTER FIVE

When Mel left Lillian's house, he had caught a cab down to Fourteenth Street, where he had hired a van and a helper. The helper turned out to be a gangly, pimply faced Irish kid. Mel took one look at him and turned back to face the owner. "Come on, man! I told you last week that I needed somebody to help me lift some real heavy shit. Is this the best you could do?"

"That's my son, Ian. He's only sixteen but he's strong. You'll see."

Ian just stood there. Mel looked at his watch. It was 8:55 A.M. No time to argue. He nodded in Ian's direction. "Let's go," he said with disgust.

Melvin said nothing to the kid as the van careened up Tenth Avenue toward Dan's apartment. He hated moving boxes and furniture. It reminded him too much of his father.

Debra had often told him the story of their parents. Harry and Simmie Jordan had married in 1953, but theirs was no church wedding. Harry had driven Simmie from their hometown of Santee, South Carolina, to the courthouse in Columbia. They exchanged the basic vows before a judge, then went back to Harry's house, where Simmie cried all afternoon. She had wanted at least a small reception at her parents' home, but Harry had been adamant. He said that he wasn't totally sure the baby was his. One sign of fuss or celebration, he told Simmie, and he was pulling out. For good. So she simply fingered her new wedding band and held her hand up to the dim light in their closet-size bedroom.

Simmie was glad to have Debra to occupy her daytime hours when Harry was working at the furniture-moving company. Harry took a real interest in Debra, even though he still didn't love his wife. For Harry, nothing was too good for Debra, his precious baby girl who looked just like him. Simmie, in turn, hated the little girl for taking away what little attention Harry used to pay her. The family moved to New York, where Mel was born four years later.

Mel, named after his maternal grandfather, had been born shortly after Debra's fourth birthday. Even though Harry, Simmie, and their tiny daughter were all brown skinned, the boy was coal black. Since Mel was so dark, Harry felt that his wife had been unfaithful. He could barely stand the sight of Mel and made sure that the boy knew it.

Simmie adored her son, but she died from a heart attack when Mel was only twelve years old. Soon after, Harry took off, leaving his two children to be raised by an elderly aunt.

Mel shook his head to clear away the dismal memories as he and Ian waited for Adrienne to buzz them into the building.

When Mel walked into Dan's apartment, he could feel the tension.

Mel kissed his wife and grunted a hello to his in-laws. He pointed a finger at the kid's chest. "His name is Ian. He's going to help me and Dan with the lifting."

"You know that old bureau that I've been keeping my CDs in?" Adrienne asked Charlene.

"Go on, take it, girl," Charlene said grumpily.

Mel wondered briefly what they had been arguing about.

Since Adrienne and Dan still hadn't finished taping the boxes when Mel arrived, he and the kid had to help them. Mel had to give Ian an extra twenty dollars for his time and it really pissed him off. The five of them worked in silence until every box was taped.

As Mel and Dan loaded the bureau into the van, it almost slipped from their grasp. This would have meant serious injury for the slightly built white boy who was holding up the other side. When the vehicle was finally ready to go, Adrienne and Dan squeezed in the front next to Mel. Charlene and Ian rode in the back.

As the blocks sped by, Mel felt as though he were headed toward a jail cell. To calm himself, he tried to think about the past few months.

Debra's place meant old-school music, dancing, card parties. Ahead of him lay a closed world with two people trying to find their place in it as the tiny ghost of a third hovered over them. He was sure of only two things. He still loved Adrienne, and his get-high days were over. There was no way any marriage could last if one partner was using drugs. From now on, he would stick to rum.

It was a silent ride. Mel couldn't think of anything to say, and he figured that everyone else picked up on his somber vibe.

When the van pulled up in front of the new building, they all clambered out. Adrienne and Charlene waited on the stoop and watched the three men struggle once again with the huge bureau. Mel saw the front door open. A tall man with butterscotch skin appeared and stood watching alongside Adrienne and Charlene. He was wearing jeans, boots, and a bomber jacket. *A big man*, Mel thought. *That's good since we could use some help.*

"Hey, man, could you give us a hand?" he yelled.

The man trotted down the steps and grabbed an edge of the bureau. Adrienne went up to the second floor to unlock the door, and the four men grunted and gasped their way up the stairs and into the apartment. They set the bureau down in what was to be the living room. After a couple of trips back out to the van, all the boxes were in as well. Mel shook the stranger's hand. "I'm glad you came along, man. Thanks a lot."

"No trouble at all. I live on the first floor in the back."

"You must be the cop," Mel said bluntly.

The guy laughed. "I hope there's more to me than that. My name is Ed Winsome. Welcome to the building."

Mel introduced everyone, and then Adrienne gestured to Dan and Charlene. "Come on, let me show you the place."

"Do you like it?" Adrienne babbled nervously as they walked

through the rooms. "I thought I could buy a navy blue leather sofa like Mel always wanted. We could put it on this wall. What I want to do is recapture the homey feeling of our old apartment while at the same time creating something new."

Mel smiled at Adrienne, realizing that she was anxious, too, and concentrated on maneuvering the bureau into the space where Adrienne wanted it. Mel moved some more boxes, then straightened up. His back hurt. He groaned.

"Are you all right?" Adrienne asked.

"Yeah, baby. I'm just getting too old for this shit."

"Don't worry," Adrienne said. "I don't see us moving out of this apartment for a long time."

"I'm glad to hear we're not moving soon, baby, because my back feels like it's about to quit on me." Mel laughed lightly.

"I have to be going now," Ed Winsome announced.

The other two men and Charlene headed for the door, too, murmuring their good-byes as Mel pressed Ian's payment into his skinny hand.

When everyone had gone, Mel pulled out his knife. "I'll cut the tape on the boxes, and you figure out where to put things, okay?"

Adrienne smiled. "We have one bureau and nothing else. There's nowhere to put anything yet."

It was the truth. Mel sighed. "Okay. Do you have some blankets? We can't sleep on this hard-assed floor."

Adrienne looked at the boxes. She pointed at three that were clustered in a corner. "Try those." Mel slit the tape on one box and peered in. "Makeup," he said, bewildered.

Adrienne hastened to his side and pulled on his arm. "A gal's got to look good," she joked nervously.

Mel knelt down and removed each item. Five tubes of mascara, ten tubes of lipstick, ten lip liners, six packs of false eyelashes, five bottles of White Diamonds perfume, three pumice stones, nine bottles of nail polish and four packs of Fashion Fair foundation. Every item in the box was still in its original package—unopened. Mel blinked and looked up at his wife, who was anxiously wringing her hands.

"What does this mean, baby?"

"I like to buy on sale, Mel."

Mel slit the tape on the next box. There were three blankets and a radio. A big book lay at the bottom. Mel lifted it out. It was their wedding album. But that didn't make sense, everything they owned had been destroyed in the fire.

"Did you have an extra album at Dan's house or something?"

Adrienne shook her head. "No. Mama sent me hers."

"That was nice of her."

"Yes, it was," Adrienne agreed softly.

Mel spread the blankets. Adrienne plugged in the radio.

They lay on the floor and turned the album pages. They looked so happy in the photos. It was hard for Adrienne to believe that so much had happened since the wedding.

"We used to be happy, right?"

Mel smiled enigmatically and stood up. "Let's dance."

Adrienne put her arms around her husband's neck, and for Mel, the clock went back four years to their first date. They had rocked to the mournful strumming coming from the guitar of a no-talent blues band in a dinky Greenwich Village barbecue joint. Everything around them had seemed to sparkle. Mel held Adrienne tightly, wanting to weep because his carelessness had shattered the beautiful life they had once created.

"I love you, Mel."

"I love you, too, baby."

CHAPTER SIX

It had been more than six months since they slept together. The only light came from a table lamp that Charlene had no longer needed, and it cast a bright circle that illuminated Adrienne and her husband as they fumbled out of their clothes. When they were both naked, Adrienne closed her eyes. Her husband's hands roamed over her body. She wanted to caress him back, but every time she started to lift her hands, something hard twisted within her chest. Was it because Mel's touch was so cold? Or maybe it was that Mel's eyes were lifeless, his lips clamped tightly shut. He looked as if he had just been sentenced to life in prison. He mounted her but didn't have enough of an erection to enter, and she could sense his shame.

"Mel, don't worry about it."

He climbed off and lay on his back. They both stared at the ceiling. "You're cold as ice. That's what the fuck is wrong."

Adrienne knew he was right. She didn't feel an ounce of desire. Ever since they had rented the apartment, Adrienne had daydreamed about being with him. She had visualized every moment of their lovemaking. The most exciting part of each of those scenarios had been the instant when the past receded into an infinitesimal dot and she was consumed by a passion so deep that it seeped into Mel's bones and transported them both into frenzied ecstasy. Instead, Mel's fondling felt like the reassuring pats and hugs she had received from her family in the awful days before Delilah's funeral. His charcoal-colored semihard penis became the image of a tiny, limp human being. Adrienne felt she could not say all of this out loud without destroying what little chance they had of rebuilding their marriage. So she just took his hand and whispered, "I'm sorry."

He sighed heavily. "Do you know where my cigarettes are?"

"So you're going to give up. Just like that?" Adrienne knew she was being unreasonable, but she couldn't think of anything else to say.

Mel turned over to face her. Now his eyes looked angry. "Let me tell you something, baby. This floor is hard, and my thoughts are all fucked up, too, so let's just try and get some sleep. Okay?"

Silent tears coursed down Adrienne's cheeks as Mel got up and fumbled around for his cigarettes. He finally found them and sat smoking in a corner on the other side of the room. As the ringlets of smoke curled through the air, Adrienne wondered if Mel had ever tried to kick the habit after the accident. How could he stand to light a cigarette after what had happened to Delilah? She sighed heavily. The road ahead was not going to be a smooth one.

"Mel, we'll get through this. Right?"

Adrienne fell asleep waiting for him to answer.

CHAPTER SEVEN

Mel woke up first. He looked down at his sleeping wife and felt like a complete shit. Last night's disaster wasn't entirely Adrienne's fault. He had felt nothing except sadness as Adrienne fumbled out of her clothing, and a wave of remorse had washed over him when he first touched her naked body. Had he lost his heat for Adrienne? If so, why hadn't he been man enough to admit it rather than blaming her? He groaned out loud because he didn't have the answer to either of those questions. The noise made Adrienne turn over. He looked around the huge living room. Nothing but boxes. And he had no money in the bank and didn't get paid until next week. Since he was a loner who didn't have any personal friends outside of Debra's crowd, there was no one he could ask for some extra cash. What a mess.

Maybe a hot shower will clear my head, he thought. He stood up, wondering which box held the washcloths, towels, and soap. The memories of their other beautifully furnished apartment came flooding back. A ragged sob escaped from his throat as he stood there in the bare, chilly room. He tenderly wrapped the blankets around his wife, got dressed without washing, and sat smoking in a corner until she woke up.

They slept on the floor for a week, and although they didn't actually make love, at least Mel could snuggle Adrienne in his arms, and she would hold him close throughout the night.

The furniture store delivered their black-lacquered bedroom furniture the following Saturday. A queen-size bed, two night tables, a chest of drawers for Mel, and a mirrored dresser for Adrienne. After everything was in place, they grinned at each other. Adrienne hugged him around the waist, that first night forgotten. They still worked well together. It felt like old times.

"Let's get these boxes out of here," Mel said.

"No," Adrienne answered quickly. "I have a better idea. You got paid yesterday. Go buy us a television set with the money we have left while I unpack."

"There's a lot of work to do here, baby. I should help."

Adrienne smiled brightly. "You can flatten all the empty boxes and take them outside when you get back."

Mel stood on the front steps. He felt very confused and a little desperate. Adrienne seemed secretive in some way. It was obvious that she had wanted to get rid of him a few moments ago. Why? He walked to the corner of Thirtieth Street and hesitated. Adrienne had rushed him from the house, so she shouldn't mind if he took his time getting back home. Debra would still be sober since it was only noon. He could take the Eighth Avenue bus uptown and pay her a visit. He could talk things out with her in a roundabout way. His sister had a way of looking at things and figuring out how to start fixing whatever was wrong. She had pulled him out of the dark and back to work when he'd given up on life. She and her crazy friends had made him laugh again. Yeah, he would go see Debra. She could also go downtown and help him pick out a nice TV.

*　*　*

Big Boy opened the door and gave Mel an angry, hateful look. Before Mel could ask what the hell his problem was, the giant stomped past him and Mel heard his footsteps thundering down the stairs. Debra kicked the door closed once Mel was inside and then sat down heavily in a kitchen chair.

"What's wrong with that crazy bastard?" Mel yelled.

"Sit your dumb ass down!" Debra roared.

Mel sat. He wondered if everyone in the world had gone crazy.

"Listen, Mel. I'm tired o' yo shit."

"What shit are you talkin' 'bout?" Mel asked.

"What you go and fuck wit Lillian for? And then you leave her bed and go straight back to Adrienne?"

Mel dropped his head in his hands. Damn, no wonder Big Boy was so mad. "Lillian knew I was married," he said weakly.

"Separated. She knew you were living here with me and that you and yore wife was separated. Don't give me any bullshit, Mel, cuz I ain't in the mood."

"Aw, damn. Lillian is a grown woman. She knows better than to hit the sack the first time a man takes her out."

"'Aw, damn,' my ass. Lillian came by here one night lookin' for your worthless ass, and I tole her you had moved out that same mornin'. Had been planning the move for a week. Poor woman broke down cryin' right here in my kitchen."

Mel couldn't think of anything to say.

"What did you go back with your wife for if you wanna fool around wit' other women?"

Mel flapped his hands helplessly. "It was my last night of freedom, Debra."

"That's a dumb-assed reason. What the hell was you thinkin?"

"I guess I wasn't thinking, Debra." All of a sudden he felt tired. "Got anything to drink?"

Debra glared at him.

"Please. Debra I'm goin' through a lot right now." He breathed a sigh of relief when his sister went to get the rum.

They poured two healthy drinks and Mel turned on the radio to an oldies station. The disc jockey was playing "I'll Be Around," by The Spinners.

"Damn. This song brings back some good memories," Mel said as he sat back down. "House parties, red light bulbs . . ."

Debra interrupted his reverie. "Grow the fuck up, Mel. That's your problem right now. Always lookin' back or feelin' sorry for yourself."

"Look, Debra, I'll go talk to Lillian and make things right. Okay?"

She snorted. "There ain't no way to make it right, but you could be man enough to say you're sorry."

Mel said nothing. He had no intention of calling Lillian and they both knew it.

Debra wouldn't let the subject go. She fixed him with a penetrating stare. "What I wanna know is how you figured you could get away with it?" She paused. "And now that Big Boy is pissed, where am I supposed to get this month's rent from?"

"Don't worry, Sis, I'll give you the rent when I get paid." Mel said gently.

Debra's body relaxed, and the worried frown left her face. She poured another drink for each of them. "Thanks. Now, tell me what you doin' up here so early in the day."

"I want you to go with me to buy a TV set."

Debra shook her head. "Ann is comin' over for me to braid her hair. I can't leave the house. You and Adrienne supposed to be doin' stuff like this together anyway. What's the matter?"

"I don't really know what our problem is." Mel confessed. He didn't tell his sister that he had not yet been able to get it up for his wife. No man would admit to that. It was humiliating beyond words.

They both fell silent as Mel wrestled for words. Debra went to the refrigerator and pulled out a loaf of bread and some baloney and cheese. Without saying a word, she made four sandwiches, thick with mayonnaise.

Mel said, "Being locked up in the house with her is gonna keep me remembering the fire. When I was living here with you, I didn't think about it all the time."

"That's real bad, Mel." Debra shook her head sadly. "For both of y'all."

Mel shifted in his chair. "I want to erase that day from my head."

"No such thing as erasin'."

"Bullshit. If I stayed away from everything that reminds me of Delilah"—he felt a tightness in the throat as he said her name—"it would all fade away just like we got out of Daddy's mind after he left."

"How do you know we got out of Daddy's mind?"

"Must have," Mel shrugged, "or he woulda come back."

Debra patted him on the arm. "I'm sorry you feelin' so bad, Mel."

Mel gave her a grateful smile. "Thanks. You know I wanted us to get back together, but somethin' just tells me Adrienne is itchin' to have a baby, and I don't ever want to try again."

Debra swallowed some meat and bread. "Did you tell her that?"

"No."

"Why the hell not?"

"I can't."

Debra's eyes narrowed. "That ain't gonna work."

Mel was relieved to hear the doorbell ring. It was Ann. Mel drank steadily and popped his fingers to the tunes as the women set up a makeshift beauty parlor right before his eyes. He remembered when Adrienne used to sing around the house, back when they were first married. After she'd told him about her old dream, he'd coaxed her into singing some of her best blues and jazz for him. She had a nice voice, strong and rich with feeling, not like some of these no-singing little girls they blasted on the urban hip-hop radio stations. Adrienne sang for real, straight from the old school—and she'd looked sexy doing it—but it had been a long time since he'd caught her humming or singing.

Ann took out a bag of store-bought hair and placed it on the table while Debra found a pair of scissors and a comb. When all the items were in place, Ann removed the green do-rag that covered her head and sat down on the floor between Debra's knees. Debra started working, and, in the party atmosphere that didn't end until the liquor ran out, Mel forgot all about the TV and Adrienne.

Ann looked up at Mel. "You got money? We need another fifth."

The rum had depressed Mel, and his thoughts were running in melancholy directions. He needed a little something to lift his spirits just this one last time. He wondered if Little Jimmy was at his post yet.

He staggered to his feet. "I'll be back," he said.

The jerking movement of the elevator made him want to throw up, but he took a couple of deep breaths and the sensation passed.

It wasn't completely dark yet, so Little Jimmy wasn't there. Mel was standing in the spot, trying to figure out his next move, when he noticed a kid watching him intently a few yards away. He couldn't have been more than twelve years old.

"What you know?" Mel asked.

The kid shrugged. "Nuthin'."

"Come on, man, don't play with me."

The kid sauntered away casually, and Mel followed him. They went back into the projects to a building on the other side of Debra's. The apartment was on the third floor. When they got off the elevator, the kid pointed at a door down the hall and took off.

Mel knocked, and a sly-looking woman in her early twenties opened the door. "The kid sent me," Mel whispered. He had paid and turned to leave before he realized that the envelope was only half full.

"Hey, this ain't gonna work," he complained. "Somebody already tapped this." Since he was halfway drunk, Mel didn't realize just how loud his voice was. A skinny guy who had been lying on the sofa jumped up and ran toward Mel. "Get out," he commanded.

The liquor had robbed Mel of his common sense. "Fuck you," he said.

The skinny guy punched him in the face, knocking him flat on his ass. He leaped to his feet and struck the guy with a right to the jaw, followed quickly with a blow to the stomach that made him double over in pain. Mel reached into his coat pocket. Shit! He had left his knife with Adrienne so she could open the boxes. As the guy straightened up, Mel kicked him in the stomach, knocking him backward and onto the floor. Mel jumped on the man and started throwing lefts and rights.

The woman's voice stopped the fighting. "I got me a gun here, and I'ma shoot you right in the back of the head if you don't get the fuck out of here right now."

Mel stood up and turned around to face the woman, who was indeed holding a pistol, her finger on the trigger.

Mel flung open the front door and hauled ass down the stairs. Back on the street, he realized what a lucky break he'd just had. Unfortunately, he had lost the coke during the fight, so he headed for the liquor store and bought another fifth of rum.

Debra opened the door, and her eyes widened in horror. "What happened to you?"

Mel pushed her aside. "Guy tried to mug me," he lied. He handed Debra the liquor bottle and headed for the bathroom to take a look at his eye, which was beginning to swell, and at his lip where his front teeth had cut it.

CHAPTER EIGHT

As the front door closed behind Mel, Adrienne leaned her tired body against it and breathed a sigh of relief. She couldn't let him help with the unpacking, because two of the boxes held brand-new baby outfits that she didn't want him to see until she got pregnant.

Before the fire, Adrienne had hated shopping. The crowds, too few dressing rooms, rude salespeople—it all had discouraged her. But after losing all her belongings, she had started buying clothes to replace those she had lost. And it escalated. The items had to be better than those she had lost, and then the game went up another notch. Then she started charging clothes and other items that she didn't have the cash for. Now, her credit card payments were overdue.

Adrienne looked at her watch. Mel would probably walk to Thirty-fourth Street and take a cab back. Adrienne had unstacked a couple of cartons and rolled up her sleeves when the phone rang. Damn! She had an hour and a half at most.

"Hey, girl." It was Charlene.

Adrienne was elated. The two women had not spoken in a week, since moving day. If Charlene was taking the time to call, that meant she wasn't mad anymore. "What's up?"

"Not a whole lot. Dan is doing a wedding today, so I have the house to myself."

"So do I. Mel went to buy a TV set."

"How are things between you two?" Charlene asked cautiously.

Adrienne sighed. "We got off to a bad start, but it will get better. We have some furniture now, so it's a lot more comfortable, but sometimes it still feels like we're strangers."

"Don't worry," Charlene said gently. "Just take things nice and slow."

"Yeah, I guess so." Adrienne said. "Can you do my hair next Saturday?"

"Sure. Is everything okay at work?"

Adrienne suddenly remembered the strange scene with Lloyd Cooper. Charlene listened quietly until Adrienne finished the tale.

"Now, that is some weird stuff," Charlene laughed. "And you really don't remember him at all?"

"No, but he did mention my new last name, so that means it has been at least four years since he saw me."

"True." Charlene was silent for a moment. "I love a puzzle. Let's think about this. He said that your calling him 'sir' was a switch. That means he wasn't a high roller before."

"Well, he couldn't have been a scrub, either," Adrienne answered dryly. "Nobody can climb the corporate ladder *that* fast."

"Hmmm. What if you knew him, like, ten years ago?"

Adrienne thought about that. "I was working a lot of temp jobs in between gigs. It's possible that he worked at one of those companies."

Charlene laughed. "See? He was probably working in the mailroom."

Adrienne started laughing with relief. "The mystery is solved."

"Wait a minute. Didn't you say he was from Chicago?"

Adrienne's heart sank. "Shit. You're right. I've never been to Chicago. What I really can't understand is how I could forget meeting any man who looks like that. The brother is fine with a capital *F.*" Adrienne could still remember the look he gave her after his presentation. She tried not to think about it as Charlene continued.

"We need more clues," Charlene said, sounding excited. "I hope he calls you soon."

"Whatever," Adrienne said dismissively. She didn't have any more time to talk about Cooper. "Charlene, I've got to unpack some boxes before Mel gets back. Can I call you later?"

"Why didn't he stay to help you?"

Adrienne hesitated. "I passed a store a few weeks ago, and there were some real cute baby outfits in the window. I bought four of them and . . . well . . . Mel wouldn't understand if he knew, so I sent him away."

"Aw, honey," Charlene said gently.

Adrienne could feel Charlene's pity, and it made her uncomfortable. She wished she could tell Charlene how she really felt, but she didn't want to talk about it. She didn't need anybody feeling sorry for her, not even Charlene or Dan. She'd wallowed in self-pity long enough, and Adrienne was determined move on. She promised to call soon, then got off the phone.

She slit the tape on the first box and wished that she and Mel could have hot, steamy sex like they used to. She wished they were once again trusting and easy with each other. She had not slept with anyone else during their separation, even though a few men had tried to date her. She'd never even been tempted. Adrienne had been too preoccupied with her grief to care about dating.

Had her celibacy been a mistake? Had she dried up and lost her womanhood? How long would Mel stay in a sexless marriage?

Her mind churned with these and other disturbing thoughts as she continued to open the boxes.

By 5:00 P.M., Adrienne had unpacked all the boxes and put everything away. Exhausted, she lay across the new bed and fell asleep, wondering why it was taking her husband so long to buy a television set. The ringing of the telephone woke her up.

"Hi, Adrienne. How you doin'?"

Adrienne sat up and rubbed the sleep out of her eyes. It was pitch-black outside. "Fine, Debra. And you?"

"I just wanted you to know that Mel is here so you don't get worried or nothin'."

"What time is it?" Adrienne asked, annoyed.

"Goin' on ten."

"Ten!" Adrienne shouted. "Put Mel on the phone, please."

"I can't. He's passed out drunk in the back room," Debra said flatly.

Adrienne took a deep breath to push back the anger that was starting to bubble inside her stomach. Why didn't Debra tell her that in the first place? "What did he do with the TV?"

"I dunno what you talkin' about."

"Debra, he left the apartment at noon to go buy us a TV set."

"Well, he didn't do it. Mel got here around twelve-thirty and he's been here ever since."

"What?"

"You heard me right."

"Don't you and your damned friends do anything up there but drink?"

Adrienne heard a hissing sound from her sister-in-law's lips. "Lissen here, heffah. It's none a yore business what goes on in my house. I didn't drag Mel up here. In fact, I'd appreciate it if you come and get yore drunk-ass husband up outa here."

Adrienne jerked her chin up. "Fine. I will."

She slammed the phone down before Debra could reply.

It took a long time for the bus to show up, and then it seemed to crawl up Amsterdam Avenue. Adrienne reached Debra's house almost an hour after the phone call.

Debra opened the door and glared at her without saying a word.

"Good evening," Adrienne said coolly. As crazy as she was, Adrienne knew Mel loved his sister, and she didn't want to make things worse by standing there arguing with her.

Debra stomped off into the kitchen as Adrienne went to the back bedroom. Mel was sprawled on his back, his eyes tightly closed. She shook his arm, but he didn't move. Debra came in carrying a pitcher of water. Without missing a beat, she threw half of it in Mel's face. He didn't move. She threw more water. He sputtered and flailed about. Then she punched him in the chest. "Git yore ass up!"

Mel opened his eyes. Debra hovered over him with Adrienne

peering angrily over her shoulder. Mel groaned at the sight and closed his eyes again.

"I know you awake now, Mel. Git up or the next water you feel will be boilin' hot."

Mel managed to pull himself up on his elbows. He opened his eyes again. The light bore into his pupils. It burned. His head throbbed.

"Your wife is here to pick you up."

Adrienne stepped forward and grabbed him by one arm. "What happened to your face?" she asked.

Mel opened his mouth to explain, but his tongue was stuck to the roof of his mouth. "Thirsty," he croaked.

Debra thrust the pitcher at him. He snatched it from her hand and drank the rest of the water in huge gulps while his wife and sister gazed at him in pure disgust.

"Get up, Mel. Let's go home."

Mel slowly eased his body off the bed. It looked as if each movement was painful. He moved unsteadily once he was in a standing position.

"I'll walk y'all outside and help you get a cab," Debra said to Adrienne.

"How did Mel bust his lip?"

"Didn't happen in my house" Debra replied. "He went to the liquor store and it was busted when he got back. Said he got mugged."

Mel stumbled after the two women, apparently too drunk to realize how thoroughly pathetic he looked. The cold air helped, but he promptly passed out again as soon as he and Adrienne climbed into the backseat of the cab.

He slept all the way home. When the cab stopped in front of their building, Adrienne paid the fare and shook her husband. "Mel, get up. We're home." He didn't budge. She shook him some more.

"Come on, lady. I ain't got all night!" the driver yelled.

Adrienne opened the door, hoping a cold blast of air would wake Mel up. It didn't work. "He's drunk, and I can't get him up!" Adrienne called to the driver. "Can you help me?"

"Hell, no! I could get sued if he falls or something. Jesus Christ! Why do I always get the fucking wackos?"

Adrienne bit her lip. Mel was too heavy for her to lift. "Is there a problem here?" It was a man's voice.

Adrienne watched as the man's legs moved to the driver's window and he repeated the question.

"What is this? A setup? You two know each other?" The driver's voice was shaking with fright.

Adrienne squinted into the darkness, trying to see the man's face.

"Calm down. I'm a cop."

Adrienne leaned out the door. It was Ed Winsome. He smiled when he saw her and moved quickly to the back door. He peeked inside. His skin was a light golden color. His features were too rugged for him to be handsome, but there was kindness in his face and his voice was gentle. "Is your husband sick?" he asked politely.

The car was reeking with liquor, and Ed Winsome had to smell it. She nodded, grateful to him for his discretion.

"Get out," he said quietly.

Adrienne climbed out and watched as he pulled Mel's legs out the door. He reached in again and, with a grunt, pulled Mel's shoulders forward. With a few swift motions, he had Mel out of the car and was half carrying, half dragging him to the building. Adrienne slammed the door. She was about to apologize to the cabbie, but he roared away. Sick with embarrassment, Adrienne kept her head down and led the way. Once they were in the apartment, Ed managed to catch her eye. "Where should I put him?" he asked.

Adrienne mumbled, "The bedroom," and then stood waiting by the front door. She heard a thump and wondered if Ed had thrown Mel onto the bed rather than placing him there gently. Ed came back.

"Thank you."

Ed kept his gaze averted. "It was nothing." He waved a good-bye and left.

CHAPTER NINE

When Mel woke up the next morning, Adrienne was dressed for work. She was wearing a red two-piece suit and stepping into a pair of black heels. There was a chunky black piece of jewelry around her neck. She looked good. He sniffed the air. Her perfume smelled good, too. Her back was facing him as she leaned on the dresser to check her makeup. Their eyes met in the mirror.

She whirled around to face him. "So, you mind telling me what yesterday was all about? Your eye is as big as a basketball, your left jaw is puffed up, and we don't have a TV set."

Mel's head felt like it was stuffed with cotton; his stomach was burning and hollow. "I got mugged," he mumbled. He couldn't believe it when Adrienne moved briskly to his side of the bed and leaned over. Her face was inches from his. "I don't believe you. Anyway, what were you doing at Debra's house in the first place when you were supposed to be out shopping?"

Had the girl lost her mind, getting all up in his face like that? No matter what he had done, he was still the goddamn man. "Back up, Adrienne," he said tightly. She moved backward a little, but there was still fire in her eyes. Mel couldn't blame her for that, but he couldn't tell Adrienne how he really got hurt. What would he say? *I was just trying to buy a little cocaine and got beat down in the process?* Instead, he tried to remember the ride home. He couldn't get past the two women shoving his limp body into the cab. How had Adrienne managed to get him upstairs and into bed? "We don't have time to talk about all that. You'll be late for work. The TV set will be here when you get home."

"Not so fast, Mel. Do you know what you've done?" She didn't wait for an answer. "When we got home, I was trying to get you out of the cab, and the driver was cursing a blue streak because you wouldn't move. Luckily, that cop who lives on the first floor came along. He dragged you out of the cab and carried you into the apartment. It was so embarrassing."

"Aw, damn, Adrienne. I'm sorry."

Adrienne looked at her wristwatch and grabbed her purse. "This is really serious, Mel. I'm getting tired of all this damn drinking. You better get it together." She left the apartment, slamming the door behind her.

Damn! The cop had carried him upstairs! Now Winsome would be watching his every move. Why couldn't Adrienne see that he just didn't have the energy to live respectably anymore?

Mel groaned and stared at the ceiling.

CHAPTER TEN

Pedestrians pushed and shoved a depressed Adrienne out of their way as she shuffled through the streets on her way to work. As usual, the briefcase that contained her lunch and a newspaper bumped against her leg, but she didn't bother to tuck it under her arm. What difference did it make if her pantyhose got ripped or not?

She ran into Sherry in the lobby.

"Talk about stormy Monday," Sherry observed. "You look like hell."

"Thanks," Adrienne said dully, removing her coat.

"That red suit is smashing, though!" Sherry smiled.

The elevator door opened with a *ping* and the two women pushed their way in along with half a dozen other people.

"My sister is flying in tonight from Los Angeles on business. It'll be great to see her even if it is just for two days," Sherry said.

The elevator door opened on the twenty-ninth floor, and the two women got out.

"What kind of work does she do?" Adrienne asked politely. She was furious with Mel, distrusted Sherry, and was in no mood for this casual office chitchat.

Sherry smiled broadly. "She's a fashion designer. If the phone rings and a woman asks for Sherry Green, it's for me. I don't want my sister to know that I still use Ingles as a last name."

Adrienne nodded without interest, and the two women entered unit 6 to start the day's work. At eleven, Adrienne's phone rang. It was her boss, Regina Belvedere.

"Adrienne, I need to see you right away." Regina's tone was crisp, and Adrienne dashed into her supervisor's office.

Regina Belvedere's slim, manicured hands were folded on the desk. Her eyebrows were knitted into a frown, and her eyes were cold. "I see you've gone out of your way to impress our new president."

"What?" Adrienne gasped.

"Sit down, Adrienne." It was an order. Adrienne sat. Regina leaned back in her chair, and her eyes turned to slits. "Sherry says that you two know each other from somewhere else and that you actually paid him a visit. Is that true?"

That heffa would say something, Adrienne thought, then told Regina about Lloyd's strange reaction at the staff meeting and their odd encounter in his office. "I've heard his voice somewhere before," she finished lamely.

Regina tapped a pencil against her cheek for several seconds before she spoke. "I believe you. Go back to your work, and I'll let you know if I hear anything else about the matter."

Adrienne was almost out the door when Regina spoke once more. "Think hard about where the two of you might have crossed paths before, and don't forget to tell me as soon as you remember. Okay?"

Adrienne nodded as she fled from the room, wondering why Lloyd Cooper's actions were so important to Regina. Gossip was rampant at Parton, Webster & Elliott, and as usual, Sherry Ingles was the ringleader. Sometimes it got so bad that the atmosphere felt more like a high school than a corporation. It was the one thing Adrienne hated about the firm.

Back at her desk, she stared into the small picture of her and Mel that rested in a heart-shaped frame. It had been taken during the first summer of their courtship. She smiled weakly. *Are we ever going to be as happy as we were when that picture was taken?* The grinning couple in the photo seemed to mock her as they embraced lovingly against the background of endless sea. Even the stuffed zebra she clutched in her arms, the one he had won for her on that Coney Island trip, seemed to know secretly of their fate, with its big pink sewn-on smile and lifeless button eyes.

Mel had proposed the following Christmas. He had appeared at her apartment unannounced. "I was just on my way out," she told him. "I'm going Christmas shopping."

"Wait, I'll go with you," he said. "We can walk down Fifth Avenue and go to Macy's."

"Macy's it is," she replied quietly.

Fifth Avenue was ablaze with lights. On both sides of the street, pedestrians hustled in and out of the expensive stores while taxicabs weaved in and out of traffic, trying to avoid getting caught up in a jam.

The store was crammed with blissful shoppers carrying parcels and choosing gifts. One department had a huge Nativity scene set up, with the baby Jesus in the manger surrounded by miniature statuettes of his mother and villagers. The whole display was festooned with holly, cranberries, nuts, tinsel, fruits, and dozens of ribbons.

Adrienne squeezed Mel's hand. "Isn't it beautiful?" she breathed.

But Mel wasn't looking at the Nativity scene. He was staring down at their hands, which were clasped together. "Yes, Adrienne," he murmured, "it's really beautiful."

Then he got down on one knee, pulled a ring from his pocket, and said, "I love you, Adrienne; please marry me."

The shoppers applauded. Adrienne was so surprised, she couldn't answer right away.

"Aw, come on, sweetheart. You can't turn me down in front of baby Jesus."

A woman in the crowd said, "This is just so romantic."

Adrienne said yes.

Adrienne put her head in her hands and rubbed her eyes gently to catch the tears that were beginning to form. Now her marriage was troubled, and she had a problem at work, too. Who the hell was Lloyd Cooper and why was he acting so strangely?

And on top of it all, she still wondered what had really happened to Mel the night before.

When she came back from lunch, there was a message on her desk to call Lloyd Cooper. She was not in the mood for more intrigue. She decided to go see the president instead of calling. When she appeared in front of his secretary's desk, Adrienne's face was flushed. A few strands of hair had come loose from her French roll and flew lightly around her face.

"Is Mr. Cooper available?"

Sally Gomez pressed a button on the intercom and listened for a second. "Yes. He'll see you right away."

Adrienne stalked past her without a thank-you and turned the knob on Lloyd Cooper's door. He stood up, came toward her with a welcoming smile, and motioned Adrienne into the visitor's chair. Her courage started to wane as she sank into the plush seat. Who did she think she was, barging into an executive's office just because she was at odds with her husband? Adrienne shrank further into the seat.

"Did you want to speak to me, Mr. Cooper?" she asked meekly.

Lloyd Cooper grinned at her, his cheeks dimpling, but when she didn't smile back, he cleared his throat.

"I'm sorry that our last meeting was interrupted and that it has taken me so long to get back to you." His voice softened. "It's really good to see you again, Adrienne. My God, it's been over seventeen years!"

Adrienne felt bad about not remembering this man who was so obviously happy to see her, but she had to tell the truth before the situation became embarrassing. "That's really nice to hear, Mr. Cooper, but do you mind telling me where we crossed paths all those years ago?"

He gave her a teasing smile. "The High School for Performing Arts. We were really tight during senior year. Why don't I go find us some coffee? Think about graduation day while I'm gone, all right?"

He left the room without waiting for an answer.

Adrienne relaxed. She couldn't remember any boy named Lloyd Cooper, especially not one as fine as him, but it had certainly been an unforgettable year.

Senior year for the High School for Peforming Arts Class of

1982 got off to a bad start when the beloved typing teacher dropped dead from a heart attack, in the classroom, right in front of thirty-five students who were so busy typing *The quick brown fox jumped over the lazy dog* that they didn't even hear the body hit the floor.

Then, in December, a group of boys from another school crashed the Christmas dance. When the resulting melee was over, three students had to be hospitalized for various injuries. Thankfully, after the New Year, the streak of bad luck came to an end. The students focused on college applications or talked about becoming famous. Adrienne had visions of a seven-figure music contract and platinum albums, the tokens of a successful recording career. Spring brought excitement over the upcoming senior prom and graduation; fall offered the first sample of reality.

Adrienne heard a bumping sound at the door. She shook her head to clear the memories and opened it. Lloyd was holding a silver tray. There were two cups, spoons, a pitcher, and a small jug of cream. "I had to kick the door," he said, smiling. "My hands are full, and Sally is away from her desk."

Adrienne helped him arrange the items on a side table and unwrapped two pastry buns that were in a covered dish. "This is really nice," she said shyly, forgetting that she had finished lunch only a short time earlier.

They each took a cup of coffee and a pastry. He met her eyes as they both sat back down. "So, do you remember me now?"

Adrienne took a sip of her coffee, trying not to let his watchful eyes unsettle her. "A lot of things happened to me during senior year, Mr. Cooper. I'm sorry, but you're going to have to refresh my memory."

"'The top bunk is mine, but Noney won't mind if we sit on hers,'" he whispered without taking his eyes off her face.

Adrienne gasped, gripping her mug. Only she and LaMar Jenkins were in the room when that sentence was uttered more than a decade ago.

"When I first saw you that morning in the conference room, I thought my mind was playing tricks on me." Lloyd said gently.

Adrienne blinked in confusion. "What do you mean?"

He laughed. "Didn't think old LaMar Jenkins would make anything of himself, did you?"

* * *

The graduation ceremony was held on a Friday morning. Daddy, who was a subway conductor and never really dressed up, was struggling with his tie. Mama ignored his loud swearing as she set the table for a breakfast that everyone was too excited to eat. From her bedroom, Adrienne heard the doorbell ring and then her Mama's surprised greetings.

"Adrienne! LaMar is here!" Mama shouted.

Adrienne gave her hair a final pat and rushed toward the front door.

Daddy sighed grumpily. "Did he bring his parents for breakfast with him?"

Adrienne shushed him. "Stop. He might here you. LaMar doesn't really have parents."

Her daddy frowned. "I didn't know that. Well, go on out there and see what the boy wants."

LaMar looked so sad standing in the foyer, stuffed into a frayed suit that was way too small, that even her daddy stopped yelling and struggling with the tie.

"Hey, LaMar," he sad gruffly and gave the grossly underweight boy who was a head taller than him a hearty slap on the back.

"Good morning," LaMar answered, but his eyes were glued to Adrienne, who was coming toward him dressed in a white sheath dress with matching pumps.

"Where are your sisters?" Mama asked.

LaMar straightened his shoulders and held his head high. "My family couldn't make it. I'm by myself. Can I ride along with y'all?"

Mama and Daddy exchanged a puzzled glance. What kind of people stayed home from a high school graduation when their kin was valedictorian?

"Sure, son," Adrienne's daddy answered. After all, if LaMar hadn't tutored Adrienne in math for the past year, she might not be graduating at all, and if she did math half as well as she sang, she might not have needed him.

Breakfast was a pleasant affair even though Dan, who was only twelve years old at the time, kept complaining about having to wear a tie, and pulling at it until Mama slapped him on the hand to make him stop.

After the ceremonies, the family posed for pictures and then headed to Howard Johnson's restaurant for lunch. No matter how much Mama and Adrienne begged LaMar to come, he resisted. "Sorry, I have to get home to Brooklyn. Everybody will be waiting for me."

Adrienne knew that LaMar's pride would not let him accept the free lunch, and he certainly had no money to chip in. He pulled Adrienne away from the group to talk privately before he left.

"Look, I know you don't need me anymore," LaMar said. "But I'd like us to stay friends. Can I come see you tomorrow?"

"Sure, you can," Adrienne said warmly.

Adrienne was home alone the next day when LaMar dropped by. When she opened the door, he stumbled in looking distraught. Adrienne led him into the living room and sat beside him on the sofa.

"What's the matter, LaMar?"

"I tried to jump the turnstile to get on the train, but I stumbled and fell down. I almost got arrested for it, but the cop was nice. He just told me not to do it again. It was stupid. Noney has enough problems right now without me getting into trouble. I feel so sorry for her."

Adrienne patted his hand. "Don't worry, LaMar. One day you'll have plenty of money and you can buy your sister a great big house." She smiled widely, hoping her words would chase away the bleak look in his eyes.

"You don't understand. After next week, I won't have any sisters. Noney said some social workers came snooping around yesterday. She told them our Mama was out shopping, but they've heard that before. If Mama isn't there Monday when they come back, they're gonna take my little sisters and me away to God knows where."

Adrienne was confused. "But you're grown and headed for college. It doesn't make sense."

He shrugged helplessly. "Noney is the only one they can't touch. I won't be eighteen until the second week in January. They'll put me in a group home until then. When Noney told me all this, I just had to get out of the house. I started walking to Manhattan, but I got tired. That's when I tried to jump the turnstile."

Adrienne was silent. LaMar in a group home! This was awful. Something had to be done. She wondered if her parents could give LaMar some advice or, even better, take him in. But what about his sisters? They were the light of his life. Adrienne had seen pictures of the girls. Noney was nineteen, Denise twelve, Pam eleven, Annie nine and the baby, Brenda was seven. None of them had the same father. Their mother was a drug addict who had run off with her current lover and left them almost three years ago. Since then, the Jenkins children had kept to themselves, afraid that if any adults found out the truth about their home life, they would be forced to separate. Only Adrienne, and LaMar's landlord, an elderly woman with a kind heart, knew their secret.

"How did this happen?" Adrienne asked tearfully.

"Brenda did it. She said something to a teacher yesterday about Noney crying cuz she didn't sell enough reefer and was worried about the rent money."

Adrienne started hugging him, but he pulled away. There was a strange look in his eyes. "Adrienne, I can't do nothin' for them, and I'm the man of the house." He wiped a sleeve over his eyes.

Adrienne patted him on the back. "Let's get out of here, LaMar. My parents and little brother will be back soon, and I know you don't want them to see you like this."

LaMar had a lot of pride. He stood up quickly. "No, I don't. I'll call you when I can."

Adrienne shook her head. "I'm going with you."

"Where?" he asked, throwing up his hands.

"To your house," she said firmly. "I'll talk to Noney, and maybe she and I can figure this thing out. There must be something we can do."

"I can't let you see my house, Adrienne."

"Don't be silly, LaMar. I'm your best friend." After the words came out, Adrienne realized they were true. LaMar had stopped being just a math tutor a long time ago. She had actually become quite fond of him over the past few months and often shared her girlish hopes and dreams with him while he hung on her every word.

"I'm going to get my graduation money and take it with me," she declared, and ran into the bedroom to get it.

Grimly, the two young people set out for LaMar's home in Brooklyn. Adrienne blinked back tears when Noney let them in. She was a tired-looking girl who looked Adrienne up and down as though she hadn't seen clothes that weren't ragged in a long time. Her manner was almost shy as she said hello and forced "the brood," as she called her sisters, to do the same.

There was no sofa. "The springs busted a long time ago," a solemn Annie told Adrienne, "so we threw it out in the alley."

It was a three-bedroom apartment. Noney and LaMar shared one of the bedrooms. LaMar took Adrienne into that room, which was neat and clean and furnished with various odds and ends that Adrienne guessed had been scavenged from Dumpsters. The only whole piece of furniture was a bunk bed.

"The top bunk is mine," LaMar said, "but Noney won't mind if we sit on hers."

Adrienne knew that even though LaMar had refused the free graduation lunch offered by her parents, he would never be self-ish enough to turn away a gift for his sisters. So they sat on the lower bunk. "Call Noney in here and give her this," Adrienne said. She opened her purse and removed a $50 bill, which she pressed into LaMar's hand. "They all look hungry. Tell her to buy some food. How can you think straight if you're hungry?"

LaMar kissed her on the cheek. "I'll be right back."

Adrienne heard whispered conversation, a lot of scampering around, and then LaMar came back. "They all went with her to the grocery store," he said.

Adrienne couldn't help the emotion that welled up inside her chest and rose up to close her throat. She had never known just how bad LaMar's home situation was. She leaned on his shoulder and cried for him. When his tears joined hers, they lay down on the bed. One kiss led to another, and when his bony fingers undid the buttons on her blouse, she did not protest. When his hand cupped her breast, she didn't have the heart to let him down. He kissed her deeply and unzipped her pants. Consumed with pity for the one person in the world who knew her deepest secrets, she let him undress her. He knew that it was Adrienne's first time and tried to be gentle, but he was inexperienced, too, and he hurt her more than was necessary.

That night Adrienne told her parents the whole sad story of LaMar and his family. "Please, Mama, can he stay here until his birthday in January? It's only seven months away," Adrienne begged.

Surprisingly, they agreed. "The group home will only destroy a good kid," her daddy said.

Since LaMar didn't have a phone, Adrienne couldn't call him that Saturday night to tell him the good news.

On Sunday morning, the Montgomery family piled into the car and went to Brooklyn. The door to the Jenkins apartment was standing open. The elderly landlord was just coming out of it. Something about the woman's expression made Adrienne clutch at her chest. "I'm looking for LaMar," she blurted out.

The old woman sighed sadly, and her eyes filled with tears. "The city paid them a surprise visit. A bunch of social workers and cops came and got 'em. I don't know where dey gone." The old woman had hunched her shoulders and shuffled back across the hall.

* * *

Adrienne's jaw dropped as the full weight of what Lloyd Cooper was saying to her impacted her brain. Her legs felt wooden, and a feeling of dread coursed through her body as his eyes bored into hers.

"Close your mouth, girl, and stop staring."

"It isn't possible. I don't believe it. How . . . ?"

"How did I become this gorgeous specimen of a man?" Lloyd's voice was mocking, with a slightly bitter undertone.

Adrienne massaged her temples. She looked at him closely, trying to find in the handsome, talented, and confident man who sat before her a trace of the neglected teenage boy with the thick glasses, terrible acne, and shoulders that always appeared slumped with defeat.

"You can't be Lamar Jenkins," she protested. "Things like this just don't happen in real life. It can't be true," she said.

His eyes, which begged for understanding, assured her that it was.

It was too much. Adrienne was not sure whether to scream, run, or both. Her eyes widened. She shook her head as her stomach tightened. "I don't believe that you're LaMar Jenkins."

"You're right. I'm not LaMar Jenkins. Not anymore. It's a long story, Adrienne."

When Adrienne didn't respond, he shoved his hands in his pockets and sighed. "I only look different on the outside. Inside, I'm still the same person that you knew so many years ago."

"Then why did you change your name?" she whispered hoarsely.

"I'll tell you that and a lot of other things when the time is right. You know, we have a lot of catching up to do, Adrienne, but not here at work."

"Really?" Adrienne asked, incredulous. "I think when you sleep with a woman and don't pick up the phone to call her for the next seventeen years, she is entitled to an explanation as soon as you run into him." Adrienne couldn't keep the sarcasm and hurt from spilling out of her voice. She felt overcome by the memories.

Lloyd recoiled as though someone had socked him in the jaw. "Oh, no, Adrienne! It wasn't like that. Jesus!" he said, staring at her intently. "Is that what you've been thinking all these years?" He knelt in front of her chair. "Adrienne, I had to leave. Don't you remember? I had to spend time in a group home until I turned eighteen. You didn't know me then, but I was a very angry, bitter young man after my experiences there. But I never forgot your kindness all those years ago, never. A lot of times it was the memory of you and your family that kept me going."

"Oh, LaMar!" Adrienne said sadly.

He reached up and patted her shoulder. "Now I've upset you, and I didn't mean to." His voice grew brighter. "I'm so very happy that our paths have crossed again."

Adrienne managed a bewildered smile. "I'm glad to see you, too." *I guess,* she thought.

And then they hugged.

Adrienne tried to reconcile the man who now held her with the boy he had once been. Things at PW&E had certainly grown more interesting now that the new president had arrived.

PART TWO

QUICKSAND

CHAPTER ELEVEN

Mel was driving the M15 bus going east across 125th Street. He braked to a stop in front of the Grant Housing Projects on Amsterdam Avenue and sighed as he lowered the steps for two blue-haired old ladies. One of them had a cane, but instead of paying attention to where she was going, she busily chatted to the other. The cane slipped, and she fell slightly forward. Mel helped her into a seat and was rewarded with a smile. The other woman settled in next to her, and Mel was back on the road again, wondering if his mother would have needed a cane in her old age. It was something he would never know. At the next stop, three teenage girls got on carrying a radio that was blaring. The lyrics were filled with obscenities.

"Turn it off!" Mel said as they dipped their Metro Cards into the slot.

One of them sucked her teeth. The other rolled her eyes.

"I'm not turnin' my radio off," said the second one.

"You will or get off the bus," answered Mel.

"You can't do that," said the first one. "We already paid."

They walked toward the back of the bus, the music still booming. Mel shut the engine off and spoke to his passengers over the loudspeaker. "We will sit here until either that radio is turned off or a police car pulls up to find out why I'm not moving." He pulled out a newspaper and pretended to read. Within seconds, hot angry words flew at the girls from the impatient passengers. A male voice shouted, "Don't y'all know today is Valentine's Day? If I'm late gettin' to my woman over on Fifth Avenue, somebody's ass is mine!"

Suddenly there was no more music. Mel grinned and turned the ignition. The ride was smooth until he hit Lenox Avenue. A long line of people was waiting for the bus, and he sighed as they filed on. Soon there would be standing room only. A woman got on pushing two small girls ahead of her. When she looked up to put her money in the slot, her eyes met Mel's. He gulped and wished he could make himself invisible.

"Hi, Lillian. Are those your kids?"

"Yes, they are," she replied, and she just stood there staring at him. The wounded expression made him wince.

"I'm sorry," he said simply.

Lillian shot him a look that was an odd combination of hate and pride, shooed the kids toward the back, and followed them without saying a word.

Lillian must have gotten off the bus through the back door, because Mel didn't see her leave. But she was one of the two people on his mind when he clocked out at the terminal and headed home. How was he going to play cards at Debra's house as long as Big Boy was still mad at him? What if Lillian showed up?

He made a quick stop at Circuit City for the television set. They offered delivery within twenty-four hours, but Mel lugged the nine-teen-inch TV home by cab and set it up in the bedroom, hoping that Adrienne would forgive his behavior from the night before.

Mel dashed back out of the house for food and flowers. There wasn't much time. Adrienne would be home in two hours. A broad smile crossed Mel's face as he shoved the apartment door open with his shoulder. His hands were filled with bags. He had purchased a dozen pink roses, a bottle of champagne, two red candles, cold shrimp, honey barbecue chicken, a container of potato salad, and a chocolate layer cake for dessert. He couldn't wait to see the look on Adrienne's face when she got home and saw the spread set up in the living room. He took a quick shower and changed into a pair of red sweatpants and a matching T-shirt.

After laying out the food on the coffee table, he turned out the living room lights and sat down to relax and wait for Adrienne.

He nervously checked the freezer to make sure the champagne and glasses were chilling properly before he sat down on the couch, anxiously waiting for his wife to put the key in the door. A few minutes went by, and then he heard the sound of her keys jingling. He rushed to greet her.

"Happy Valentine's Day, baby," Mel drawled as he grabbed Adrienne tenderly around the waist. Smiling, he took her by the hand and led her toward the living room.

He switched on the light. "Take a look around, baby!"

Adrienne took off her red blazer and laid it over the sofa as she eased her way toward the romantic dinner Mel had prepared for her. "This is so sweet, honey. How thoughtful of you. Very nice," she said absently while strolling into the bedroom.

Very nice? Mel thought angrily. After all the work he had put into this evening to make it perfect, and the best she could do was "very nice"? Feeling foolish and disappointed, he followed her into the bedroom. She was taking off her work clothes and humming softly to herself. It took a moment for her to realize he was standing in the doorway. He didn't recognize the tune.

"Are you going to eat this food?" he asked stiffly.

Adrienne glanced at the open door leading to the living room. "Sure. Let me take a shower first." She bent over and slipped out of her shoes.

"Why are you acting so cold?"

She pulled herself together and gave him a tremulous smile. "I'm sorry I acted so crabby when I came through the door. I was thinking about the new president at work. Believe me, it is one strange story."

"Well, it must be something for you to turn down all this." Mel pulled her close to his chest, his hands resting on her curvy hips. "Why don't you tell me about it tomorrow?"

She gave him a sexy smile and wrapped her arms around his neck. Mel smelled like warm cinnamon. "Okay, baby. Why don't you tell me what you have in mind?"

Mel swept her up and carried her to the bed. They could heat up the food later.

CHAPTER TWELVE

Adrienne and Dan had spent their early years in the Crown Heights section of Brooklyn. However, when Adrienne was entering junior high, drugs took over the street. Their father soon moved his family to Manhattan. He made good money as a subway conductor, but in order to afford the rent on the two-bedroom apartment he found on Tenth Avenue and Fiftieth Street, he had to work double overtime. The family rarely saw him after they moved. He was always just getting in from work or leaving to go to work.

Since their mother was always at home or at the school doing volunteer work for the PTA, Adrienne and Dan couldn't get away with much. No attending after-school centers, going to hooky parties, smoking reefer, or cutting class for the Montgomery kids. As a result, they were well mannered and earned excellent grades. When it was time for high school, Adrienne auditioned for the High School for Performing Arts and was accepted.

As he grew older, their father was still always working. When he was around he managed only to frighten Dan with his constant demands that he "straighten up and act like a man." Mama smothered and fussed over her son as if he were made of glass. It was only with Adrienne that Dan could relax and be himself, until he met Charlene.

*   *   *

Adrienne rang Dan's bell three times. There was no response, and she was about to leave when her brother finally answered the intercom. "It's me, Adrienne." As Adrienne rode the elevator upstairs, she wondered if she had interrupted her brother and Charlene in bed, even though it was one on a Saturday afternoon.

Dan came to the door, and Adrienne peeked anxiously over her shoulder. "Is Charlene here?"

Dan laughed and stood aside to let Adrienne pass. "Yes. She is in the bedroom, on the phone with the cable company. They have us on hold, and we're afraid to get off. You know how long it takes to get through to them."

Adrienne shivered as she unbuttoned her coat. "Dag, it's windy out there." She tossed her coat and pocketbook onto the coffee table and flopped down onto the sofa. Dan excused himself, went into the kitchen, and picked up the extension. For the next few minutes, he and Charlene took turns arguing with a cable representative over the bill for over three hundred dollars that they had received. Adrienne didn't pay attention to the details.

There were two big pots on the coffee table. One was filled with fat green beans and the other was for the discarded ends. Adrienne sat rubbing her hands together to warm them until Dan and Charlene got off the phone.

Dan finally came back and sat cross-legged on the floor. Charlene joined them. She gave Adrienne a hug. "It's about time you came to see me. I'll do your hair as soon as I get these beans cooking on the stove. Why don't you help me?" Charlene flopped down on the sofa beside her sister-in-law and the two women started in on the beans.

Dan said. "You look like you're about to burst, Adrienne. What's up?"

So Adrienne told Dan the Lloyd Cooper story. When she finished talking, his mouth was hanging open in astonishment.

The three lapsed into silence for a moment, and then Adrienne kicked off her shoes and went to the kitchen in her sweat socks. She opened the refrigerator. "Let's see, it's too early for a beer." She took out some crackers and a can of soda. "LaMar looks great, and he was thrilled to run into me again."

Dan laughed. "Why any man would remember you past fifteen seconds is beyond me."

Adrienne stuck her tongue out at him. "Cut the little-brother jokes, Dan. Anyway, I can't think about it anymore. That's how I almost spoiled a nice surprise that Mel put together for me last night. I had Lloyd on the brain when I walked through the front door."

Dan said, "I can't wait to see LaMar. He was such a wuss. Always sitting at the kitchen table mooning after you."

Adrienne blushed. "Will you forget about Lloyd for a minute? I have a real problem."

"There's *more* drama going on in your life?" Charlene asked incredulously.

Adrienne sighed. "Yeah." She told them about Mel, the TV set, and the story he had given her about being mugged.

"I knew there was something wrong with Mel," Charlene said.

"You were right about Mel's drinking," Adrienne said softly. "I think it is out of control, but he doesn't even realize it."

Charlene shook her head sadly. "Poor Mel."

Adrienne could feel tears welling up in her eyes. "Poor Mel? What about me? I can sense Delilah's presence sometimes."

"I'm sure Mel does, too, Adrienne," Charlene replied.

But Adrienne wasn't so sure. She wondered if Mel thought about Delilah as much as she did.

Charlene patted her on the back. "Buck up, honey. Remember, you're a former prom queen. Blink back those tears and smile."

Adrienne was embarrassed by the praise. "Girl, please. When I was in show business, I met a whole bunch of former prom queens. I wasn't special anymore. Plus, they were a whole lot tougher and scrappier than me. I guess that's why I didn't make it."

Dan changed the subject. "Did Mel report the mugging?"

"I don't believe Mel was mugged at all, but since I can't get a handle on what else might have happened, I have to leave it alone."

Charlene smiled at her husband and pointed at him with a long string bean. "Dan better not try no shit like that."

Adrienne poked Charlene in the ribs. "Husbands and wives have always toughed it out in our family. We're a loyal bunch, so you're stuck with Dan."

Charlene sucked her teeth. "Every clan has a divorce somewhere on the family tree."

Adrienne shook her head. "Not on my mother or father's side."

"Whatever. Dan is a good man, and he better stay that way or we'll end up in the Jordan history books as the first couple to throw in the towel."

"Mel had the place looking real nice last night; there were flowers and good food. So tonight Mel and I are going to Nell's. My treat."

Dan laughed. "Nell's is a nightclub for young people. It's hard to picture you and Mel out on the dance floor rocking to hip-hop music."

"Tonight they're playing old school jams. So we'll be okay."

"I hope you have a good time," Dan said.

Adrienne rubbed her hands together nervously. "We're going to dance, drink, and have a good time. Everything is going to be perfect."

*   *   *

The evening was far from perfect. The trouble started right after dinner. Mel washed the dishes and lay down on the bed. He used the remote to click on the TV. "I'm gonna watch the game," he said.

Adrienne could see that he was in a lousy mood, so she tried to cheer him up. She tapped him lightly on the leg. "Aren't you going to iron your clothes first, honey?"

He sighed, not bothering to hide his irritation. "I'm not in the mood to go dancing."

Adrienne spoke softly. "We need to have as much fun as we can, Mel."

The look on her face stopped him from asking why. She was trying to look cheerful, but he could see the desperation in her eyes. Adrienne never asked much of him, and for the most part, she let him do what he wanted to do. If going out tonight would make her feel a little better about herself, well, he guessed he could manage it. But Mel still didn't feel like dressing up, and bumping and grinding around a bunch of young bloods barely old enough to remember "old school" wasn't his idea of fun. He clicked the TV off before the game started and he could change his mind. "I hope this DJ plays some good music," he said as he dragged himself over to the ironing board while Adrienne dressed.

By eleven, she was looking good in a clingy white skirt that fell right above her knees, accenting her long legs. She wore a sheer white blouse with a white tube top underneath, silver jewelry, and matching heels. Adrienne knew she looked good, and Mel's approving glance confirmed her opinion.

Mel was decked out in a pair of creased dark-gray slacks and a light-gray silk shirt. He refused to put on a tie. "It's too uncomfortable," he grumbled.

Adrienne wore her evening cape, and Mel put on his black dress coat.

They took a cab down to Fourteenth Street. Nell's was packed. They worked their way through the crowd and waited at the bar until two seats became available. Adrienne's heart was heavy; Mel hadn't said a word since they left the house. She put on a brave smile and squeezed his hand. He responded by ordering drinks for both of them and tapping his foot to the music as he turned to watch the well dressed men and women who were gyrating to Will Smith's "Getting Jiggy Wit It."

"I thought you said this was old-school dance night," Mel grumbled.

"It starts in a few minutes, Mel. Please be patient."

"Well, I hope it starts soon, 'cause this music 'bout to get on my nerves."

Adrienne didn't answer. When the drinks arrived, Mel swiveled around to watch the dancers and sipped his rum and Coke with a grimace on his face.

Adrienne drank her sloe gin fizz quickly and slid down from the barstool. "I want to dance," she said flatly.

They danced two songs before the disc jockey played a slow jam. It was a real old tune called "Sideshow" by a group called Blue Magic. Mel held Adrienne close. "This song brings back a whole lot of memories," he murmured.

Adrienne sniffed. They hadn't known each other when "Sideshow" was a hit song, so he was obviously thinking of someone else.

When the song ended, Mel's expression was unreadable.

"Who are you thinking about?" Adrienne demanded.

"It's not a 'who,'" he answered. "I was remembering a time when my life was carefree and happy."

They were poised at the edge of the dance floor when Mel spoke. Adrienne felt tears well up, but she blinked them back and squared her shoulders. "Perhaps you'll be happy again someday, but right now I want to go home."

"I'm sorry," he replied. "I didn't mean that the way it sounded."

"Really? Well, it sounded like you meant it," Adrienne said, staring at him under the strobe lights. "You know, I don't understand you. If you really didn't want to go dancing with me, you could have stayed your ass at home."

"Look, Adrienne," Mel said, raising his voice. "I told you from the get-go that I didn't feel like going, but you was the one standing there looking pitiful. I told you I didn't mean it that way, and you need to let it rest."

"I'll let it rest, all right," Adrienne said, pulling her purse under her arm. She tipped the bartender and started heading for the door. Angry, Mel followed behind her, weaving through the crowd of dancers who were swaying blissfully to the music.

When they pushed past the line of couples still waiting to get into the club, Adrienne stood on the sidewalk, forcing back the tears. Mel wouldn't even look at her. He stood in the street and held his arm out, signaling a cab.

The cab ride home was silent, and that night, Mel and Adrienne slept back to back.

CHAPTER THIRTEEN

Mel was lying on his back with the radio playing softly on the nightstand beside him. His hands were folded behind his head as he stared at the ceiling. Adrienne had questioned him again about the "mugging," and he had lied his ass off. But now that the episode was over, he was really scared. He had meant it when he vowed to leave drugs alone. Yet once he and Debra's girlfriends had finished off the liquor, the craving for cocaine had been intense. Had he developed a drug problem during the horrible months after the fire? Mel had known a lot of dudes who had believed it when they said, "I can stop whenever I want to." Most of them were either dead or in jail. He shivered even though the bedroom was warm. A phone call interrupted his gloomy reverie.

"Wassup, little brother?" Debra asked playfully.

"Not a hell of a lot. Adrienne just went to work. I'm gonna go back to sleep. Gotta be at work at four."

"When you comin' to see me?"

"I dunno," he muttered. "I doan want no shit with your old man, and it seems like he's always at your house these days."

"I see. Well, stop by the bar, then. Okay?"

"Sounds good."

After they hung up, Mel started to call Adrienne at work just to chat but then changed his mind. She would pick up on his gloomy mood, and it might ruin her day. He turned over, went back to sleep, and sank into a familiar dream.

*   *   *

The welcome home party was jumping, and the champagne flowed like water. Adrienne's family—Aunt Patsy, Aunt Clarice, and Aunt Ellie, who had all come up from Dietsville to celebrate—mixed, stirred, fried, and laughed in the kitchen as they kept the chicken, greens, and macaroni coming. Debra and her friends were everywhere dancing and shouting over the loud music that boomed over the Jordans' new sound system.

Neighbors from Adrienne's old building came with their grandchildren, and even her former roommates showed up. Everyone under fifty and over thirty clapped and sang along with the Gap Band's "Burn Rubber" as those too old or too young to remember the noisy song mumbled among themselves in disapproval.

Mel and Debra drank cup after cup of rum and Coke as they passed out handfuls of pink-ribboned cigars to celebrate Delilah's birth. The infant didn't let the party disturb her. Closed off in her parents' room, she slept quietly in a white, lace-covered bassinet that her grandma had bought her, fists held tightly against her cheeks.

Adrienne, still a little tired from Delilah's birth the week before, sat in the living room watching everyone have a good time. There was a strained smile on her face as she waited patiently for the celebration to end. Then the screams rose in Mel's ears. Higher and higher they became, until he found himself looking into a singed bassinet to find nothing but ashes where his angel had once slept. The guests, who had been wearing party clothes, were suddenly draped in black. They swarmed around him with their sorry, tear-streaked faces. A white man sprang up with a shovel in his hand, and everyone was transported to Delilah's gravesite, where the man proceeded to dig the hole that would put Mel's baby in the ground forever. Rain suddenly poured out of the sky, drenching everyone with such force that Delilah's charred little lips popped out of her mouth and landed on the ground next to Mel's foot.

*   *   *

Mel sat up shaking from the nightmare, his face damp with perspiration and tears.

CHAPTER FOURTEEN

Adrienne had just booted up her computer and started on the day's work when her phone rang.

"Media Services," she said crisply.

"Hi, Adrienne. How are you?"

It was Lloyd Cooper. Adrienne's heart skipped, but she kept her composure. "I'm fine. And you?"

He sighed. "I'm in the midst of an apartment hunt, and believe me, it isn't fun at all."

"I know exactly what you mean. It took weeks for me to find something decent in Manhattan. At least you'll get help from the company."

"That's true," Lloyd agreed. "Every week I get a list of ten empty spaces that sound just perfect. I make time in my schedule to view the place and it turns out to be either a dump or a cubbyhole."

"What are you looking for?"

He paused. "I want a three-bedroom duplex on the Upper East Side of Manhattan, with a doorman."

"Where are you living in the meantime?"

"At the Parker Meridien Hotel."

"Not bad."

"Parton, Webster will pay for the suite for another month or two, but I don't want the search to take that long. I'm practically living out of a suitcase, and I miss my belongings. They're all in storage back in Chicago."

"I'm sure you'll find something soon."

"I'm sorry that I made such a mess out of our first meeting." Lloyd said quietly.

Adrienne could hear phones ringing around her, feet scurrying up and down the hall, peals of laughter, and the whir of the printer as it spewed out documents. But none of these ordinary office sounds could distract her from the knowledge that Sherry Ingles had stopped typing and was eavesdropping on her conversation.

"It was quite a shock, but I'm all right now."

"All right enough to have lunch with me today?" he asked.

"Ah, sure," she said cautiously.

"How about one o'clock at the Four Seasons?"

"That'll do," Adrienne answered casually.

"Great. I'll meet you there. We could walk over together but I don't want to start tongues wagging. Okay?"

"Okay. Bye."

For the rest of the morning, she worked like a woman on automatic pilot. There were so many unanswered questions. Where were LaMar's sisters? How did he end up in Chicago? Was he married? Did he have any kids? When Regina or Sherry tried to make conversation with her, all they received in return was a blank stare and a monosyllabic answer to their remarks. After a while, they left her alone.

Adrienne turned heads as she entered the restaurant. Lloyd stood up until she was seated.

"How was your morning?" he asked, sitting down.

"Pretty good. Yours?"

"Great. I just saw a terrific apartment this morning. It's not a rental, though. I'll have to buy it."

Adrienne wanted to ask what the cost was, but that would have been rude. "Congratulations!"

"Thanks. Hotel life just does not agree with me. The place I found is on East Seventy-seventh Street. It's a three-bedroom duplex with a den, eat-in kitchen, and formal dining room. I'll have to do a lot of business entertaining, so it's just perfect."

Adrienne didn't know what to say, so she took a sip of her water and then gazed at him thoughtfully. "Do you mind if I ask you a few questions?"

Lloyd signaled a waiter and turned back to face her. "Let's order lunch first. Are you in a hurry?"

"I don't mind so long as you give me a late pass when we get back to work."

He chuckled. "After lunch, I have a meeting across town, but I'll write the pass on a napkin and you can present it to Regina Belvedere with my apologies."

"That should go over well," Adrienne said dryly.

"If she gives you a problem, let me know."

A pale, thin young waiter eagerly approached the table clutching his pad.

"Welcome to the Four Seasons; may I take your order, please?" he asked with practiced enthusiasm.

"What would you like?" Lloyd asked, examining the single-card lunch menu.

"I'm not sure; how about the salmon?"

"Excellent choice. But then, you always had good taste. I'll have a steak, medium rare, and a Caesar salad."

Adrienne blushed and nervously cleared her throat as she passed the waiter her menu.

Lloyd chuckled. "I'll have a cranberry juice with seltzer."

"The same for me."

The waiter flashed another winning smile. "I'll be back in a moment with your drinks."

Lloyd placed the card down and smiled.

An uncomfortable silence fell between them. "Let's play a game," she finally said.

He cocked his head to one side and stared at her. "What kind of game?"

"Let's see if we can fill in a little of the seventeen-year gap since we've seen each other."

He agreed. "Great idea. I want to know all about your life, and

I'm sure you have a million questions for me. So, we each get to ask three questions. First you, then me, and so on. Okay?"

Adrienne's stomach tightened. There was no way she was going to talk about Delilah. "I'll go first," she said cheerfully.

"Okay."

"How is Noney, and the rest of your sisters?"

His face looked pained. "I don't know, Adrienne."

"You haven't found them yet?" Adrienne asked, astonished. "Have you thought about hiring a private detective to find them?"

He hesitated. "Yes, but there is something very important to consider before I could take such a step."

Adrienne wondered what could be more important in life than finding your family, but Lloyd looked so upset that she decided not to pursue the subject. "Your turn."

"All right. Tell me why you opted for corporate life instead of the bright lights of stardom."

Adrienne shook her head. That would take more than a lunch date to explain. She still couldn't explain it to herself. "I didn't decide on corporate life," she began. "I tried to make it as a singer and failed. Corporate life seemed like the most sensible alternative."

The waiter arrived with their drinks, and they sipped quietly for a few moments before Lloyd wiped his mouth delicately. "Hmmm," Lloyd said, "I'm surprised."

"Surprised about what?" Adrienne asked, intrigued.

"You. It's just that it's not like you to give up." Adrienne didn't respond. "I remember when I was tutoring you in math. You didn't let anything stop you, no matter how hard or difficult it was to you. You were focused. And optimistic. That's what I liked most about you. And your beauty."

"Seventeen years is a long time to try anything," Adrienne said, blushing.

"Is it?" Lloyd stared at her, his brown eyes seeming to stroke her skin. Adrienne shifted in her seat.

"I believe the ball is in your court."

"Okay." She thought for a moment. "What really happened that last weekend?"

After a strained silence, a silence filled with dread and desire, Lloyd began to speak.

"On the morning after graduation, I left the bedroom that I shared with my older sister Noney and went into the kitchen. Noney was toasting bread and trying to make sure that each slice received a scrap of butter, since it was almost gone and there was no money to buy more. She also had a pot of water boiling with our last three teabags in it. Breakfast for the brood is what she called the meal."

Lloyd smiled bitterly before continuing. Adrienne lowered her eyes. "Poor Noney," she said. Lloyd nodded in agreement.

"Noney's hands were shaking as she apologized to me because she and the rest of the brood had missed my graduation. There wasn't enough carfare, you see. I comforted her and went to get my other sisters in order. They were fighting over who would get to use the bathroom first. I barked out orders at them until they were all washed and sitting at the kitchen table. I kept watching Noney as she ate, wondering why her hands were shaking and why her face looked even sadder than usual. After cleaning up the kitchen for her, I made the younger children go outside so I could find out what was going on."

Lloyd took a deep breath. Adrienne sat very still.

"The news stunned me. Unless we could produce a Mother within forty-eight hours, the authorities were going to step in and split us up. Worse, Noney and Pam were both in the early stages of pregnancy." Adrienne's eyes widened at this news. They were both so young—and alone. "I was suddenly sick and tired of the whole lot of them. I felt a sudden, violent hatred for my promiscuous mother. I had to get out of the house. Without saying another word to Noney, I set out to walk to your house in Manhattan."

His lips went down at the corners and his face creased into a frown. When he spoke again it was through clenched teeth. "I hated it when you insisted on returning home with me. For years, I remembered the look of shock and disgust on your face when you saw my living conditions. It stripped me of the last of my pride. When you gave me the money to buy food, I wanted to toss it back in your lap, but that would mean no food for the rest of the weekend, and I couldn't do that to my sisters. Especially since two of them were pregnant. So I took it."

The waiter came to the table with their food, but by that time Adrienne's appetite was gone. She hadn't realized Lloyd felt like that, and from the bitter tone of his voice, it didn't seem as though his pain had lessened over the years. She felt ashamed. She didn't mean to hurt him. She was only trying to help. Lloyd stared down at his plate of salmon, and his voice dropped to a whisper. Adrienne had to lean forward to hear the rest of the story.

"I had not planned to seduce you. I just needed someone to hold me. When you didn't say no to my advances, I was very surprised. When we were making love, I believed that you were really in love with me. I thought that we could go through college together and build a life. We could get married, have fun, raise a real family, and love each other just like your parents did. The fantasy blew up in my face as I walked you back to the subway. You made a remark that wasn't about love at all. I can't remember your exact words, but it was clear that what we'd just shared was pity sex. My beloved Adrienne had given up her virginity because she felt sorry for me. I wanted to die."

Waves of emotion washed over Adrienne. She cried softly into her napkin.

"After kissing you good-bye, I went back to the apartment. It was crawling with cops and official-looking folks who separated me from my sisters. All of us were taken away. I haven't seen my family since.

"Don't cry," Lloyd said. "The past is gone, and I'm a long way from that."

Adrienne blew her nose and struggled to regain control of herself.

"Enough about me," Lloyd said briskly. "I'd like to hear about you. Are you happy?"

"Yes . . . well, I will be."

"What a curious answer. When will you be happy?"

"My husband and I are having some problems. I will be happy when they are resolved."

"Are you sure they can be resolved?" he asked. "Sometimes two people come to a fork in the road, and the only thing left to do is go in opposite directions."

"I'm trying to avoid that." Adrienne answered. "Lloyd, I just want to say that I'm sorry for anything I've ever done to hurt you. Please believe me."

Lloyd gave her a wan smile. "I know that, Adrienne. You were just a kid. Neither of us knew anything about life or love. Now, please stop sniveling and tell me about Dan. I thought about him a lot over the years. He always seemed so meek. The exact opposite of you. How did his life turn out?"

Adrienne wiped her eyes and blew her nose again. "Dan is fine. He graduated from City College with a degree in history and then went to a trade school to learn photography. He's married now. His wife, Charlene, is a social worker."

"That figures," Lloyd said, a strange grin on his face.

Adrienne felt uncomfortable. "What do you mean by that?"

"Oh, nothing," he said, reaching for his drink. "It's just that I would not have expected any less for Dan. It sounds like he has lived the perfect life."

Adrienne didn't know what Lloyd was getting at, but she wasn't in the mood to press it further. She picked at her salmon and watched him eat. The odd lunch date could not end soon enough.

*   *   *

Late that night, as Adrienne lay in bed waiting for Mel to come home, she went over every minute of her lunch with Lloyd. There was something cold and remote about him, but that was really none of her business. She admired the way he had dragged himself out of a hopeless situation and built a successful career. He was also an old friend who had power and influence at her place of employment. Since she was too old for a singing career, maybe God had sent LaMar back into her life so that she could make a second grab at the brass ring. But why would God do that for her after she had failed as a mother and wasn't setting any records in the wife department either?

Adrienne fell asleep with that question floating in her mind.

CHAPTER FIFTEEN

The bar didn't have a name. It was located in an abandoned tenement off 135th Street. The outside was so scrawled with graffiti that it was impossible to discern the building's original color. Years ago, people had lived in the apartments upstairs, but now every single window was broken, and trash littered the stoop. The front door had been cemented shut to prevent squatters and drug users from getting in, but if you were brave enough to take a short walk through the back alley, there was a black door with a small pane of glass in the middle.

To get in, a customer had to ring the bell and wait until one of the barmaids peered suspiciously through the glass. If she didn't recognize the face, the bell went unanswered. It was as simple as that. If the door opened, the customer followed the barmaid down a short, dark hallway, where a man with a handheld metal detector stood in front of another door. There was a cardboard box sitting on the floor beside the man. If you were packing any kind of weapon, it had to go in the box. No one had ever been dumb or high enough to refuse to put their knife or gun in the box. Mel dropped his switchblade without being asked and followed the young barmaid, whose name was Tina, down a short flight of steps and through a second door that led into the bar where Debra and her friends eked out a living. Tina turned and smiled at him as they entered. "Ain't seen you here in a long time, Mel. Where you been hidin'?"

Mel swatted her on the backside. "Busy workin', Tina. You stayin' outa trouble?"

She giggled and sashayed over to the jukebox without answering.

Mel blinked so his eyes could adjust to the dim room after the bright streetlight. He noticed that there were only about ten customers in the gigantic space. The joint wouldn't start jumping until it was dark and the other businesses on the street had closed up for the night.

He took a stool near the door and waited while Debra slapped down a mug of beer in front of a young guy who seemed to be talking to himself. She sauntered over and stood in front of Mel, her hands on her hips and a friendly grin on her face.

"Well, well, well. Look what the cat dragged in."

Ann, who was washing glasses at the end of the bar, waved a soapy hand at him. Belle was wiping down the counter. She wiped her way to stand beside Debra.

"Tina's feedin' quarters into the jukebox. Damn," Belle said.

"Hey, Tina!" Debra hollered. "Nobody wanna hear that rap mess, all right?"

"I sure as hell don't need it," sighed Mel. "All that noise gives me a headache." He liked the song that was playing now, "The Midnight Hour," by Wilson Pickett.

Tina answered the older women without turning around, "I hate this old fogey music." She punched some numbers into the jukebox and stomped defiantly behind the bar. She said something to Ann, who laughed loudly.

"So, what you drinkin', Mel?" asked Debra.

"Same as always. Rum and Coke."

Debra went away to fix the drink, and Belle watched the jukebox as if it were about to come alive. She continued to complain about Tina.

"That girl can't be no more than nineteen or twenty and been in jail three times. It doan make no sense at all."

"Belle, leave that girl alone," Mel said.

She slapped his arm with the wet towel and laughed. "How come you don't stop by Debra's and play cards no more?"

Belle stared right into his eyes and her cheeks puffed up as she tried to look seriously concerned instead of just plain nosy. Mel knew that meant she knew all about the trouble between him, Big Boy, and Lillian. Before Mel could think of an answer that would put her in her place, lyrics from the female rap group TLC rollicked out of the jukebox. Belle headed toward Tina, hollering and cursing with every step.

Debra pulled up a stool. She had made a drink for herself, too. Mel took a sip of his and winced. It was a hell of a lot more rum than Coke.

"Listen at what those young girls are saying," Debra said with disgust.

The bass line was booming, but when Mel listened closely, he could understand that the lyrics were saying that it was okay for a young woman to beg a man for sex if she was feeling hot enough.

Mel grinned at the lyrics and at the way Tina, the dive's youngest barmaid, began to shimmy as she mixed a Long Island iced tea for her customer. Debra lit a cigarette.

"Tina loves that song," she snickered.

Mel could hear Debra's feet doing a *tap-tap-tap* on the rungs of the stool. "You like it, too." He laughed.

"Yeah. I don't like rap, but I can damn sure dig this one."

Tina started chanting along with the record, Ann joined in, and Belle scowled at both of them before giving up the fight.

Since there were no windows in what was essentially the basement of an apartment building, the place reeked of stale cigarette smoke, cheap perfume, and liquor. The walls were bare except for the space right above the liquor bottles. That wall held pictures of Martin Luther King, Malcolm X, and John and Bobby Kennedy.

Mel drank silently while Debra watched him. He glanced at his watch. 7:00. He had finished his route two hours ago.

"You know what today is?"

"Yeah," Debra answered sadly. "Mama's birthday."

"I was thinkin' about it today while I was driving the bus. I'm one year older than she ever lived to be."

"I think about that shit every day," said Debra. "I watch people come in and outa here all the time that I know ain't takin' care of themselves but they still alive. Mama never took a drink or a smoke in her life, and God only gave her thirty-nine years on earth."

Mel nodded. "God is impossible to figure out."

The abrupt death of his mother had been a cruel blow. At her funeral, he had stood before the open coffin in stunned disbelief, unable to cry. For two years after she died, Mel had been paralyzed inside. Then, one day during his freshman year in high school, he was sitting in English class as the teacher was reading James Baldwin aloud. It was a passage that had to do with love torn away without warning. At that moment he felt the sorrow, the agony, the dreadful separation. He ran from the classroom, out of the building, and home to Debra. He needed to make sure she was still alive. Without her love, he would have felt completely alone in the world, with no firmly fixed place to head for and no idea how to get there. Their aunt had made no secret of the fact that she wasn't happy about having them around. She didn't like young people, which was why she had never married or had children of her own. Debra let him cry on her lap, murmuring softly, "I knew this day would come. You'll be okay now." The next day he went back to school and finally noticed the girls who had been trying to get his attention for quite some time. He also made a couple of male friends. All the guys talked about was girls, an old seventies movie that had just been released on videotape called *The Mack*, and its charismatic star, Max Julien.

Mel saw *The Mack* three times at his friend's house that month and started to walk like Max Julien, talk like Max Julien. He became popular, and it made him feel good about himself. Debra was so happy to see him smiling and laughing that she even defied their aunt and worked after school to buy him some clothes that made him look as much like a lady-killer as possible. The girls flocked to him. It wasn't long before he had sex for the first time, and by the end of freshman year he was tired of looking at tits and asses. Years later he would cringe in embarrassment at photos of the fourteen-year-old boy he had been, all dressed up in flashy clothes in imitation of the famed celluloid pimp.

Debra poked his arm, returning his thoughts to the bar and the drink in front of him. "Look behind you," she whispered. "I think you got a fan."

She walked away to wait on some men who had just come in, as Mel turned to see what she was talking about.

The woman advancing toward him with a huge grin on her face was about five feet two, with dyed blond hair that she wore short and slicked to her head. Her lipstick was ruby red, and her eyebrows jet black. Her eyelids were streaked with blue eye shadow. She was wearing tight black leather pants and a yellow turtleneck sweater. Her perfume was cheap and overpowering. Mel shuddered as she slid, grinning, onto the stool beside him.

"Tina say you Debra's brother."

"Tina told you right."

"Debra's brother got a name?"

"My name is Mel, and I ain't in the mood for conversation."

The smile turned to a grimace. "To hell wit' you."

She jumped off the stool and stomped over to the pay phone, but Belle was standing in front of it. "Go outside if you wanna make a call," Belle told the woman.

Mel watched the woman leave the bar in a huff and kept his eye on Belle. She dragged uneasily on a cigarette, and her left arm, which hung free, quivered tautly. Her eyes darted around the room, and she glanced suspiciously at the last three men who had come in. She puffed a last drag of the cigarette and dropped it to the floor, grinding it beneath her heel. She was about to walk away when the phone rang. "Where the hell you at?" she asked. "You still comin? . . . Make that three hours. . . . Yeah . . . Uh-huh . . . I said all right, damn it . . . See you in a few." She put the phone back on the hook, and their eyes met. Her eyes said, *You didn't hear nuthin'*, and his answered, *I damn shore didn't.*

She went back behind the bar to wait on the three new customers. Mel ordered another drink and waved Debra over to join him.

"You still gonna help me out on the rent? Big Boy's showing his ass over what you did to Lillian, and I'm stuck."

"Yeah." Mel stood up and pulled out his wallet. "I got paid today so I can help you out, but I wish you wasn't so dependent on him. Can't you find a job in a regular bar?"

Debra took the money and jammed it into her bra. "I been thinkin' about that."

"Don't just think about it. Make a move."

She nodded in agreement and then changed the subject. "We miss you at the games."

Mel grinned. "I'll be back when things simmer down a little bit. I don't wanna have to kick your man's ass."

"Ain't nobody fightin' in my house," Debra said sharply, "and you can't duck Lillian forever."

"I don't have to. She got on my bus last week with two little kids."

Debra's eyes widened as he described the brief encounter. "I would have slapped the shit out of you," she said when he finished.

Mel shrugged. "That's cuz you ain't got no class."

"Maybe not, but your face would still be on fire."

They shared a laugh and a lot more drinks before Mel staggered home.

CHAPTER SIXTEEN

Adrienne woke up in the morning to find Mel stretched out beside her, his inert frame still in the blue uniform he had worn the day before. The only sound in the room was Mel's deep snores. He and the room smelled like old booze. She felt like kicking him once to get him off the bed, and several more times to roll him right on out of the house and into the streets, where he obviously wanted to be. Instead, she punched him hard in the chest, more to ease her frustration than to wake him up. Mel responded to the blow by jerking slightly. His eyelids twitched and his face turned sideways as he settled back into slumber. Adrienne remembered that the baby used to react the same way if she or Mel made a loud noise while Delilah slept in her crib. Mel's face was just an older, harder picture of his daughter's. All of a sudden, Adrienne didn't want to kick Mel anymore. He was the only part of Delilah she still had.

She craned her neck to look over his body at the clock. It was almost 8:30, which meant she was running late. She jumped out of bed and went to brush her teeth. The bristles were soft and slid across her teeth without offering any real resistance to the food particles that could be lodged between them. That meant it was time for a new toothbrush. She had read somewhere that bristles were supposed to be stiff. She spit out the toothpaste, rinsed, and then poured mouthwash into a Dixie cup and let the minty green liquid fill her mouth. It tingled the inside of her cheeks.

Even though she made a great deal of noise getting ready for work—slamming drawers, running water for a shower—Mel never moved. She left without kissing him good-bye.

Lloyd called her late in the day. "I'd like to talk to you about something. Can you stop by my office?"

"I've got to finish a report for Regina. I'll call you tomorrow."

Lloyd chuckled. "I'll wait here until you're done."

It was after six when Adrienne got to his office. His face lit up as she walked in. He stood up, walked around his enormous desk, and gestured toward the sofa. "Let's sit there," he said. "It's a lot more comfortable."

She sat.

"Would you like something to drink? Coffee? Tea? Soda? Hot chocolate?"

"Hot chocolate."

"I'll be right back."

He returned with two PWE mugs filled with the hot liquid and sat down beside her. "You look positively wounded tonight. Is Regina working you too hard?"

Adrienne shook her head no, picked up her mug, and took a sip.

"Your hands are trembling," he said. "More problems at home?"

Adrienne sighed. "Something like that. How did you guess?"

"I've done enough time in bad relationships to know the signs."

Adrienne steered the conversation away from herself. "Do you have a girlfriend now?"

"No. I went through a bad breakup a few months ago."

"I'm sorry."

Lloyd crossed one leg over the other. "So am I. Patricia is a lawyer. We would have made a great team."

Adrienne wanted to know if they had been planning to live together or get married, but she decided not to pry. Instead, she asked him another question that was on her mind. "What should I call you?"

Lloyd chuckled, put a finger to his lips in a motion for silence, and got up. He walked tall and erect, like Peter, her Hunter College love. Funny, she hadn't thought of Peter in years. He had been a studious and attentive suitor who was unable to understand her decision to leave school and join Starship. They had argued until there was nothing left to say, then drifted apart.

Lloyd closed the door and sat back down before answering. "At times like this, you can call me LaMar if you want, but in public it's Lloyd."

Adrienne waved a hand. "Forget it. Too complicated. I'll stick to Lloyd."

He accepted that with a slight nod of his head.

"I'm really proud of you, Lloyd," she said gently.

"Thanks. Sometimes I can't believe that I actually made it."

He was a handsome man. The horrible acne that had earned him the nickname "Pimple Jenkins" in high school was gone. The thick, black-rimmed glasses were gone, too. Adrienne figured he must be wearing contact lenses, because nothing could have fixed LaMar's terrible vision.

"I owe a lot of my success to you and your family."

"Why do you say that?" Adrienne asked in amazement.

He explained that she had been his only friend back in the old days, when he was lonely, penniless, and scared. "At your house, there was warmth and affection. You guys showed me what real family life was all about. Patricia and I were going to raise our kids in an atmosphere just like that."

So Lloyd had intended to marry his ex-girlfriend.

They were quiet for a few moments, and then Lloyd broke the silence. "What did you expect married life to be like?"

Adrienne laughed. "That's the easiest question you've ever asked me. I expected that Mel and I would have a loving, happy union, just like my parents have."

"Patricia's folks are still together. Maybe she would have known how to make it work," Lloyd said.

"What is it you wanted to talk to me about?" Adrienne said, trying to lighten the atmosphere.

"I want to talk to you about a job, but first let me tell you something about your boss," Lloyd chuckled. "I've had women come

on to me before, but that Regina Belvedere gives new meaning to
the word *shameless*. She made an appointment to see me one day,
and while I wondered what it was about, I didn't want to be rude
and refuse her. So she comes in and sits down across from me
with her skirt hiked up so high, I could see her panties. I didn't
say anything, but the possibility of a false sexual harassment
charge did cross my mind. Well, Regina sat there talking about
ways that she could be a valuable member of the PWE Multicultural team, and all the time, she's licking her lips and playing
with her hair. When I'd heard enough, I called in Sally Gomez. I
told Regina that I wanted Sally to take notes so that I could consider her request for a transfer later on. She fell for it, but I had
no intention of hiring a woman like that. The only reason I called
Sally in was to have a witness in case Regina someday says that I
came on to her or something. Anyway, about three weeks passed,
and I ran into her on the street. She starts batting her eyelids and
stuff like that. I told her that I had considered her proposal but
that my team was already chosen and there was no more room for
additional staffers. I was polite, but she got the message. Now I
hear that she wants to start her own company and take the Puerto
Rican girl who sits with you along with her."

"What Puerto Rican girl?"

"Sherry."

"Sherry Ingles isn't Puerto Rican, and she wouldn't like it one
bit if she heard herself described that way. Her ex-husband was
Hispanic, and that's how she got the name. Sherry is actually
Jewish."

He laughed. "Sounds like she kind of looks down on Latinos.
No wonder the marriage didn't last."

"That's what I think, too."

"Well, since Regina may be leaving, I thought you might consider coming to work for PWE Multicultural."

Adrienne didn't show her excitement. "What about Sally?"

He shook his head. "I'm not talking about a secretarial job,
Adrienne. I'm negotiating with a woman named Mallory Guest. If
all goes well, she'll be the creative director for PWE Multicultural.
She'll need a secretary and a talent manager. I figure you for the
latter position."

"I don't know what a creative director or a talent manager does," Adrienne admitted.

Lloyd looked at Adrienne. "A creative director supervises the artistic side of an advertising campaign," he said slowly. "Mallory understands television and radio production as well as what makes an effective print ad. Do you follow me so far?"

Adrienne nodded. "Yes."

"So," Lloyd continued, "Mallory will supervise all the writers, producers, and artists who work on the ads and commercials."

"Where would I fit in?"

"A talent manager is in charge of the actors, singers, dancers, and models. You'll deal with their agents, set up auditions, make sure they get paid properly, and a host of other things that I don't really know about. Mallory will explain how she wants you to handle the job." Lloyd leaned back in his chair. "You interested?"

A new job meant a pay raise and a chance to get out of debt. "Very, very interested, but why are you offering me the job? I'm sure there are other people who are far more qualified."

"Let's just say that I owe you a favor."

Lloyd winked at her as if they shared a secret, and then his eyes fell on a book that was sticking up out of her tote bag. He pulled it out.

"What are you reading?"

"*After the Garden*, by Doris Jean Austin."

He leaned back against the sofa, his long legs stretched out in front of him. "What is it about?"

"It's about this young, innocent girl who has been sheltered by her grandmother after her parents died. Her grandma wants her to be a teacher, but she falls in love with a boy from the wrong side of the tracks and ruins her life completely."

He read the book jacket in silence.

Adrienne asked, "Do you like the story?"

Lloyd rubbed his eyes as he handed her back the book. "I feel sorry for the grandmother. It's hard letting go of a dream." Adrienne noticed the note of strain that came into his voice.

Adrienne took the book from him. "I know all about that scene," she replied. "My mother was real mad when I left college to join an all-girl singing group."

She told Lloyd that instead of praising the singing gift God had granted her, her mama had said, "All singers and actresses have to sleep with lots of men to get famous. You weren't raised like that."

"I'm sorry to hear that you didn't finish school, Adrienne. What did your father say?" Lloyd asked.

Adrienne's chuckle was bitter. "Daddy seemed bewildered. He said, 'You mean I worked like a dog all those years for nothin'?'" She did a gruff imitation of a man's baritone.

Lloyd's expression was unreadable.

Adrienne continued. "I thought the music industry would welcome me with open arms."

"Because you're gorgeous?" Lloyd asked softly.

"No. Because I was voted 'most talented' *and* 'most beautiful' in my high school yearbook," Adrienne laughed. "I was still riding high on that. It all seems so naive now."

Lloyd shrugged. "Sure, it was. Still, it must have been exciting."

"It was in the beginning," Adrienne admitted. "We called ourselves Starship. There was me, a woman named Lisa, and her cousin, Shawna."

"Did you have a manager?"

"No, but that was okay. Lisa was a good businesswoman. We worked steadily for three years. Mostly singing background vocals for other groups. Nothing major-league, but at least we didn't have to get day jobs, so it was real nice."

"Wow! I'm real impressed."

Adrienne smiled her thanks. "It was hard work, but we had fun."

"What happened?"

"Shawna fell in love with a drummer from another band and followed him to the West Coast." She took a deep breath. "Not long after that, Lisa met someone. They dated for a while and then . . . and then he and I made a mistake."

Lloyd's lips twitched. "So, you aren't perfect."

"It's not funny, Lloyd." Adrienne mumbled. "I hurt a friend, and it was wrong."

Lloyd nodded. "Yeah, sleeping with your friend's man is pretty bad, but it sounds like you paid the price."

"You got that right. She threw both of us out of her life. I missed her for a long time."

Lloyd patted her on the back. Adrienne felt her back stiffen, then relax under his touch. She was too close to him, close enough to smell his musky cologne. "I know how you feel. Wouldn't it be great if we could turn back the clock and erase our mistakes?"

Delilah's image flashed through Adrienne's mind, stilling her thoughts, and she shivered. "Oh, God, yes," she agreed.

Adrienne was surprised at herself. She had never told anyone before about what she had done to Lisa. And she had never responded so much to another man, not since she'd been married to Mel. There was something about Lloyd's presence and the melodic sound of his voice that made Adrienne feel safe, warm, and comfortable. She made a mental note to be careful. She had to watch herself around him. Lloyd wasn't the shy, young, awkward man she'd known when she was in high school, and she was no longer a curious virgin. They both were grown now, full of their own needs. No matter how her body responded, in spite of her, she didn't want Lloyd thinking she could fulfill his.

She hunched over, her arms resting modestly on her thighs. She was conscious of his eyes hovering around her hem. His attention flattered her. It had been some time since Mel had looked at her that way. "I deeply regret dropping out of college," she said, reminding herself not to compare the two men.

"I'll see that you get a chance to go back someday," he said.

Adrienne looked up and saw that Lloyd was smiling. She could not remember the last time she'd felt so completely relaxed.

* * *

When she got home, Mel was sitting on the living room floor watching TV.

Adrienne smiled at him. "Hi, honey, how are you?" she asked, dropping her briefcase on the floor.

"Hey, baby," Mel said, his voice empty of feeling. His right leg was shaking.

Adrienne kissed him on the cheek. "What's the matter?"

"Adrienne, there is something you ought to know."

"What are you talking about?"

He hung his head like a whipped dog. "I spent my share of the rent money, Adrienne. Debra was in a jam, and I had to help her."

Adrienne just stared at him.

Mel stood up and went into the bathroom, locking the door behind him.

She went to the door and screamed. "The rent is due tomorrow!"

He muttered something unintelligible.

"What?" she shrieked.

"I know that," he yelled back.

Adrienne pounded on the door. "Come out of there, Mel!"

"What for? You're only going to keep on screaming!"

"Come out and look me in the face like a man!"

The door opened, and he stood there with his hands hanging limply at his sides.

"I wanted to tell you, Adrienne, but I didn't know how."

"How are we supposed to pay the rent?" she whispered.

"The landlord will just have to wait. We'll double up next month," he said.

Adrienne sank down on the foot of the bed and put her head in her hands for a moment. She felt an overwhelming sense of disgust, which made her mouth twist and her nose turn up as though she smelled something bad. The bedroom suddenly felt like a prison, and the setting seemed to belong in some macabre cartoon.

He sat beside her and began talking earnestly. "Please try to forgive me, Adrienne." He gave her a tremulous smile.

Adrienne didn't smile back.

"Adrienne, I'll make all this up to you. I swear."

"Leave me alone, Mel. To tell you the truth, I'm beginning to think getting back together was a mistake."

Mel froze. "Please don't leave me, Adrienne."

She looked at him scornfully. "If anyone walks out that door, Mel, it will be you. And the locks will be changed before you hit the corner."

Mel knew that it was his fault they were short on the rent, but now she was taking it too far. He stood up. "Change the locks? What makes you think I'm gonna let you put me out of my own house? Are you outa your muthafuckin' mind?" His chest was heaving as he waited for an answer.

Adrienne's mouth quivered, and her eyes narrowed. "You act like you don't want to be here anyway! All you do is drink at that damn bar. I'm sick of it."

Mel tried to backtrack. "It isn't like that."

"You've sunk as low as a man can get, Mel Jordan. And do you know why?" Mel didn't answer, his fury rising.

"Because you spend so much time with lowlifes, that's why!" yelled Adrienne.

"Things will get better," Mel said weakly. "Remember how it used to be between us?"

Adrienne actually had the nerve to rise from the foot of the bed, place her hands on her hips, and push her face so close to his, their noses were almost touching. "Yes, I do, but you know what, Mel? I'm getting real tired of remembering those days every time you fuck up. And you've been fucking up a whole lot lately."

How could he let a woman step to him in such a manner and curse him to his face, and still call himself a man?

The blood in his veins felt hot. Beads of sweat appeared in his mustache. Adrienne's mouth was moving, but he could not hear what she was saying. When he spoke, his voice sounded as if it were coming out of a wind tunnel located far away. "Back up, Adrienne, and the next time you jump up at me, you better be able to whip my ass."

Adrienne had the good sense to walk away. She was almost out of the bedroom when she turned around to have the last word. "I'm not paying one penny more than my share of the rent, so I guess you're gonna be driving the fuck out of that bus."

She went into the bathroom and slammed the door so hard, several of the stick-on mirrors in the hallway fell and shattered on the floor.

Mel's craving for cocaine had never been stronger.

CHAPTER SEVENTEEN

Adrienne sat cross-legged on the floor of Charlene's living room. Charlene used a pick to untangle Adrienne's wet hair as she listened to the tale of the missing rent money.

"How dare he just give away our money?" Adrienne fumed.

"If Dan was down and out, what would you do?"

"I'd help him, of course."

"So?"

"So, Mel still should have talked it over with me first."

Charlene put the pick on the coffee table and opened a jar of Bergamot hair grease. "Next time I do your hair, I'll have to give you a touch-up. These roots are gettin' kinda tough." She began to part Adrienne's hair in small sections, greasing the scalp as she went. "It's true that Mel was wrong not to say anything," Charlene admitted, "but honey, it may be that Mel has gotten out of the habit of making decisions as a couple."

"In just six months?"

"Six critical months."

"Go ahead and say it, Charlene."

"Say what?"

"That I shut him out when he needed me most."

Charlene stopped greasing. "I can't do this, Adrienne. It's just too draining. Let's talk about something else."

"I'm sorry, Charlene. It's just that there's so much going on, and I don't know what to do about Mel. We're not talking. Not about dinner, not about TV, the news, work, nothing. It's like I'm sitting up in that apartment with somebody I don't even know anymore. I don't know what to do."

Charlene held the comb and looked at her sister-in-law. "I told you. Both of you need counseling. Get some help in talking about Delilah."

Adrienne sucked her teeth. "Charlene, Mel is not going to tell nobody his business. Maybe his sister, but not a therapist. And me, I don't know if I'm ready to talk about it either. It's too painful now."

"Well, maybe that's what you need to do. Talk to Debra. She might be able to tell you something that can get you and Mel talking again, you think?"

"Debra?" Adrienne said, surprised. "I was actually thinking about that, but not exactly what you have in mind. I think Debra's part of the problem. And if not her, definitely her trifling card-playing friends. Ever since Mel moved over there, he's been slipping further and further away from me, and you know Debra and I don't get along. I can't imagine what she'd have to say to me. But let's talk about something else."

Adrienne searched her mind for something more pleasant to discuss, but the only positive thing that had been on her mind lately was Lloyd. "Lloyd said that he's going to help me get a promotion."

"Girl, that is terrific. Tell me about it."

Adrienne told her all about the lunch, the new position, and that Lloyd seemed to be suffering over the breakup of a bad relationship. "I bet Patricia is a siddity, bourgeoisie sistah," Adrienne said.

"Why do you think that?"

"Because Lloyd is one uptight, buttoned-down brutha, that's why. He never seems totally relaxed."

Charlene put the cap back on the grease jar and brushed Adrienne's hair thoroughly. "Well, let's help him unwind a little. What do you think about inviting Lloyd over for dinner? I'd love to meet him, and I know Dan is dying to see him."

"I like the idea. Let's do it after Easter."

"Good. I'll make shrimp scampi and get some wine. We can do it on a Saturday night when Mel doesn't have to work. It'll be a real celebration."

CHAPTER EIGHTEEN

For the next two weeks, Mel took all the overtime he could get to make up the rent money. Today things weren't going well at work. The traffic was light, and there was no snow or rain to make the tires skid or impede his vision, but his bus had a fault in the Metro Card slot. With every third or fifth passenger who slipped a card in, the machine would hold on to it and make a whirring noise until Mel banged it with his fist. Once the card popped out again, the passenger would stare at it suspiciously. "Did it take extra money off the card?" each would ask. By the time Mel's shift was over, he was weary and his hand was killing him. He called Adrienne from the depot. The phone rang three times before she answered.

"Regina Belvedere's office."

"Hey, baby, I'm finished for the day. I'm going to stop off and see my sister. I'll be home late."

"Don't come home drunk tonight, Mel."

Adrienne was stretched out on the navy blue leather sofa when he came in. Her eyes were closed. Mel noticed that the checkbook, some stamps, and open bills were scattered on the coffee table. Now that he'd had a few drinks, his bad mood was gone. He leaned over and kissed her on the forehead. "Hey, baby."

She opened her eyes and looked at him sadly. "Hey."

As Mel headed to the bedroom, he wondered why Adrienne's mood was so somber. After a hot shower, he pulled on his robe and went back to the living room. She was sitting up, staring at nothing. He sat down and put an arm around her. "What's the matter?"

Adrienne sighed and leaned close to him. "I'm going to have to declare bankruptcy."

Mel was shocked at her answer. He swept up all the bills and went through them. MasterCard: $2,600. Visa: $2,500. American Express: $1,000. Discover: $1,500. Bloomingdale's: $750. He couldn't go on. He put the bills back on the table.

She followed his gaze and sighed once more.

Mel was amazed. "Adrienne, how did you get in so much debt?"

"Shopping."

"I know that, baby. What I meant was, didn't you see that you were headed for trouble?"

She didn't answer.

Mel thought about Adrienne's dresser drawers and bulging closet. "You got to stop buying so much clothes and cut up all those charge cards." He peered at her intently.

"That's not all," she said dully.

He took her face tenderly in his hands. Her eyes were red, like she'd been crying. "Tell me everything," he said gently.

And it all came tumbling out. "Every time you walk out the door, I wonder if you're going to come home drunk or not. Why do you spend so much time at that bar where Debra works? Are you cheating on me?"

He shook his head. "No. There is no other woman."

She relaxed a little. "Then why do you drink so much? Tell me what you're running away from?"

"I don't know what you mean," he stammered.

"I want you to get professional help before you become an alcoholic."

Mel hesitated. "I don't need to do that, baby."

Adrienne started to cry, and Mel looked at the bills. "If you file for bankruptcy, your credit will be ruined." He stroked her hair as she sobbed.

There was no answer for a moment. Mel realized that his wife had a serious case of the blues and that she was going to cry about anything and everything that had ever gone wrong in her whole life. *She's probably crying about Delilah, too*, he thought sadly. But he couldn't even bring himself to say his child's name aloud.

So he just cuddled Adrienne and stared at the bills on the table, and wondered how they would ever get out of the hole they were in.

* * *

The bills were still on Mel's mind when he got off work the next day. He decided to stop off for a drink to take his mind off his troubles before going home. When Mel walked into the bar, he took one look at Debra's face and knew something was wrong, but he waited until his drink arrived before asking what it was.

Debra huffed, "Look at that high-yella bitch over there!"

Mel turned in the direction Debra was pointing. A fat, light-skinned woman with dyed-red braids was sitting with Tina, the young barmaid. The fat woman had several earrings in each ear, and Mel figured that the hair had to be fake because it hung to her waist. Mel couldn't see her face clearly from where he was sitting, and he didn't want to.

"Who is she, and why you callin' her a bitch?"

Debra took a rag and wiped the counter in front of him so fiercely that she knocked his glass over, spilling his drink.

"I ain't payin' for that," Mel said irritably. "What the hell is going on?"

Debra's voice rose. "That bitch just started workin' here, and she think she hot shit, but I ain't havin' it. Big Boy just came in here to see me, and her ugly ass was all over him."

Mel cracked up. He laughed so hard, tears came to his eyes. "Girl, get me another drink and make it a double this time," he wheezed. *There is some real, sho-nuff stupid shit going on here.* How could any self-respecting female even consider brawling over an overweight, uncouth, illiterate lout like Big Boy?

Debra slapped the drink down in front of him. "What the fuck is so funny?" she asked.

Mel swallowed a gulp of the rum, which had very little soda in it. He grimaced. "Ain't a damn thing funny, Debra, but if you gettin' ready to fight over that fool, times sure must be hard for women. That's all I can say."

Debra gave him a very pitiful look. "Big Boy helps me out a lot, Mel. You know I don't make much working in this place. Now that you moved out, I don't even have the money you used to give me. If that heffah takes Big Boy, what I'm gonna do?"

Mel backed off. "Hey, I'm sorry. Just remember something. If Big Boy hears you're sweatin' this, he's got you by the tit, and he'll drag you around in the dust. Act like you don't give a fuck, and that fat fool won't be goin' nowhere. Now put a smile on your face and pull yourself together. Me and my wife are coming to your house for Easter dinner next Sunday, and I don't want you serving me no half-raw shit just because you been feelin' too blue to cook it right."

Debra said, "Aw, shut up, Mel," and then she started to laugh.

Someone was missing from the scene. Mel gazed around the bar. "Where's Belle?"

"Belle went to jail," Debra said matter of factly.

Mel wasn't surprised. "What for?"

Debra said that Belle had helped two dudes plan a holdup of the bar. "The robbery happened a couple of hours after you was in here the last time," Debra informed him as she tapped her feet to the music that was blaring from the jukebox.

Mel remembered the strange way that Belle had acted that night when she was on the phone, and he hoped that the criminal justice system kept her ass behind bars. Some people were too stupid to be walking around loose.

"Debra, lemme ask you somethin.'"

Her feet stopped tapping. "What?"

"It's about me and Adrienne."

Her feet began to tap once more. "What's goin' on? She pregnant?"

Mel stared down into his glass. "No, thank God. It's just that sometimes we act like we really want to make it. Then, a week later, things feel like it's all over between us. How can we fix things, flip-flopping like that?"

Debra waited for him to continue. When he didn't, she said, "Maybe what's broken can't be fixed."

Mel wanted to tell Debra that there was a lot more on his mind. Things like the worsening financial situation in his household, and how liquor wasn't the high he craved. No matter how much he drank, it didn't come close to the effect that coke gave him. Sometimes he wanted to throw his passengers off the bus, point the vehicle west, and drive nonstop until he reached Little Jimmy. The feeling was worse now that Adrienne had shown him all of her bills.

Mel didn't say any of these things. He swallowed the rest of his drink.

"When we first got back together, I didn't really want to be there." He shrugged. "Something changed inside me around Valentine's Day, and now I want us to make it. Trouble is, Adrienne ain't the same no more, but I'm not ready to throw in the towel just yet."

Debra said nothing, and after a few minutes, Mel changed the subject. After drinking steadily for the next few hours, he threw some money on the counter, blew a kiss at his sister, and staggered out the door.

When he got home, Adrienne was lying on the sofa reading a magazine. Her eyes lit up when she saw him. "I was trying to wait up for you," she said.

Mel staggered to their room without answering, fell across the bed, and then everything went black.

CHAPTER NINETEEN

On Easter morning, Adrienne woke up to an empty bed. Mel had worked a double shift and wouldn't be home until late afternoon. Just in time to get dressed and go to his sister's house, where they were having dinner. Adrienne thought about the long, silent hours that stretched before her. She felt very restless. She surfed the television channels, watching a few minutes of each program before going on to the next.

By noon, she was tired of lying in bed. She showered, dressed, and then decided to put on some music and clean the house. She thumbed through her CD collection and finally chose *Al Green's Greatest Hits*. She turned on the stereo at full volume and vacuumed the bedroom while singing along to "I Can't Get Next to You." *You hit the nail right on the head, Al,* she thought grimly. Ever since she'd told Mel about her bills, his attitude had gotten worse. He was brooding and silent for long periods of time and he was drinking far too much.

She was still in a foul mood after vacuuming the whole apartment. Al Green had moved on to "Tired of Being Alone" when Adrienne attacked the refrigerator. She took all the food out, filled a pail with soapy water, grabbed a sponge, and started scrubbing the inside vigorously.

Adrienne knew that a husband had a right to expect his wife to spend time with his family, but the fact that he was always shutting her out these days made spending Easter with his tacky sister and her useless friends a monumental sacrifice. Adrienne didn't like Debra, because Debra had never really accepted the fact that Mel had ditched some woman named Rose the day after he'd shown up to install Adrienne's telephone. She wondered briefly if Debra would overlook this and talk with her, woman to woman, about whatever was going on in her brother's life.

By 3:00 P.M., the apartment was spotless. Adrienne was pulling clothes from her closet in search of a casual outfit to wear for dinner when her parents called.

"Happy Easter!" Mama said.

"Same to you," Adrienne muttered.

"What's wrong?"

"Nothing."

"How is Mel?"

"Fine."

"Good. Put him on the phone and let me say hello."

"He's at work, Mama. I'm expecting him any minute. We're going to Debra's house for dinner."

"Oh," Mama said knowingly. "That's what the matter is." She chuckled. "I know Debra is a little rough around the edges, but she's got a good heart and that's all that matters."

Adrienne wasn't so sure. Daddy picked up the extension before she could reply. "Hey, baby girl!"

"Hi, Daddy. How are you?"

"Fine." His voice boomed through the receiver. "You cooking today?"

"No. Mel and I are having dinner at his sister's house, and I'm not looking forward to it."

"If you plan for misery, that's what you'll get. Make up your mind to have a good time and everything will be all right. Okay?"

Adrienne smiled, knowing her father was right. "Sure, Daddy."

"Good. I'm gonna hang up now." Adrienne heard a click, then her mama's voice. "Well, we just called to wish you a good day, baby."

Adrienne hung up the phone just as she heard Mel's key in the door. He looked tired.

He planted a perfunctory kiss on her cheek.

"Mama just called to say 'Happy Easter.'"

His face relaxed. "That's real nice. Debra's expecting us at four-thirty, so we better get moving."

Adrienne forced herself to smile and went back to the closet as he headed for the shower.

* * *

Adrienne wrinkled her nose at the smell in the elevator of Debra's building as they rode up to the thirteenth floor. She stood in one spot, not wanting her shoes to touch any litter or get near the puddle of urine that lay in a pool between her and Mel. She was beginning to feel slightly nauseous when Debra opened the door with a welcoming smile.

Mel started popping his fingers as soon as they walked in, because Debra's apartment was jumping to the sound of one of his favorite records, "The Big Payback," by James Brown. "Hey, y'all!" he exclaimed as he headed toward the back room with their coats.

Adrienne remembered her father's advice and smiled widely at the folks who crowded the small living room. She walked into a wall of funk and heat as she squeezed herself onto the sofa between two women who looked vaguely familiar. It smelled as if Debra had been cooking chitlins.

Debra stepped into the center of the room. Adrienne could tell she'd had a lot to drink. "Everybody, this is Adrienne, Mel's wife." She then pointed out each person to Adrienne. "You know Big Boy. And that's Ann sitting next to you. On your other side is Tina. She done took Belle's place at the bar where I work."

"Belle is in jail," Big Boy informed Adrienne.

"You do remember Belle, don't you?" asked Debra.

Adrienne shook her head. She didn't remember anyone named Belle. As Debra went into a lengthy description of what Belle looked like, Adrienne wondered why everyone in the room was so dressed up. They all looked as if they were heading for some tacky nightclub. Big Boy was actually wearing a suit!

Debra rattled off a few more names of people in the room, and

Adrienne forgot them instantly. They were all either neighbors or coworkers of Debra's. After a few minutes, they all forgot about her. Mel was dancing and throwing back drinks. Debra alternated between checking on the food and sitting playfully on Big Boy's lap, and the young girl named Tina kept complaining about the music. "Don't ya'll have anything that wasn't made in the Stone Ages?" she asked.

"What you know about the Stone Ages, girl? I didn't think you stuck around high school long enough to even hear about anything like that!" Mel shouted.

Tina stuck her tongue out at him, everyone laughed, and the party went on. Somebody turned on "Ain't No Stoppin Us Now," and Adrienne stepped out of the way as they began moving the chairs and the coffee table out of the way so they could all dance. She looked over and saw Debra darting back into the kitchen, and wondered if this might be a good time for them to speak.

Adrienne moved past a couple who were dancing, drinks in hand, and nodded at Mel, who was deep in conversation with an old friend. She ducked into the cramped kitchen, where Debra was busily chopping up onions.

"Hand me that butter knife over there," she said, barely looking up.

Adrienne didn't really want to touch anything, but she took the knife and started to run it under the tap water.

"Just hand it to me, Adrienne. It's clean," Debra said, exasperated. "I swear, you just as prissy as they come."

"Debra, I didn't come in hear to argue with you."

"Well, whatchu come for, then? 'Cause I know you didn't come in here to wish me no Happy Easter."

Adrienne didn't know how to begin. She was beginning to think this was a bad idea.

"I was wondering if Mel had said anything to you."

"What you say?" Debra asked, shouting above the music. She was busily making a salad.

"I said, has Mel said anything to you—about us? I mean. We hadn't been talking much, and, well, it just seems like he has a lot on his mind."

"I guess he do. Hell, his baby gone, and something like that, you just can't blink and jump back on your feet."

Adrienne couldn't believe how blunt Debra was—or that she was acting as though Mel were the only one who was suffering, too. She didn't know how to respond without causing a scene, so she just glared at Debra, watching her mix up the salad.

"And Adrienne," Debra said softly, "don't be over there lookin' crazy. I ain't got no kids, but I was a girl once, and I know how much you love your little girl. It's gone take some time, Adrienne, maybe a whole lot of time, 'fore you and Mel and work through that kinda loss." She watched Adrienne staring at her, mistrustful. "But if you don't want to lose him, too," she continued, "I think you better just chill and don't play him so close. Mel a grown man, and prissy as you is, you know how these men do," Debra said slyly.

Now what does that mean? Adrienne wondered as Debra stuck her plump finger into the bowl and licked it, checking the salad's taste.

The music seemed to grow louder, and Adrienne felt a headache coming on as Debra sucked the last bit of blue cheese dressing off her finger and held the bowl in her hand.

Just when Adrienne thought she couldn't take another minute of the gathering, Debra slipped out of the kitchen and stood in the doorway. "Dinner is served," she said grandly.

Ann and Debra filled the plates in the kitchen, and Tina passed them out to the crowd in the living room. Everyone ate with their plates on their laps and drinking glasses at their feet. There were the traditional Easter foods—ham, fried chicken, collard greens, and macaroni and cheese—but there was also roast beef, cornbread made from scratch, homemade apple pie, and caramel cake. Adrienne was picking at a little bit of everything when Mel sat down beside her and began to eat as if he hadn't seen food in months.

"Why you not eatin', baby?" he asked.

"I'm not feeling too well," Adrienne lied softly. *Debra's words had sunk into the pit of her stomach.*

He stopped eating for a moment. "Yeah, you do look strange. We can leave in a little while if you want."

Adrienne nodded. They were talking quietly about how tired he was from driving all night and half the day, when Adrienne felt Mel stiffen beside her. He choked on a piece of ham, and she pounded him on the back as he reached frantically for his drinking glass. "What's the matter?" she asked. Before Mel could answer, Big Boy's voice clamored over the music. "Well, what a surprise! Look who's here. If it ain't my favorite cousin!"

Big Boy was taking coats from a woman and two small girls. The woman was wearing a green dress in some kind of shimmery fabric, and the neckline was so low, it almost reached her nipples. She was wearing two huge gold earrings in each ear, and a lot of bracelets. The two little girls were wearing ruffled pink dresses and black patent leather shoes. The woman whispered something to them, and they waved shyly at Mel.

"Mel, you remember Lillian, don't you?" Big Boy shouted. There was no mistaking the glee in his voice.

Mel stiffened beside her. "Yeah," he muttered.

Big Boy helped his cousin into a chair and then looked at Mel again. "Well, it would seem to me that a man could say hello if he remembers somebody."

Mel said, "Hello Lillian," without taking his eyes off his plate.

Big Boy grinned widely and whispered in his cousin's ear.

"What cute kids," Adrienne said. "Do you know them?"

"No," he said shortly. "I only seen 'em once when they got on the bus with Big Boy's cousin. I met a lot of people when I was staying here."

Why did Mel sound so defensive? Adrienne sighed. His moods were so unpredictable lately. She felt someone staring, and when she looked up, the woman in the green dress was looking at her with unabashed curiosity. Big Boy did the introductions, and Adrienne thought there was an odd gleam in his eye.

"Lillian, I think you know everybody here except Adrienne." Adrienne smiled. "Hello."

"Adrienne is Mel's wife," Big Boy added.

Now there was no mistaking Mel's discomfort. He was practically as green as Lillian's dress. There was a lot of rustling around as Lillian and her children found places to sit. Adrienne saw

Debra grab Big Boy by the arm and tug him toward the kitchen. She looked angry. Lillian now looked upset as well.

"Mel, what is going on?"

"I don't know what you talkin' about."

Adrienne didn't know what she was talking about either, but then Ann started whispering in Tina's ear. When she finished, the young girl let out a whoop and they both looked earnestly from Lillian to Mel to Adrienne and back again.

Debra and Big Boy came back. They had obviously been fighting, because Debra rolled her eyes at him and made a point of sitting as far away from him as was possible in the tiny space. Adrienne watched as Lillian again murmured to her children. They both nodded obediently and walked over to stand in front of Mel. The taller one piped up. "Hello, Mr. Jordan. Mama wants to know when you comin' back to our house."

No one was talking. Adrienne's eyes met Lillian's, and the woman's chin went up. She gazed back at Adrienne in open defiance. Adrienne started to think the unthinkable.

"The little girl asked you a question, Mel. Why don't you answer her?" Adrienne said calmly. "She wants to know when you are coming back to her house."

Mel gave the child a smile. "I don't know, sweetheart."

The children skipped back to their mother. Mel glared furiously at Lillian, and the woman stared back. There was malice in her gaze.

Debra leaped to her feet. "Let's play some cards y'all, and turn up the music—it's too quiet in here!"

Adrienne watched as everyone started moving around, taking plates to the kitchen and mixing drinks. Big Boy grabbed Lillian and started dancing.

Adrienne looked at the little girl and wondered what Mel had been doing in her mother's home. The child had big eyes like Delilah. She remembered one night when Delilah was about three weeks old and wasn't sleeping well at night. She kept waking up and crying until Adrienne finally took her out of the crib and into the living room. She settled into an armchair with the infant in her lap. "Shush, sweetie, Daddy has to get up at six. He only has two more hours of sleep. Be a good girl for Mommy. Don't wake Daddy up."

She had been so exhausted from taking care of the baby all day and most of the night that she was close to tears. She must have fallen asleep, because the next thing she knew, Mel was gently taking Delilah from her arms. "Go get some rest, baby," he said. Adrienne gave him a kiss of gratitude, and Delilah just stared at them both with big brown eyes that matched her father's.

Adrienne rubbed her temples. "Mel, what were you doing in that woman's house?"

"Putting up kitchen shelves with some of the other guys."

"I don't believe that."

Mel shrugged. "If you want to cause a scene for nothing, I can't stop you. Just go on over and ask her."

Adrienne's pride would not let her do it. "The only place I'm going is home. Right now!" Her head was starting to throb. The pain was so intense, she just wanted to go home, take some aspirin, and lie down in her bedroom with the lights off.

"Sure, baby," Mel answered easily. "Let's get our coats."

Adrienne stood up and followed Mel. She turned her nose up at Lillian as she passed. The look told the cheaply dressed tramp that if her game plan had been to cause trouble in Mel's marriage, it had failed. It told the floozy that all she had done was make a fool of herself.

Over the next two days, Adrienne kept thinking about Lillian and her two little girls. As she walked out the door for work one morning, she wondered for the hundredth time if Mel had slept with Big Boy's cousin. No, Mel would never be physically unfaithful to her, but he hadn't told the whole truth, either.

By the time she sat down at her desk, Adrienne had faced a cold, sad fact. Her marriage might not last, and if they were headed for divorce, she shouldn't be thinking about getting pregnant. It was time to start using some sort of birth control.

CHAPTER TWENTY

M el drove along his route, thinking about Easter dinner. If he could have wrapped his hands around Lillian's throat and choked her to death without fear of going to jail, he would have done so without hesitation. What kind of funky shit was that she had pulled on him? How could she use her kids to get even with him for not sticking around to be her man? No matter what Debra said, she had willingly climbed into bed on the first date with a man she knew was legally tied to someone else. He thought about going to her house and telling her stupid ass exactly what he thought, but then he decided that such a step would only make matters worse. She would make sure that Adrienne found out, and how would he explain that? Not that Adrienne had bought his story anyway. He had seen the truth in the grim set of her jaw the following morning.

Mel felt that Lillian's antics had forced the hidden tension between him and Adrienne out into the open. Now it was just a matter of time before war was officially declared. Until then, he could only do just what he was going to do now: drive the bus, grab a drink after work at the bar, and go home to wait for the inevitable explosion. A drink would calm his nerves, slow his thoughts down to a pace where he could handle them. Slow them down just enough to help him stave off the other desire that seemed to be getting stronger. No, what he needed was a stiff drink, not no more of that coke. Mel concentrated on the black road ahead of him, on the hellacious New York traffic and taxi drivers, and tried hard to steer his thoughts away from that pretty white dust.

CHAPTER TWENTY-ONE

Adrienne selected a black Italian two-piece pantsuit from her closet and a Valentino scarf from her dresser drawer. She had purchased both at an upscale discount boutique called Le Firme, on Fifty-seventh street between Fifth and Sixth Avenues. The suit had been marked down from twelve hundred dollars to six hundred dollars, and the scarf had been a steal at only thirty-five dollars. She wriggled into the suit, feeling a delicious sense of anticipation. As she pulled her Bleecker Satchel coach bag from the top shelf of her closet, she glanced at another pile of bills that were stacked neatly beside her accessories, and hastily closed the door. Mel had worked the night shift and wasn't home yet.

She walked quickly through the chilly morning air and reached Parton, Webster & Elliott a few minutes early. Sherry was already there, sipping coffee and reading the newspaper.

"Good morning," Adrienne said as she pulled off her coat.

Sherry looked up. "Hey! That suit is fabulous!"

Adrienne smiled. "Thanks."

She hung up her coat in the hall closet and settled down at her desk. There was a note from Regina Belvedere asking about the status of several projects. There had been no further word from Lloyd Cooper, and Adrienne didn't know if he had spoken to Mallory Guest about her or not. After she booted up her computer and retrieved the information for Regina, she e-mailed Lloyd a message that was deliberately worded to conjure up memories of senior year. She really needed the extra money that a promotion would bring so that she could pay off her bills.

Girl voted Most Likely to Succeed still waiting for the chance to prove it.

Never mind that she was hardly a girl and hadn't been for a long time. She clicked *Send* and waited several minutes but there was no answer. Feeling disappointed and foolish, Adrienne settled into the morning's work. At 11:00 A.M., a little box appeared on the screen.

Adrienne Jordan has one unread message.

She clicked on her E-mail. The message was from Lloyd Cooper.

Are you available for dinner tonight?

Adrienne chuckled.
"Are you all right?" asked Sherry.
"Yes," Adrienne said quickly. Sherry was entirely too nosy.
Sherry pressed for more information and even walked over to look at Adrienne's computer screen. Adrienne waved her away before she could read the message and then typed her reply:
Yes, as long as the food is well done. No sushi.
Regina Belvedere bounced into the bull pen and smiled warmly at the two of them. She was wearing a dark-green suit that set off her red hair and pale-green eyes. Adrienne thought that her supervisor's skirt was a little too short for the office, but at least she had shapely long legs to carry it off. Regina placed a hand on Adrienne's shoulder and glanced idly at the screen.
"Is that Lloyd Cooper's name that I see?"
Adrienne sat angrily as Regina read the message and Sherry watched them both with frank curiosity.
"Can I see you in my office?"

Adrienne sighed and followed Regina past Sherry and out of the bull pen.

As Adrienne took the visitor's chair and Regina settled in behind her desk, she noticed that Regina's smile was still frozen in place but that there was wariness in her eyes.

"Adrienne, what is that E-mail all about?"

"It turns out that Lloyd Cooper and I went to the same high school. He has invited me to dinner for old times' sake." She didn't try to hide her annoyance at Regina's prying questions. Now that she knew Regina's true character, it was hard to treat her with respect. "May I go now?"

When Regina nodded, Adrienne went back to her desk and started working on the status report that Regina had requested. Adrienne sighed, wishing that she had been less frosty with her manager. Even though Regina had turned out to be a scheming tramp as far as men were concerned, she had been very understanding when Adrienne returned to work after the accident. It had been hard for Adrienne to venture out into the world after her isolation. Regina had been kind, thoughtful, and compassionate about her terrible loss.

Adrienne went back to Regina's office to explain that her interest in their new president was strictly professional.

"Why didn't you tell me when you found out who he was?"

It was a good question. Adrienne just shrugged. "I don't know."

Regina grinned. "It doesn't matter."

The two women smiled at each other and the crisis was past.

For the rest of the day, Adrienne did her assignments like a woman on automatic pilot. Her mind churned with reflections on the mystery that was LaMar Jenkins/Lloyd Cooper. *I'm going to really press him about the new job tonight,* she decided.

Adrienne thought about how she would approach the subject as she ate lunch at her desk. The ham sandwich she'd brought from home tasted like cardboard. When the phone rang, she jumped to answer, thinking it might be Lloyd.

"Hey, baby, it's me," said Mel.

"Oh."

"Damn. I'm glad to hear your voice, too," he answered irritably.

"I'm sorry. It's been a busy morning."

"Okay." He changed the subject. "What do you want for dinner tonight? It'll have to be something quick and easy, because I'm already tired and I've got four more hours to drive that damned bus."

"I have to work late. I won't be home for dinner."

"Okay. I'll miss you, though. See you when you get home."

"Bye."

"Adrienne, before you hang up, there's something I have to say."

"What?"

"I love you."

"I love you, too."

Adrienne didn't hear from Lloyd until 4:45 P.M. He called from the company limousine, and his voice was low. "I'm parked right outside the building. Let's not talk about the past in the car, okay?"

Adrienne agreed. Lloyd was obviously a man who liked to keep his private life undercover. He was probably worried that the driver would hear something embarrassing about his youth and mention it to another executive.

They drove out of the city in silence. Lloyd seemed to be in a bad mood. His brows were drawn together, and his bearing was stiff. Adrienne stared out the window feeling uncomfortable while Lloyd sat beside her, reading *Advertising Age*. She could tell from the sound of the paper rattling that he was having difficulty concentrating.

"Where are you taking me?" she finally ventured timidly.

"A town called Hastings-on-Hudson. There's a nice quiet restaurant there with excellent food. I think you'll like it."

It occurred to Adrienne that Mel might call the job. "I have to call my husband."

He gave her the phone without saying anything. The line rang a few times, and then the answering machine picked up. "Mel," Adrienne said, "you won't be able to reach me at the office. My boss and I are taking the project with us, and we'll work on it over dinner. Don't worry, I'll take a cab home."

When Adrienne gave Lloyd the phone back, his mouth was

twisted into a sardonic smile. "Women," he spat. "You've changed, Adrienne. I can remember when you were a terrible liar."

"I'm not lying," Adrienne snapped. "You are my boss, and I'd like to learn more about what is going on at PWE Multicultural."

"There are different ways of lying. Your husband will think that you're out with Regina Belvedere. Am I correct?"

Adrienne smarted under the criticism. "I don't think you're in a position to lecture me about how I've changed, Mr. Whatever-your-name-is."

He chuckled. "Touché, my dear."

* * *

Le Chateau was an elegant French restaurant tucked away on a side-street between a florist's shop, which was closed, and a posh boutique for children. The doors of Le Chateau were mahogany with solid-brass door handles. Lloyd opened the door for Adrienne and she gasped at the sheer loveliness of the interior. The color scheme was slender ribbons of pale blue and soft ivory. This pattern curled intricately throughout the marble floors and on the walls. There were only ten tables in the place, and the damask-covered chairs were ivory to match the tablecloths. Two ivory candles burned at each table.

After the waiter took their orders, filet mignon for Lloyd and coq au vin for her, Adrienne unfolded her napkin, laid it across her lap, and smiled engagingly at him. "It's been so long since I heard from you. I thought you'd forgotten all about me." Her remark was just supposed to be a coquettish icebreaker, so Adrienne was surprised at Lloyd's emotional response.

"It's funny, Adrienne, but I feel like you and I have somehow changed places."

"What?"

"You come across as lacking confidence and fearful of life in general. Like I used to be long ago."

Adrienne felt like going home and leaving Lloyd to his stupid thoughts of yesteryear, but it would only hurt her in the end. Lloyd was wealthy. All she had was a depressed husband whom she needed to pay half the household expenses while she dug herself out of a mountain of personal debt.

"I can't be a seventeen-year-old girl anymore, Lloyd," she said gently.

"I didn't expect you to be. But you were so strong-willed, vivacious, and ready to take on the world. I refuse to believe that the old Adrienne has disappeared forever."

Adrienne knew that if Lloyd had come back into her life just a year earlier, he wouldn't be so disappointed. It was as though Delilah's horrible death had removed the stuffing from her insides. But that was not a story she was ready to tell him.

"It's like you're surrounded by some kind of mist."

"We're different people now, Lloyd, and that is as it should be. Now, stop talking crazy like that and let's talk about something else, like why you changed your name."

The waiter came back with their dinner. Lloyd didn't answer until the waiter had arranged their plates and departed.

Lloyd grimaced. "Your tone is very judgmental. How many black men with low-class ghetto names like LaMar Jenkins have you ever seen running a Fortune five hundred company?"

Adrienne shook her head. "None, I guess. But you shouldn't have to give up such a big part of who you are to get ahead."

His brows were furrowed again. "Nonsense. People do it all the time in show business. Cary Grant's real name was Archibald Alexander Leach. If a record company had presented you with a five-million-dollar contract, and the only condition was that you change your name to Patti Pularski, what would you have done?"

Adrienne couldn't think of anything to say. Lloyd had made his point. They both knew what her answer would have been.

"That's what I thought." Lloyd sounded triumphant.

"Eat your food," Adrienne said gently. "It's getting cold."

She searched her mind for something pleasant to talk about, but she was so surprised by what Lloyd had said that she gave up and just ate. After a while she said, "This is delicious."

Lloyd took another bite of his filet mignon. "They cook a mean steak, too."

"How did you find this place?"

"John Elliott and his wife bought me here my first night in town." Lloyd grimaced. "Speaking of John, he isn't very happy with me these days."

So that's why she hadn't heard from Lloyd in so long. "Why not?"

He sighed and wiped his mouth. "On the day Mallory Guest was supposed to sign our contract, she asked me a question and didn't like the answer I gave her. So now Ms. Guest is thinking things over. She isn't sure about the job anymore."

Adrienne's heart sank. That's why he was in such a bad mood. It looked as though she was going to stay stuck in the secretarial bull pen. "Can you tell me about it?"

Lloyd shrugged. "Why not? Mallory read the contract and then asked if PWE Multicultural will use the art, production, and writing personnel that we currently have on staff. Her voice sounded edgy but I ignored it. I told her that the person I hire will have to recruit a whole new staff of talent."

"What did she say?" asked Adrienne.

"She said that the new creative director would have to raid the staffs of African-American-owned advertising agencies to find the qualified people."

Adrienne frowned. "That's terrible."

Lloyd was clearly taken aback, but he recovered quickly. "*Raid* is a pretty strong word," he replied smoothly. "I prefer to think that PWE Multicultural will simply invite interested parties to join our team."

"I'll bet she didn't like the sound of that any better than I do."

"No, she didn't," Lloyd admitted. "She said if every mainstream ad agency follows this trend, the African-American-owned ad agencies will cease to exist."

"Would you really let that happen?"

"I had not given any thought to the issue until Mallory raised it, but I certainly don't want that to happen. I told her a small fib to buy myself some time to think. I told her that I had considered the possible ramifications, but I wasn't prepared to discuss my solution with her until she took the job."

"You should have been a politician. Go on."

"Mallory smiled like a game show hostess and said that unless she agreed with my solution in advance, she wouldn't be joining PWE at all."

"So now you're trying to come up with a solution?" Adrienne guessed.

"I need Mallory Guest to sign that contract so I can move on to some other plans that I have. Hell, I would like to just start the search for a creative director all over again," Lloyd said irritably, "but John Elliott is hell-bent on having her."

"Why?"

"Mallory is the creative director for Smith and Geren, which is PWE's main rival. She's won many Clio awards for her cutting-edge advertising campaigns, and she's a real smart woman."

"She may be smart in her field, but Mallory Guest under-estimates black people," Adrienne replied.

"Meaning?"

"If this trend, as she calls it, does start hurting the African-American ad agencies, they'll find a way to turn the situation around before any permanent damage is done. You can be sure of that."

"How?"

"I don't know how, but our history is proof that they will. Black folks have always made a way out of no way."

Lloyd smiled gently. "Yes, but her point was that I am a black man and that they shouldn't get a dirty trick like this thrown at them by one of their own."

Adrienne hadn't thought of the situation in that light, but she realized that Mallory Guest was right. "She has a very good point."

Lloyd sighed. "I was the only African American at Lewis and Wyse, and the only time you saw a brown face at PWE Chicago was when the mail guys came by." He laughed, but it was a hollow sound. "I'm not accustomed to dealing with these type of issues since I've never worked with my own kind before."

Adrienne didn't like his choice of words. What did "these type of issues" really mean? Could a boy from the ghetto grow up to be an Oreo?

"What are you thinking right now?" Lloyd asked abruptly.

Although Lloyd Cooper looked worried and vulnerable at that moment, Adrienne knew that underneath that image was LaMar Jenkins, a male of iron will who could set a goal for himself and meet it come hell or high water. She had no doubt that Lloyd would get Mallory Guest to come and work for him.

"I was thinking that you shouldn't give up, Lloyd," Adrienne lied quickly. "Why don't you ask her how she wants to handle the hiring and let her do it in her own way?"

Lloyd's eyes brightened. "You are absolutely right! Finding the talent to get the job done properly is her problem, isn't it? A simple answer to the problem!" His voice became husky. "You were always good for me, Adrienne. I'll see that you learn a lot from Mallory Guest if I can get her on board. With your theater background, you should do quite well in the networking and business-entertaining arena."

They grinned at each other.

"I think I'll order a bottle of wine; would you like that?" he asked.

"Sure."

Lloyd signaled the waiter and then looked at Adrienne. "White or red?" he asked.

"Red."

Lloyd gave the waiter a name and year that meant nothing to Adrienne, and then smiled at her. "So, when am I going to see Dan?"

"Very soon. Charlene and I are planning a dinner at their place. You are the guest of honor."

Lloyd seemed pleased. "I look forward to it."

Adrienne smiled. "I'm surprised you have such fond memories of my brother. He was such a little pain in the ass when we were trying to study."

"I liked the whole scene. The beautiful daughter. A pesky little brother. A mother and father who worked, kept the place clean, cared whether their kids went to school, and served hot, nutritious meals seven days a week. It felt good. Sometimes I even pretended that I was part of the household. The smart, geeky older brother."

"Sounds like a TV show."

"Better."

"Well, you're a bigger success than Dan or me. We're both proud of you."

"I'd trade everything I have for some decent childhood memories."

Adrienne didn't know how to answer such a sad assertion, so she told him about her years as a theater major at Hunter College, about the years of job-hopping from one corporation to another while trying to become a singer, and about meeting Mel. "I'm afraid my life doesn't match yours for drama," she ended.

Lloyd cleared his throat. "I'm glad to hear it, Adrienne. I always hoped that you were happy." He smiled at her.

"I'm okay," Adrienne said dryly, "but you should be over the moon. I'm dying to know how you did it," she said, smiling. "So tell me the rags-to-riches story that will be in bookstores everywhere soon."

He watched her coolly as he chewed his food precisely. *Now, that is the LaMar Jenkins I remember*, Adrienne thought. *Meticulous in every detail.* She waited until he'd chewed every bit in his mouth; then he reached for his wine.

"It's not a lot to tell," he began. "I think our stories are pretty much the same—I mean, in terms of our determination to live at least a few of our dreams. When I finally got out of that awful juvenile center, I was determined to get to college, by any means. I didn't have any money, and because of what my home situation was like, I didn't work closely with the guidance counselors during my senior year to narrow down some of those scholarships and select the school that would be best for me—and my sisters. I'd always assumed that the girls and I would be together, and I didn't want to travel too far away from them, no matter how much money they offered me, but when they separated us, all those early plans went out the window." He paused, taking another sip. Adrienne listened intently.

"I took a few temp jobs at first, just to get on my feet, but I knew where I needed to be was in college. I didn't even have enough to go to a two-year state college associate degree program, so I did what most young brothers do, especially when they don't see many other real prospects. I enlisted myself into the armed forces, namely, the Air Force."

"The Air Force?" Adrienne was shaking her head in disbelief. "LaMar—I'm sorry, Lloyd, you mean you actually joined the army?"

"The Air Force."

"Air Force, Army, Navy, Marines, you know what I mean. I don't believe it."

"Why?" he asked, bristling up a bit. "You don't think ole Pimple Jenkins had it in him?"

Adrienne recoiled at the taunt that had caused her old friend and tutor so much grief. But as she looked at him now from across the elegant table, she knew that Lloyd Cooper was as far from a Pimple Jenkins as anyone could be.

"I'm sorry you had to go through that, Lloyd—"

"Oh, don't be sorry for me," he said, cutting her off. "I doubt any of the guys I grew up with are making more than forty K a year, if that. They'd be lucky to make even a fraction of what PW&E is paying me."

With my meager thirty K, I wonder what Lloyd thinks of me, Adrienne thought. Surely he knew she wasn't pulling down the big ducats from the secretarial bull pen.

"But the rest of my tale isn't all that riveting. I served my duty in the Air Force, acquired some great skills, had the government pay for my college education, graduated with double degrees in marketing and business management, enrolled in Harvard's MBA program, and worked my way up the corporate ladder; and today, well, I'm fortunate enough to have you share your beautiful company with me."

He went back to eating, and after a minute Adrienne excused herself and sought refuge in the ladies' room. After relieving herself, she repaired her lipstick and then leaned forward against the sink to stare into the mirror. What was she doing? He knew she was married, and yet he never missed an opportunity to show her just how much more than friends he wanted to be. Would Lloyd expect her to sleep with him in return for his help? Was he really a sellout, as Mallory Guest apparently suspected? There were no answers in the mirror, so she went back out into the dining room.

Lloyd's eyes lit up as she approached the table. He stood up and pulled her chair out for her. Adrienne liked that he behaved as a gentleman. She gave him a smile. "Thanks."

"You're welcome." He sat back down. "Now, tell me how your mom and dad are getting along. They were wonderful to me during senior year. I'd love to see them also."

Adrienne soon had Lloyd cracking up as she told him all about her parents' new life down in the tiny town of Dietsville, Alabama.

Lloyd ordered another bottle of wine. And then another. The evening passed by so swiftly that they were both half drunk and startled when the waiter came over and said that the restaurant would be closing in a half hour.

Lloyd paid the bill, and as they walked through the parking lot toward the company car, he said, "I'm going to get you out of the secretarial pool as soon as Mallory signs that contract."

Adrienne gave him a quick hug of gratitude.

Lloyd's smile was blissful as he took a step backward slowly. For a minute Adrienne thought he might lean in and kiss her, but he backed up and straightened his tie. He started to say something and then changed his mind. To hide his feelings, he stuffed his hands deep into his pockets and walked quickly to the car with his head down. It was exactly what LaMar Jenkins used to do whenever he was overcome with emotion. Adrienne followed.

*   *   *

When Adrienne got home, her step was buoyant and her eyes were glowing. The magical quality of the evening's events made her want sex. She practically danced into the bedroom, where Mel was under the covers watching a made-for-TV movie. "Where the hell have you been?" he demanded. "It's almost midnight and I called your job. Nobody answered the phone."

"Hello, my love," she shouted breezily while tossing her coat and purse on the floor.

"Don't be 'hello lovin' me," he said, frowning at her. "Not when you waltzing in here at midnight like some trick in the street. I said, where you been?"

Adrienne just smiled and let out a blues wail, *"Oh, you never get nothing by being an angel child. You better change your ways and get real wild . . . "* She began unbuttoning her blouse and kicking off her heels.

"Adrienne," Mel said, confused. "Adrienne, what the hell are you doing? What's gotten into you?"

"'Cause wild women don't worry," she sang, *"wild women don't have the blues . . . "* She shimmied out of her skirt, revealing a black garter belt and silky panty hose. *"Wild women . . . "*

Before Mel could say another word, she threw herself on top of him and gave him a resounding kiss on his full lips. She bit the bottom one slightly, grazing it with her teeth.

Mel looked surprised for a moment, but he recovered quickly. He rolled her over so that she was now lying beneath him. "Hello to you, too, baby," he murmured. "You know, you a trip."

Their lovemaking was hot and heavy and wild that night—just like old times.

CHAPTER TWENTY-TWO

Mel woke up the next morning feeling like a new man. The previous night had not just been about sex. There had been genuine love between him and Adrienne. *Maybe God has decided that I've suffered enough,* he thought. The idea made him smile, and he stroked Adrienne's bare back tenderly until she opened her eyes.

"Is it time for work already?" she groaned.

Mel kissed her forehead. "Yes, but you must have one hell of a hangover. Why don't you call in sick?"

"I can't. Regina has a report that I have to start on today or she'll miss her deadline."

"Okay. I'll get you some Alka-Seltzer and dry toast. That and a shower should help a lot."

They smiled at each other and Mel squeezed her hand. She squeezed back, and the sensation made him feel weak with relief.

The next few weeks passed by in a delicious blur. Mel continued to work double shifts to catch up on the rent. He didn't go to the bar, and Little Jimmy never crossed his mind.

He was giving Adrienne a foot massage one evening when a long-forgotten wish resurfaced in his mind.

"Adrienne, did you ever think about leaving New York?"

She cocked her head to one side and gave him a sweet and

quizzical smile. "Sure. Part of my whole performing bug came from a desire to see the world. London. Tokyo. Nigeria. Scotland."

Damn. He wasn't thinking that big. "I meant leaving New York to live in another American city."

Adrienne stroked his hair. "Do you have a particular city in mind?"

"Yeah. When I was young, I wanted to live someplace that was always warm. If I never see another flake of snow again, it'll be way too soon. What do you think about moving to Miami?"

She paused. "I don't know."

Mel rubbed some more baby oil on her right foot, then slipped a white cotton sock onto it. "What about Los Angeles or Phoenix?"

"Los Angeles sounds better."

"Why?"

She shrugged. "Bigger city. More jobs."

Yeah, that made sense. "Do you think we could do that, baby?"

Adrienne sighed. "I can't think beyond that pile of bills in my closet, Mel. Will you ask me again when they're all paid off?"

Their eyes met. She leaned down, and they exchanged a kiss. Mel wondered silently if his marriage was really back on track, or if God was just playing some kind of game with him.

PART THREE

GOOD-BYE TO YESTERDAY

CHAPTER TWENTY-THREE

From the look on her supervisor's face, Adrienne was expecting bad news. She sat down on the edge of the chair and wondered what was going on.

Regina flung her red hair from her face in one fluid motion and waved a piece of paper in the air. "I have a memo here from Human Resources. You are being offered a promotion."

Adrienne grinned broadly.

"The job title is talent manager, and you'll be reporting to Lloyd Cooper, but I'm sure you already knew that." She waited for Adrienne's response, and when Adrienne didn't rise to the bait, she continued. "The starting salary is fifty thousand dollars per year."

Adrienne gasped. That was twenty thousand more than her current salary. She could pay off her bills in no time. "Are you sure?"

Regina wordlessly handed the memo to Adrienne. "See Mary Gibbons in Human Resources to complete the paperwork."

Adrienne stood up. "Thanks, Regina."

Regina's smile was frosty. "Good luck to you, Adrienne."

Adrienne was headed out the door when Regina called out behind her. "Oh, one more thing. As soon as you're done in Human Resources, Lloyd Cooper would like to see you."

Adrienne rushed through her paperwork, barely listening to the Human Resources representative. Then she hurried to Lloyd's office. She stood in the doorway. "So you worked it out with Mallory Guest. I'm not surprised. Thank you for the job."

Lloyd smirked at her remark about Mallory, and then they grinned at each other just like the mischievous youngsters they used to be.

"When do I start?" she asked.

"Is tomorrow morning soon enough?"

*   *   *

The next morning, Adrienne stood silently in unit 6 and watched the men from Office Services load two cardboard boxes of her belongings onto a hand truck. Sherry sullenly watched the proceedings, too. "Don't forget about us chickens still cooped up in the henhouse," she said.

Adrienne smiled. "I won't forget you since I'm sure you'll be coming upstairs to visit me quite often."

She waved good-bye to Sherry and followed the workers out of the cubicle and upstairs to her new office, which was directly opposite Lloyd Cooper's. She turned on the lights and was pleasantly surprised to find that the office was decorated in alternating shades of beige and mauve, with the desk, file cabinet, and floor-to-ceiling bookcase in a light shade of wood.

After the workmen left, Adrienne sat down in her brand-new chair and twirled around, waving her arms gleefully. When the chair stopped spinning, Lloyd Cooper was standing in her doorway, a playful smile on his face.

"Hey, there, gorgeous," he said.

Adrienne placed her hands flat on the desk and assumed a crisp, professional air.

"Good morning, Lloyd," she replied.

He beckoned. "Come with me. I'll take you down the hall to Mallory's office. She's looking forward to meeting you."

Adrienne gulped nervously. "I'm looking forward to meeting her, also."

Lloyd sat down on the edge of her desk and caressed her cheek lightly with his fingertip. "Don't worry, Adrienne, I'm ready to catch you if you fall."

Adrienne pushed his finger away. What kind of payback did he expect in return for his generosity? "Lloyd, I'm a married woman," she said sternly. "Please don't forget that."

He threw back his head and laughed. "I don't expect you to sleep with me, for God's sake. You gave me pity sex once. Let's not add sexual harassment to the mix."

Adrienne was mortified. She followed him down the hallway without saying another word.

Mallory Guest had flawless caramel skin, which set off to perfection the red outfit she was wearing. She wore her long, jet-black hair in thick, glossy twists that gently swept her shoulders and framed her perfect features as though someone had sculpted her face instead of letting it form on its own. When she smiled, her straight, white, even teeth seemed to glisten and draw even more attention to her curvy red lips. She carried her body with grace and self-assurance. Like a lady who has always had everything.

"Pleased to meet you, Adrienne," she said. Her voice had an easy sweetness. Adrienne unconsciously smoothed her clothes.

Her office was beautifully decorated to resemble a studio apartment. It even had a hardwood floor instead of carpeting. A Luther Vandross CD played softly in the background. Mallory gestured toward an apricot-colored sofa. "Please have a seat. Lloyd, I'll see you later." It was a dismissal.

Lloyd left the two women alone.

They sat side by side. Mallory's hands were folded in her lap, and her gaze was questioning.

"So, you're my talent manager." The statement held a trace of mockery.

Adrienne ignored the tone. "I'm very excited about the job, Ms. Guest."

"Call me Mallory."

Adrienne didn't like the expression on Mallory's face. Besides, she had enough drama in her life. If this woman didn't want her, it was better to find out right now. "Is there a problem, Mallory?" Her tone was cold and brisk.

Mallory was cool. "I wouldn't call it a problem, but I certainly am curious about how you got this job with not a shred of experience in this area."

Adrienne stammered. "I have a background in theater and I . . . uh . . . used to, uh . . . work in show business."

A slight smile played around the corners of Mallory's mouth. "Docks Sportswear has been a PWE client for the past twenty years. Up until now, Joseph Scarpaci, the president of Docks, has been content with selling his line of khaki pants primarily to wealthy white suburbanites in the Midwest. But times have changed, and Scarpaci is a smart man. He wants to go after a new market, the African-American market, and he's committed to an advertising budget of more than fifty million dollars."

Adrienne gasped.

"Docks Sportswear will be the first client of PWE Multicultural. Scarpaci wants to make Docks Sportswear the preferred brand of leisure clothing in the African-American community. I'm going to need talented African-American art directors, copywriters, TV commercial producers, casting directors, and media planners. Which brings us to the reason you're here. I'd like to see your list of contacts."

Adrienne stammered that she didn't have any.

Mallory smiled knowingly. "I figured that," she said. "Well perhaps your *friend* can give you some leads." She made the word "friend" sound like "lover."

CHAPTER TWENTY-FOUR

Mel was furious when Adrienne finally got around to telling him about the new job. They were lying in bed with the TV tuned in to some mindless sitcom that neither was paying attention to when Adrienne told him about her promotion. Mel sat up and glared down at his wife.

"I think you're more excited about this Lloyd Cooper than you are about moving out of the bull pen."

Adrienne shifted her position so that her body was turned slightly away from him.

"Don't be ridiculous," she muttered.

Mel sensed that he was onto something. "Turn on the light and sit up, Adrienne."

She didn't move.

"Didn't you hear me talkin' to you?" he demanded.

"Go to sleep, Mel. We both have to get up early in the morning."

Mel snatched Adrienne by the edge of her nightgown and turned her around to face him. Then he switched on the light himself. Adrienne was trembling, but he didn't care. If she was going to start cheating on him with her new boss, she had every reason to be afraid.

"Talk to me, damn it!"

"About what?"

Now she was going to play dumb. "Tell me how this guy even knew you were alive. He's just started a new job as president, for chrissakes; he must have a lot of stuff to do. Why all this interest in you?"

Adrienne removed his hand from her shoulder and climbed out of bed. She stood with her back to the dresser, leaning her hands on it to brace herself. "Okay, Mel. I'll tell you, but it's a long story. Just hear me out, okay?"

Mel was bewildered. "How can it be a long story? I thought the man just got there?"

Adrienne closed her eyes, then opened them. She held up a hand for him to be quiet. "It turns out that Lloyd Cooper and I knew each other from high school." She laughed nervously. "Life is funny, isn't it?"

Mel wasn't laughing. Something was terribly wrong.

Adrienne clutched the dresser, and then the incredible tale of LaMar Jenkins/Lloyd Cooper came pouring from her lips.

Mel couldn't believe what he was hearing. Some boy named LaMar had been the first one she'd slept with. The day after it happened, he had run off and Adrienne had never heard from him again. Now, LaMar was back and working at Adrienne's company under a new name. Mel felt a stab of rage shoot through his forehead.

"Let me get this straight, Adrienne. The first man you ever fucked just gave you a job in his department. Now your paycheck is bigger than mine. So the first man you ever fucked is going to put food on my table, and I'm just supposed to accept this. Is that what you're telling me, Adrienne?"

"Mel, stop talking nasty like that. We were children. I'm a married woman now."

"And he . . . ?" Mel watched her closely. "Is he married, too?"

Adrienne bit her lip and flushed. "No. He's still single."

"Do I have the word *stupid* printed across my forehead, Adrienne?"

"What are you talking about?"

"Have you seen him outside the office yet?"

She didn't answer. Mel got scared and angry at the same time. He jumped off the bed, grabbed his wife, and shook her. "Answer me!" The flickering lights from the television illuminated Mel's face and made it appear distorted in rage.

"Yes." It was a whisper. Adrienne looked frightened.

He let her go, ashamed, and sat back down. "I don't care how much he's paying you. You're leaving that company."

Her eyes were defiant. "I am not leaving the company, and you'd better not ever put your hands on me again, Melvin Jordan."

"Or you'll do what?" he snarled.

"Stop it, Mel. Have I ever given you reason not to trust me?"

Mel thought about it. No, Adrienne had never given him reason to think she would be unfaithful—and he certainly shouldn't be the one doing any finger-pointing—but it wasn't Adrienne he was worried about. It was that brother. He knew Adrienne and he knew men, men with eyes in their heads just as good as his own. There was no way this Lloyd guy was just giving Adrienne another twenty thousand dollars to "work in his division." No, something was wrong, whether she wanted to admit it or not. He couldn't just sit back like a chump and let this man make a play for his woman.

"Besides, I need the money," Adrienne pressed.

Mel knew she was right about that. That was the foul thing. Thanks to her shopping sprees—and his little now-and-then habit—they needed the money now more than ever. When he spoke again, his voice was cold and flat, resigned. "If you're smart enough to move up in the world, you should be smart enough to know when to shut the fuck up."

He turned off the TV and went to sleep.

CHAPTER TWENTY-FIVE

Adrienne, Lloyd, and Mallory spent many hours making plans for the start-up of PWE Multicultural. There were dozens of details that had to be worked out. They decided that it didn't make sense for Mallory to be physically separated from the people who would be reporting to her, so Lloyd had an entire department moved to another floor to free up space for the new venture. The art department was put to work designing stationery, business cards, and brochures according to Mallory's specifications.

They met with PWE's computer wizard and spent hours explaining the number of desktop units, software, networks, and other technology that were necessary. When Lloyd was exhausted, Mallory was still percolating. It was time to choose furniture and divide the space into cubicles for the copywriters, technical stations for the art directors, and offices for the account executives.

Lloyd seemed bored when it came to Mallory's color swatches and fabric samples, but he listened anyway. Mallory stood in the center of what would soon be the reception area of PWE Multicultural and declared "The color scheme has to reflect our heritage. Maybe I could use splashes of red, black, and green."

Adrienne knew that Lloyd was not going to go for that. She watched as his brows creased.

"This is not our own private company, Mallory," Lloyd said. "It's a division of another. Remember that many of the clients will meet with you here, and most of them will be pretty conservative."

She flashed him a brilliant smile. "Don't look so worried. I was only teasing to see if you were listening. I'll stick with a little kente cloth and order framed African-American art for the walls."

"That's much better, but still, don't overdo it. We're here to make money, and frightened people don't write checks."

Mallory was unfazed. "People have a way of becoming unfrightened when their profits start to soar."

Lloyd threw up his hands in resignation. "Fine. How many full-time people do you need?"

Mallory shrugged. "No more than twenty on the payroll. I have an excellent Rolodex of freelancers."

"Very good." Lloyd stood up. "I've got a lot of paperwork to catch up on. Keep me informed." Mallory waved good-bye and Lloyd walked away.

She smiled and went back to her swatches. "I refuse to raid the black ad agencies. I'll fill all the entry-level positions from talented beginners at the various art schools and copywriting workshops around the city. Make a list of them and start making calls today. We'll use freelancers and small businesses for everything else."

Adrienne gazed at her in admiration. Mallory was all soft and pretty on the outside, but she had strong principles.

"I also need you to put the finishing touches on a press conference that Lloyd and I have planned to launch the new division. What you'll need to do—and quickly, I might add—is a little research. Please use the media directories in the company library to develop a list of print journalists and TV and radio producers who should be invited. By the time you're done, there should be at least seventy-five media people on the list. Make sure that equal numbers of African Americans are included. I don't want them getting the news secondhand. Sally Gomez had one hundred invitations printed, and they arrived today. Pick up the box from her and get them out by tomorrow evening."

Adrienne scribbled the instructions as fast as she could, barely keeping pace with Mallory's fast speech.

The PWE Research Center took up the entire fourth floor of the building. Behind its glass doors were hundreds of books and periodicals covering every aspect of advertising, consumer demographics, marketing, and public relations.

Adrienne approached the white, circular reception desk, and a wizened little man gave her a kind smile. His pink scalp had only three long gray hairs on it, and these were oiled and artfully swirled across his shiny pate. Adrienne wondered briefly why the little man bothered with the hairs at all. It would be simpler just to snip those strands off and go bald.

"Good morning." She smiled.

He returned her greeting with a grin and a quick pat of the hairs as though he were concerned about his appearance. "How can I help you?"

Adrienne explained the project. The little man listened and then pointed toward the opposite end of the room. "What you need are the *Bacon's Media Directories.* They list every media outlet in the United States. There's one for radio, another for magazines, and a third for newspapers. The fourth volume combines TV and cable."

Adrienne groaned. "Four volumes! That could take hours. I'll have to check them out."

The little man shook his head vigorously from side to side. "No, ma'am. Those directories can't leave the center. Sorry."

Adrienne bit her lip and thought hard. "Is the information available on disk?"

"It is, but I'm afraid we don't carry them. You'd have to contact the Bacon's company directly. Each disc will run you about a hundred and seventy-five dollars."

"That's a total of seven hundred dollars!"

"Afraid so, ma'am. You know the Bacon's directories are organized by city and state. Would you consider just Xeroxing the sections you need? The volumes are pretty heavy, but it's not impossible."

Adrienne wanted to hug the little man. "Of course! I'll come back and do it at lunchtime." She wanted to get the press list to Mallory Guest as quickly as possible.

It was after five when Adrienne was finally able to get back to the library. She found the directories and carried them over to the copier. By the time she found the pages she needed in the first volume and ran off legible copies, it was after nine, and she was bone tired.

Adrienne picked up the second volume, chose the section she needed, and kept on copying the pages even though her arms ached from lifting the heavy books.

When she delivered the press list to Mallory's office the next afternoon, the elegant woman motioned Adrienne into a chair with a simple gesture of one manicured finger. Finally, Mallory looked up. Her face was beaming. "This is perfect!" she announced. "Every name on this list makes sense. It's a wonderful mix of trade, business, and consumer outlets."

"Thank you, Mallory."

"On the contrary, Adrienne. I thank you. A press conference can't be successful unless the appropriate media are invited."

Adrienne had never been to a press conference, so she wasn't sure what the next step was, but surely decisions about the space and seating arrangements needed to be made, and perhaps refreshments ordered. It seemed to Adrienne that although the journalists would hear whatever speeches were planned, there should also be printed information for them to take away from the event. Information with plenty of detail about the new division that would expand on the points made by the speakers. She took a deep breath and shared her ideas with Mallory.

Mallory nodded. "You're absolutely right. Go ahead and put it together."

*   *   *

On the morning of the press conference, Adrienne was a nervous wreck. She sat on the side of the bed and went over her checklist before she was even able to get dressed. She spoke out loud. "Let's see, the caterer called yesterday for the final head count and to verify that I ordered bagels, coffee, tea, orange juice, butter, cream cheese, jelly, Danish, and a fruit platter. I ordered a podium, microphone, and videotape recorder. All the press packets have been placed in front of each chair at the table.

I typed up both Lloyd's and Mallory's speeches and made extra copies. John Elliott's secretary gave me a copy of his speech, and I have an extra copy of that as well."

She chose a mauve suit from her closet and put it on. She used gel to smooth her hair into a perfect French roll and polished her image with a double strand of pearls around her neck and tiny seed pearls in her ears.

"You look real nice, baby," Mel drawled from the bed.

"Thank you." Adrienne's tone was crisp. She was still mad about the way he'd behaved when she told him about the job.

"Does this mean you'll be home late again?"

"Maybe. I'll see you later."

She grabbed her coat and purse, gave him a quick kiss, and left.

Adrienne took a cab to work because she didn't want to risk any possible ruin to her outfit.

She went straight to her office and double-checked everything. The media were expected to arrive at 10:00 A.M. Adrienne crossed her fingers and prayed hard.

By ten-thirty, all the senior executives were gathered in the boardroom, which overlooked the Avenue of the Americas. The food was attractively displayed on the twelve-foot mahogany conference table. The journalists were all helping themselves to breakfast and networking. John Elliott, Lloyd Cooper, and Mallory Guest each greeted the media representatives.

Adrienne stood in a corner of the room admiring Mallory's conversational skills, flawless appearance, and polished demeanor as she worked the room. *By next year this time, I'll be just as sophisticated as she is,* Adrienne thought.

John Elliott was the first to speak.

"I want to welcome all of you to Parton, Webster and Elliott. Thanks for coming out this morning." He droned on for about fifteen minutes, and then Lloyd took over.

Lloyd was ablaze with enthusiasm as he passionately promoted his cause.

The press conference ended a half hour later, and soon only Adrienne, Lloyd, Mallory, and John Elliott were left in the gigantic room.

"Brilliant!" exclaimed John. He gave Lloyd a firm handshake. Lloyd accepted the compliment from his boss without any false modesty. His head was held high and his chest puffed out.

As the two men began to talk privately, Mallory walked over to Adrienne. She looked tired. "Thank you so much, Adrienne; everything was wonderful."

CHAPTER TWENTY-SIX

It was a Saturday afternoon, and Mel was in Debra's apartment all by himself. Debra and Big Boy had gone to Atlantic City, and his sister needed someone to wait for a package from UPS.

Mel had to go to a dinner party at Dan's house in three hours to celebrate Adrienne's promotion and to meet Lloyd. He wasn't happy about it at all.

Why should he want to be in the same room with a man who had slept with his wife? The only reason he was going to this dinner was because Adrienne had insisted.

Adrienne's job was all she thought about these days. She was reading a lot of books that had the word *marketing* in the title, and she worked late almost every night. That meant what he wanted or needed didn't mean shit. It also meant he should be able to do as he pleased.

Little Jimmy was on the corner. Mel hesitated slightly as he approached the boy. He had sworn off drugs when he and Adrienne had reunited five months ago. Was this a one-time backslide? Could he handle getting high just today and not do it again tomorrow? He shrugged off the warning thoughts. *It will serve Adrienne right if I overdose on drugs. She doesn't care about me anymore. All she does is talk about Lloyd Cooper and her promotion.*

"How much?" asked Little Jimmy.

"Half a gram."

Back at Debra's house, he sat down at the kitchen table with a fifth of Bacardi, a liter of Pepsi-Cola, and the cocaine. He took a couple of snorts. The phone started ringing, but Mel wasn't about to quit. He took two more snorts. He was floating somewhere between Pluto and Uranus. Just as he finished and took a sip of rum straight from the bottle, the phone rang again. This time he answered. It was Adrienne.

"Mel, could you bring a pound of jumbo shrimp when you come? The fish market down here was out of them."

"Sure."

"Are you all right?"

"Un-huh."

"You sound funny."

"Un-huh. Shrimp. Sure." He hung up.

CHAPTER TWENTY-SEVEN

"**I** would never have recognized you on the street," Lloyd shouted as he clasped Dan in a bear hug. "My, how you've grown." He and Dan stood in the doorway grinning at each other as Adrienne and Charlene hovered nearby. Dan motioned for Charlene to come forward.

"This is my wife, Charlene," he said.

Lloyd gallantly kissed Charlene's hand. "What a beautiful woman. It's a pleasure to meet you. Thank you for inviting me to dinner."

Charlene looked back at Adrienne for a second. "Wow! I like him already."

Adrienne and Lloyd exchanged hugs, and then he looked around expectantly. "Where's your husband?"

"Mel had to do a favor for his sister," Adrienne explained. "He'll be here any moment."

Charlene took Lloyd's coat and waved everyone into the living room. "Go on, sit down and talk."

Dan was gazing at Lloyd with unabashed curiosity. "So, I hear life has been pretty good to you, man."

Lloyd sat down. "Yes. I've succeeded beyond my wildest dreams, Dan. I only wish your mom and dad could join us tonight."

A shadow passed across Dan's face. "We can call them later if you like."

Lloyd rubbed his hands together in anticipation. "Yes, I would love to tell them my story."

Although Adrienne was proud of Lloyd, she felt a bit uncomfortable about the proposed call to her parents. This dinner was supposed to be a relaxing occasion with an old family friend. She also wanted Mel to see that Lloyd was not a threat to their marriage. If Lloyd made such a call to Mom and Dad, it might sound as if he were bragging and everyone would be uncomfortable.

Charlene pulled Adrienne's arm. "We're going to leave you guys alone for a few minutes."

The two women went into the kitchen. "Why don't you make the salad while I rustle up the pasta?" Charlene suggested.

Adrienne nodded and opened the refrigerator. She took out lettuce, tomatoes, cucumbers, green pepper, and carrots and set them all on the counter. "I need bread crumbs and salad dressing."

Charlene was filling a huge pot with water. She gestured with her chin. "Look on the top shelf of the third cabinet. I hope Mel gets here with the shrimp soon. It won't take long to make this spaghetti."

Adrienne started cutting up ingredients. "He should be here in the next ten minutes."

Charlene looked toward the living room. "It's always nice when I can connect with a part of Dan's past."

"Get the fellas something to drink. That'll keep 'em busy till Mel gets here."

"Good idea." Charlene put the pot on the stove, dropped some olive oil in the water, turned the flame up high, and left.

Adrienne could hear snatches of conversation coming from the living room. *"I'll take a vodka and cranberry juice if you have it . . . just bring me a beer, honey . . . "* There was a lot of murmuring after that.

Charlene was grinning when she came back. "I asked Lloyd to tell me what Dan was like when he was a little boy."

"What did he say?"

"Smart but a little bit of a mama's boy."

"That's true."

"Maybe so, but I don't think Dan liked his answer."

"What do you think of Lloyd?"

Charlene loaded cubes of ice into a bucket and started searching for the tongs. "Don't get mad, Adrienne, but I think you need to forget the LaMar you once knew. That boy is long gone."

Adrienne felt confused. "What are you talking about?"

"I'm saying that Lloyd Cooper seems like a man who doesn't really trust anyone. He also plays his cards really close to the vest. You'll never really get to know him again, Adrienne."

"You're wrong, Charlene. He just seems very alone to me."

"I'm sure he is, and I'll bet he likes it that way," Charlene replied sarcastically. "Why do you think he is here tonight?"

"To see Dan?"

"And?"

"I don't know, Miss Social Worker, why don't you just tell me?"

"To show the Montgomery family what he has become. He will insist on calling your parents, even if Dan doesn't bring it up again."

"I'm sorry you don't like him."

Charlene shrugged. "Don't be silly. I'm not the important person here. I'll be nice to him because he has made you start smiling again. I also admire him. I hope that at least one of the kids I deal with every day finds his way out of the 'hood. I just want you to take off the rose-colored glasses and deal with the man he has become. Not the Oliver Twist he used to be."

Adrienne mixed the salad. Charlene's words made sense. There was a lot she still didn't know about Lloyd. She would think about all that later. In the meantime, where was Mel?

Dan suddenly appeared in the doorway. "Hey, we're dying of thirst out here." He smiled.

Charlene handed him the ice bucket, tongs, and a bottle of vodka. "I'm right behind you with the juice and beer."

"Dan, what do you think?" Adrienne whispered.

"He's a little conservative but okay."

The two went back out into the living room. Adrienne laughed to herself, wondering why she had even bothered to ask Dan's opinion. Her brother could find a soft, cuddly side to a serial killer.

The salad was ready. The spaghetti was cooked. The three of them sat drinking and chitchatting while waiting for Mel to arrive with the shrimp.

Dinner was supposed to be at seven. Shrimp scampi, pasta, and salad followed by Charlene's homemade brownies for dessert.

By eight, an uncomfortable silence had settled on the group. "I don't know what happened to Mel," Adrienne said finally, "but I'm hungry."

Charlene muttered an assent, and the two women hustled into the kitchen. As Charlene warmed up the food, Adrienne snatched plates, glasses, and silverware from the cabinets and drawers.

"I should have known Mel would pull a stunt like this. He didn't want to come in the first place."

"Maybe something happened to him."

"Unless he's dead, there is a phone nearby," Adrienne said as she slammed a glass down on the countertop. "He could have called. God only knows what Lloyd is thinking. This is so humiliating."

Adrienne glanced into the living room. Dan and Lloyd were engaged in an earnest conversation, but she couldn't make out what they were saying over the music.

Charlene and Adrienne carried bowls of salad and plates of spaghetti into the dining room, and everyone took a seat at the table.

Adrienne felt uncomfortable because the conversation was strained and everyone was so determined not to mention Mel's absence.

When dinner was over, Dan said, "Let's eat the brownies." His voice was tight.

Just then, the downstairs doorbell rang. Adrienne flew to the intercom and pressed the Talk button. "It's Mel," said the male voice.

Adrienne avoided Dan's and Charlene's gazes as she stepped out into the hallway. She heard the elevator door open, and then

Mel came swerving around the corner. He held on to a wall all the way down to the apartment, grinning steadily at his wife. By the time he reached her, she could smell the gray, stained sweat suit that he had on. She wrinkled her nose in distaste and stood in front of the closed door with her arms folded.

"Let's go home, Mel. You're drunk."

"Girl, what you talkin' 'bout?" With that remark, Mel pushed her aside and stumbled into the apartment. Adrienne followed him and saw Dan and Charlene leap to their feet.

"Adrienne," he yelled while turning to face her. "Baby, I got the fish."

He held up a smelly, wet bag for her to see. He stumbled backward and then propelled himself forward again. Somehow, he made it to the sofa. He put the smelly bag on his lap and squinted at each of them.

Lloyd hastily wiped his mouth with a napkin and pushed his plate away. "I think I'll be going now. It was good seeing you, Dan. Nice to meet you, Charlene." Lloyd's hasty retreat was lost in the hubbub.

"How come there's five Dans?" Mel asked.

"Because you're drunk," Adrienne screamed.

She went to hit him, but Dan grabbed her. "Don't do that. Let him lie down on the sofa and sleep it off."

Mel waved his arms about in the air and then fell onto his side. The shrimp fell out of the bag and slithered in several directions across Dan's freshly shampooed carpet. Adrienne picked up the shrimp and took them to the kitchen.

"Mel," said Charlene, "you knew that Adrienne's boss would be here tonight. How could you humiliate her like this?"

Mel's voice rumbled up from the sofa. "Damn this shit! Adrienne! Are you gonna let this woman talk about me like that? Can't a man get some respect from his own wife?"

He sat up with difficulty.

Dan spoke to him quietly. "Mel, you've got to earn respect. Something is obviously bothering you, which is why you got drunk in the first place. Maybe you could share your real troubles with Adrienne and everything could turn out all right."

Mel turned his drunken, coke-filled gaze on Dan. "Oh, so you one of those new sensitive black men I been hearing about, huh? One of those brothers who cook, clean, and talk all day long about your fuckin' feelings. Am I right? Huh?"

Charlene jumped up. "Don't start picking on Dan."

"I can handle him," Dan replied.

Mel stood and leaned forward so that he was nose to nose with Dan. "Well . . . handle me . . . go on . . . take your best shot."

Dan stepped forward to hit Mel but Charlene pushed him back. Charlene turned on Adrienne, who was watching the scene in frozen horror. "Mel cannot stay here tonight!" she shrieked. "And after this, if you don't see that you two need professional help, I don't know what else to say to you."

CHAPTER TWENTY-EIGHT

It was bad enough that Mel had embarrassed the hell out of her last night at Dan's house. But then, before she could stop him, he had stumbled out of her brother's house and stayed out for the rest of the night!

The next day, when Adrienne left the house to go shopping, it was way past noon and she'd still had no word from Mel. Now she hoped fervently that her period would come on time. Something was terribly wrong with Mel, and it was time for her to face that. He'd stayed out all night, and she didn't know where he'd been. *He could have been laid up with some woman, for all I know,* Adrienne thought, *maybe that Lillian bitch,* but the idea made her cringe. The last thing they needed was a baby. In fact, maybe it was time to start thinking about divorce.

Waiting for the elevator in Macy's department store, Adrienne massaged her hands, which were chilly from an unseasonably blustery wind outside. Last year, New York City had had its hottest spring in seventy-five years, according to the news reports. Obviously, Mother Nature was not going to be so kind this year. Nearly everyone on the street was still wearing a jacket. An elevator opened, and Adrienne waited patiently for the stream of passengers to get off. As she rode up to the women's dresses department, her body shook with anger.

Adrienne stalked the aisles like a demon. Ever since the fire, when all her belongings had vanished, shopping was the only activity that could quiet her nerves when she got upset.

After looking at every single skirt in her size, she settled on a Scotch plaid mini. Then she saw a gray ankle-length knit with a slit up the left thigh, which came with a belt that had a big silver buckle. Next it was on to dresses. After trying on ten different dresses, she chose an uncomplicated black Norma Kamali. *But you hardly ever wear black*, a little voice whispered in her ear. She shrugged the voice away and draped the garment over her arm. She fell in love with a silk blue-and-burgundy dress and didn't even blink at the price, which was $385. She paid for the purchases and went on to another floor.

Her rage lurked right beneath the pretty smile and courteous words that she gave the salespeople who helped her. Adrienne knew that they would have been astounded to know how desperately sad and angry she felt inside.

She chose a black tank top with mesh insets and a bikini bottom: $74. Then a young salesclerk dangled a silk twill scarf in gold in front of her eyes. She simply had to have it: $195. For a fleeting second, she thought about stabbing Mel as soon as he walked through the door and making her getaway before the cops could catch her. For that, she grabbed a classic leather backpack in brown: $95.

At this point her arms were aching, but today her shopping fetish had reached its peak. A sales clerk offered to hold all of the items behind the cash register. Adrienne flashed her a smile and was off and running once more. A French purse in black, shiny calfskin with a multicolored interior was next: $170. Then a faux pearl collar with pendant and a whopping price tag attached to it: $1,050.

Adrienne thought of how angry Mel would be if he knew that she was spending so much money. The mere thought of it made her feet do a light skip of glee, and her hands latched on to a V-neck poorboy ribbed cotton sweater for $68. It came in navy, natural, gray, white, burgundy, and brown. Adrienne couldn't decide which color was best, so she snatched up one of each.

She thanked the salesclerk at the register who had held the other items and now started ringing everything up.

"Will that be cash or credit card?" she asked.

"MasterCard," Adrienne replied confidently.

The cosmetics counter fell under attack: foundation, lipstick, blush, eyeliner, eye shadow, perfume, lotion, face cream, lip gloss, mascara. The total was $600.

The jewelry section was a virtual wonderland. Adrienne indulged in a pair of sterling silver hoops for $65 and a tennis bracelet that cost $500.

"Visa." Adrienne answered the clerk's question quite smoothly.

Adrienne strolled casually around the rows of electronics on yet another floor. In front of a cellular phone display, a salesman waved to get her attention. Adrienne shifted the heavy shopping bags to a more comfortable position and stepped up to see what the handsome white man had to offer. His hair was a dirty blond, and he had bright blue eyes that twinkled as he made his sales pitch.

"No one can afford to be without a cellular," he finished. "I tell you what, if you buy one cellular phone, I'll throw in a carrying case for free. The case comes in black or brown leather. Which one do you want?"

Adrienne's anger was beginning to subside. "Give me the brown," she said dispiritedly.

With her last ounce of energy, she stopped at another counter and spent $60 on a digital AM/FM cassette player. According to that salesclerk, a young Asian guy barely out of his teens, it had auto-reverse and an extra bass system.

This time her MasterCard was denied, so she put the purchase on her Discover card.

Adrienne balanced the heavy packages and tried to hail a cab, but to no avail. Thirty-fourth Street was crowded as usual with mobs of rude New Yorkers forging ahead like a Roman legion. They bumped into, stepped on, and cursed Adrienne as she struggled through the herd to get to the next corner, powerless to defend herself. Adrienne spotted an empty cab six cars behind the others, and a glimmer of hope made her heart pump in anticipation. She couldn't wait to get off her feet and out of the zoo on Seventh Avenue.

As she struggled to get closer to the cab so the driver could see her, a group of Japanese tourists began snapping photos of Macy's. Annoyed, she pushed through them, and to her dismay, she saw a tall blonde with a cell phone in hand jump into the cab she desperately wanted. Adrienne's heart sank as she looked into the cab, knowing she would have to walk several blocks to try to get another one. She regrouped the packages and lunged forward like a linebacker through the hordes of people, her aching feet and problems accompanying her for six blocks until a taxi finally stopped for her.

When the cab pulled up in front of her apartment building, Adrienne hauled all her bags out and then checked the backseat carefully to make certain that nothing had been left behind. Her rage was spent, and she felt positively exhausted.

CHAPTER TWENTY-NINE

Mel felt as if he were lying on the slimy bottom of the East River instead of driving a bus packed to capacity with chattering passengers across 125th Street. It was raining, and his skin felt cold. He had seen the tiny Apollo Theater a hundred times, yet today it looked even more old and decrepit than usual. He was in a terrible mood. He had apologized to Adrienne over and over, but she had not said a word to him since that awful night at Dan's house. It was clear that she was fed up.

Mel grimaced at a woman who was struggling up the steps with a baby in one hand and a folded stroller in the other. He lifted the steel bar that separated him from the public, and got up to give her a hand. He took the stroller and started pushing his way through the crowd of startled passengers. "Hey!" he yelled. "I need one of you righteous brothers to stand up and let this sister and her baby have a seat!"

A teenage boy stood up, and Mel gave him a brother-to-brother palm slap and helped the woman settle in. She thanked him warmly, and Mel went back to the driver's seat wishing that women with children would just stay at home.

For the past four weeks, Mel had tried to be the perfect husband. He cleaned the house, washed the dishes, did the laundry, and kept the refrigerator's interior shiny and filled with food.

Adrienne ignored everything he did, and he couldn't blame her.

Maybe he should just walk away so that Adrienne could start over. No, that wouldn't be right. If he asked Adrienne for a divorce, it would send her spiraling back into the depression that had enveloped her after Delilah's funeral. Worse, she could have a nervous breakdown and end up as a patient in Bellevue Hospital or something. *Delilah's death was all my fault,* he thought. *Adrienne is just beginning to rebuild her life and she wants to make our marriage work. Besides, what kind of man causes the death of his only child and then leaves his wife alone to live with the memories? If I left, I'd be a worse man than my own father was.*

No, he couldn't break Adrienne's heart again. Tears sprang to Mel's eyes at his predicament, and he wiped them away quickly. It took a few minutes for him to get his emotions under control, and then he turned to greet another line of boarding passengers with a quiet, tired smile.

CHAPTER THIRTY

All the bills from Adrienne's shopping spree arrived to haunt her.

She took them to work with her one morning to call the credit card companies and confess that she couldn't pay. Her bills were neatly stacked in two columns on each side of her desk. The tears that pooled in her eyes fell in heavy drops atop her desk.

"Adrienne?"

Adrienne wiped her eyes and looked up. *Good Lord,* she thought, *I forgot to close the door!* "Yes?"

"Why are you crying?"

"I don't want to bother you with my problems."

"It's never a problem to listen to a friend."

Adrienne managed a weak smile.

"Is it your husband?"

They had never spoken about the dinner. Lloyd seemed to know that she didn't want to discuss it. Adrienne felt a crying jag approaching, but she was powerless to stop it.

Lloyd closed the door.

"Oh, Lloyd, I'm in so much debt." She waved the bills in the air in desperation.

Lloyd lifted her chin up toward him and watched the tears stream down her face.

"Adrienne, you know money is not an issue for me. I'll give you the money to pay your creditors."

Adrienne pulled away and furiously shook her head. "I could never accept such a gift. I owe too much money."

"How much do you owe?"

Adrienne continued to shake her head.

"Tell me."

She sighed. "At least twenty thousand dollars."

Lloyd rolled his eyes. "That's nothing. I'll get my checkbook and we can settle all this right now."

"Absolutely not. I can't take that kind of money from you."

"Fine. It's a loan, then. Does that make you feel better?"

"I'll think about it, Lloyd."

"May I ask you a question?"

"What?"

"Are you in debt because of your husband's problem?"

"What problem are you talking about?"

Lloyd frowned. "His drug problem."

Adrienne felt as if he had slapped her. "Are you crazy? Mel is not on drugs!"

"Yes, he is," Lloyd said firmly. "I can spot a user a mile away."

"He isn't," Adrienne said stoutly. "And you don't know a damned thing about my husband."

"It's kind of you to stand by him after all he's put you through," Lloyd said quietly.

"Kindness?" Adrienne laughed bitterly. "I'm lucky he stayed with me after what I did."

Lloyd cocked his head to one side. "Guilt?" he asked.

Part of her wanted to tell the whole sad story, but she didn't want to watch the respect and admiration fade from his eyes.

"I don't know what hurt you've caused him in the past, Adrienne, but I'll bet that debt has been paid in full a thousand times over." He shifted from one foot to the other.

Adrienne shook her head. "You're so wrong."

Lloyd cleared his throat. "I'm sorry, but I don't believe you. Please don't get mad."

Adrienne took a deep breath and decided to let the truth come out. It was better than letting Lloyd believe that Mel's erratic behavior was caused by drugs. "I'm not mad at you, Lloyd. I just wish you had known Mel before we lost the baby. He hasn't been the same since Delilah died."

Lloyd was shocked. "A baby!"

Adrienne stood up and began to pace as she spoke. The story tumbled out: her need to get away from the baby, Mel's fatigue, the visit to the hair salon, dinner with Dan, the drive home, the street in Rosedale that was clogged with police cars and fire trucks, Delilah's funeral, and her withdrawal from life.

Her phone rang, but she and Lloyd both ignored it.

Lloyd listened without interruption until she sank back down on the chair, covering her face with her hands as though she were waiting for him to pass some terrible judgment.

"Adrienne," he spoke to her bowed head. "Every mother gets tired of her child once in a while. Escaping from a crying infant for a few hours didn't make you a bad mother. It means you were a good one. Do you know how many women are in jail for child abuse? Women who probably would not have snapped if they weren't under so much pressure?"

Adrienne had never thought of her longing to get away from Delilah that dreadful day as a sign of good parenting. It was a re-markable notion, and when she met Lloyd's eyes and saw that he meant it, a gigantic weight fell off her slim shoulders.

CHAPTER THIRTY-ONE

Mel walked through the back alley, rang the bell, and waited in front of the glass so the barmaid could see his face clearly. A cinnamon-colored, oval-shaped face stared at him for a moment and then disappeared. The door remained closed. Mel rang again. After five minutes, the same face reappeared. "My sister, Debra, works here," Mel shouted. He banged on the door for emphasis. The face disappeared, and then a new pair of eyes appeared in the glass, angry eyes that turned soft when they recognized him. The door swung open. It was the guy with the handheld metal detector. "Hey, man, you tryna catch a bullet or what?"

Mel followed him down the short, dark hallway and dropped his switchblade in the box. "Naw, man. Just wanna drink like everybody else. Who is the new hoochie that was just at the door?"

The man shrugged. "Think her name is Jane or some shit like that. How you been?"

"I'm all right." Mel waved good-bye and walked down the short flight of steps, through the second door, and into the bar. He blinked to adjust his eyes to the dimness. The place was packed. There was no empty stool, so he stood at the bar, waiting for Debra to notice him amid the waving, shouting, singing, and laughing customers.

Debra finally spotted him and smiled. "I know what you

drinkin'," she yelled in his direction. "One rum and Coke comin' up!"

He squeezed himself in between the folks on the stools. When Debra placed the glass in front of him, he drank its contents straight down without stopping. "Give me another one."

"Damn! What's wrong with you."

Mel wanted to say "everything," but there were too many other men around. He would come off sounding like some kind of punk. He shrugged off her question, but she wouldn't be put off so easily. "You need something, Mel?"

Hell yeah, he needed a whole lotta shit. Like somebody to talk to about the drugs that kept calling him. He needed a place to stay since it was just a matter of time before Adrienne threw him out in the street. He needed a preacher to go to God for him and ask how much more bad luck he had to suffer through before his debt to all those women he had wronged was paid in full. He needed to hit the lottery so he could pay off his wife's bills and wipe away that worried crease on her forehead. He needed his sister to come out from behind the counter and tell him everything was going to be all right. Most of all, he needed somebody to tell him why he felt so scared and lost inside.

But the bar was crowded. Debra put two more drinks in front of him and went to serve some other customers.

In the end, Mel didn't even get a chance to talk to his sister. She kept him supplied with drinks as she worked the busy bar. Finally, he gave her forty dollars and staggered home.

CHAPTER THIRTY-TWO

Charlene answered her phone on the first ring.

"Can you do my hair?"

"Now?"

"It's okay if you can't do it."

"No. Come on over."

The evening temperature was balmy, so Adrienne decided to walk the fifteen blocks to her brother's house. She was surprised to see that a photo of Dan and Charlene, which had been taken in Hawaii on their honeymoon, was now blown up to a gigantic size and hung on a living room wall. The expression on their faces made Adrienne want to weep. She and Mel used to look at each other like that.

"When did you do that?" Adrienne gestured at the picture.

"About two weeks ago," Charlene said proudly. "Doesn't it look great?"

"Yeah."

Charlene started bustling about, gathering her hairdressing gear. Adrienne followed her as she pulled some towels from the linen closet.

"Look, Charlene, I'm really sorry about what happened the last time I was here. I've been too embarrassed to call and tell you that."

Charlene turned around, her arms filled with towels and her eyes warm with concern. "I know that, honey. How is Mel?"

"I haven't been speaking to him and I can tell that it's driving him crazy."

"That's not the answer, and you know it."

"I've been too angry with him to have any kind of rational discussion about what happened. I plan to talk with him tomorrow night. I'm giving him an ultimatum. Either he signs up at Alcoholics Anonymous or finds someplace else to live."

"That's a start," Charlene said mildly, "but it's not enough."

Adrienne didn't want to hear any of Charlene's psychobabble. There was something else on her mind. "Stop. I've got something to tell you."

"Good news, I hope?"

"Very good news. Come on, I'll tell you while you're washing my hair."

They went into the bathroom. Charlene turned the water on as Adrienne knelt on the floor with her head hanging over the tub. The cold tile was hard beneath her knees. "Why don't you and Dan have bath carpet?"

"Because you have to wrestle with them to fit them into the washing machine. Then you can't put them in the dryer because the foam rubber will melt off. The back of the darn thing has to hang over the shower rod until it is dry enough to put back on the floor. Too much work."

"Lazybones," Adrienne grumbled. "And what happened to the bath mat?"

"It was old. We threw it out."

"Don't you know it's dangerous to get in the tub without a mat in it? What if you slip and fall?"

"What if you talk about what is really on your mind instead of complaining about my bathroom?"

Warm water cascaded over Adrienne's head. There was a pause and a squishy sound when Charlene squeezed the shampoo bottle. Finally, Charlene massaged the shampoo through her hair and began to scrub her scalp with her fingertips using vigorous circular motions.

"Lloyd has offered to loan me the money to get out of debt," said Adrienne.

"What does Mel say about that?"

"I didn't tell him."

The fingers stopped moving. "How much money are we talking about, girl?"

"Twenty thousand dollars."

"What?! I know you're feeling really desperate, Adrienne, but you can't commit Mel to something like this behind his back."

"Mel didn't make these bills," Adrienne answered irritably, "and I don't expect him to help me pay Lloyd back. So it's none of his business."

Charlene refilled the pail and rinsed the shampoo from Adrienne's tresses. "Sounds like you've already decided to take Lloyd up on his offer."

"I guess you're right." Had there ever been any real doubt about it?

Charlene relathered her head. "Be careful, girl."

"If Mel finds out, I'll deal with it then."

There was a hush, and then Charlene said, "That is not what I meant and you know it. Things are starting to get way out of hand, Adrienne."

"I don't know what you mean," Adrienne replied stubbornly.

"Sure you do. This may have started off as a platonic friendship between two old high school chums, but it is turning into something else."

"No, it isn't. Lloyd knows that I am not going to sleep with him. I already told him that."

"You haven't taken his twenty thousand dollars yet."

Adrienne couldn't suppress a giggle. "Okay, you may have a point. I'll just have to make it clear to Lloyd that I'm not interested in him romantically. I'll say it just before he puts the check in my hand."

Charlene wrapped a towel around Adrienne's head and helped her to a standing position.

"Adrienne, are you *sure* you aren't interested in him, maybe a little?" Charlene asked, biting her lip. "You have mentioned more than once or twice how fine he is."

"Charlene, I ain't thinking about Lloyd, and you know I love Mel."

"I hear you, girl. I hear you, but we both know sometimes love don't have nothing to do with it." Adrienne huffed beneath Charlene's hands. She was blotting her wet hair with the towel.

"And besides," Charlene continued, "Mel won't believe you and neither do I. You practically break out in a sweat every time you say Lloyd's name."

Adrienne shook her head emphatically. "That's not true." But it was. He affected her in a way she didn't know how to understand. At first she had thought it was simply nostalgia, some desire to relive that part of her youth, do it differently; but now she didn't know what to think. Every time he touched her—even the most innocent of brushes—left her remembering something she was beginning to think was no more with Mel.

Charlene folded her arms across her chest. "Cut it out."

Adrienne could not look Charlene in the eyes, but she still refused to give in. "I enjoy his friendship and that's it."

"Pure crap. You know what I think?"

"What?" asked Adrienne.

"I think that you would like to lay your head on Lloyd Cooper's broad chest and run your hands down those sleek dark thighs." Charlene was laughing now as she blocked Adrienne's attempt to leave the bathroom. "I think that you have fantasies of him holding you in those muscular arms."

Adrienne tried to choke back a giggle but she was unsuccessful. "It sounds like my brother is the one with the problem here. You were definitely checking Lloyd out when he came over here. I'm going to call Dan and tell him all about it, right now."

"Don't you dare!" Her face grew serious. "But really, Adrienne, I know you don't want to hear it, but I *am* a social worker, and I've seen so many families go down this road, and—"

"Charlene, please. No psyche-speak now. And anyway," Adrienne said, tying the towel tighter around her head, "I have a phone call to make to my brother. He needs to know that you thought Lloyd's thighs were sleek."

Adrienne ran from the bathroom and headed for the kitchen phone with Charlene hot on her heels. They wrestled playfully with the phone for a second, and then Adrienne sat on the dining room chair as her sister-in-law rooted around in a closet and emerged with a handheld blow dryer and an electric curler. She plugged them in and took the towel off Adrienne's head.

"Don't worry, Charlene. I've got the situation with Lloyd well under control, and even if something did happen, Mel would deserve it. I don't believe he didn't sleep with Big Boy's cousin."

"We don't really know what happened between Mel and that woman. It's best not to jump to conclusions—or jump into a situation with Lloyd you may regret sooner than later."

"I know in my heart, Charlene. Anyway, I don't want to talk about Mel. And no more of this booty talk about Lloyd. I need your advice about something nice that I want to do for him."

Charlene looked wary. "What is it, and why do you want to do it?"

Adrienne settled back in the chair as Charlene untied the towel and began to comb the tangles out. "The way I see it is like this. It's going to take me a long time to pay Lloyd back all that money. Even then, it won't really mean a lot to him because he isn't going to really miss the cash in the first place. So, I'm thinking of using the Internet to try and track down at least one of his sisters. I can't think of a better way to say thank you than that."

Charlene agreed. "Well, although I don't approve of you accepting the money, that is a wonderful idea, but if you find an address or phone number, don't set up any kind of reunion. He may need to do that in his own way, on his own terms. Just give him whatever information you find and leave it at that."

"That's exactly how I planned to handle it. Do you have any tips on where to start? I've gotten lost in the Internet maze quite a few times."

"At Social Services, we use People Search. First you go on the Yahoo, click on People Search, and then follow the steps. It's really easy."

"How much does it cost?"

"It's free."

* * *

So the following week, Adrienne took the check from Lloyd, gave him a grateful kiss—on the cheek—and stayed late one night to search the World Wide Web for her old friend's family. The search engine took her to the People Search home page. It was a simple form. All she had to do was enter the first and last names, city and state, then click on "Search." The results yielded no match for the name Noney Jenkins. There were eleven matches for Denise Jenkins in the New York City area. Ten Pamelas, seven Annies, and eleven Brendas. That meant she had twenty-four phone calls to make. She was tired, but it was best to make the calls in the evening while people were at home. She started dialing.

Adrienne and Lloyd crossed paths several times the next day, but she didn't want to give him the exciting news while he had business to take care of. He would need some silence and privacy in case his emotions got the better of him. She simply whispered, "I have a secret to tell you, but it'll have to wait until after five." When he pressed her for more information, she only smiled at him mysteriously. "I'll meet you in your office at five-thirty," she told him.

Lloyd called at four. "I have an emergency meeting outside the office. Can you tell me this good news around six over a drink at my apartment?"

Maybe Charlene was right. He did expect her to sleep with him in return for the money. "Why can't we talk somewhere else?" Adrienne asked suspiciously.

A lazy chuckle came from his throat. "My God, Adrienne! I thought we were long past this issue. I just want to show off my new home, but if you really don't trust me, I'll meet you back here."

Once again, Adrienne felt foolish. "I'm sorry, Lloyd. Give me your address."

* * *

He lived in a doorman building on the Upper East Side. The lobby was bigger than the first floor of many museums. Adrienne gave her name and the doorman waved her on by. Her high heels clicked across the marble floor of the lobby until she reached the elevator. It was a smooth, quiet ride to the penthouse floor. She was shocked when the elevator door opened and she found herself in Lloyd's foyer.

He was wearing a crisp, light-blue oxford button-down shirt, a pair of ironed blue jeans, and his bare feet were tucked into Gucci loafers. He grinned at her. "Hi, there, gorgeous."

He looked so sexy in jeans that Adrienne could only mumble a "hello" in return. She peeked over his shoulder. The place looked enormous.

"Why don't I take your coat and hang it up while you have a look around?"

A white sofa on white carpet was in the living room. Several pieces of expensive art lined the walls, along with Lloyd's diplomas, but there wasn't a single picture of Lloyd at all or a woman who could have been his ex-girlfriend, Patricia. In fact, there were no photos of anyone. There was no way to peek into Lloyd's past, present, or what the man intended for his future.

He bounded into the room, plunked himself down on the sofa, and patted the space beside him. "I've asked my maid to bring us some wine, but you must sit down and tell me what's going on before I burst from curiosity."

Adrienne gave him a teasing smile. "I'm sure you'll live until I get back from your bathroom. Where is it?"

He pointed. "Up those stairs."

She climbed the circular staircase up to the second floor. The first door opened onto a bathroom that was as big as her living room. All of the fixtures including the bathtub were ivory and gold. The tub's gilded legs stood on cream-colored floor tiles with an exquisite inlaid design of the same color. There was a huge movie-star mirror with lightbulbs on all four sides that was fixed to the wall above the double sink. Adrienne was in awe. She stood in the sumptuous room and remembered the desperate young boy she had known in high school. He had dragged himself from a situation that would have defeated a lesser human. It was quite a feat, and her admiration for LaMar had never been greater.

Adrienne went down the stairs and found Lloyd still sitting on the sofa. There was a spread of crackers, cheese, and fruit on the table in front of him, along with a bottle of wine and two crystal glasses. She sat down beside him and started rummaging through her briefcase for the papers she had printed out. When she found them, she positioned her body so that they were facing each other.

"Lloyd, you have done so much for me in the last couple of months, and I gave a lot of thought to finding a special way to repay you for the job, the money, and just being an all-around caring friend. I found the answer yesterday, and I hope that these papers bring you all the happiness that you've always deserved." She extended the papers and he eagerly took them from her hand.

Lloyd skimmed the first page, and his facial expression changed from happiness to a mask of shock.

Adrienne sat waiting for the gleeful shriek and the dancing around the room that she had imagined so vividly. Lloyd read the skimpy information and then placed the papers on the sofa between them. Adrienne was starting to feel uneasy. Something was terribly wrong. Why did Lloyd seem frozen in place? Why were his eyes impossible to read? Why were his hands curling into fists? She opened her mouth to speak, but the words stuck in her throat. Her mind told her to flee, but that didn't make sense. She sat rooted to the spot, utterly bewildered.

"You decided to find my sisters." It was an icy declaration.

"Lloyd, what's the matter?"

"I've known where my sisters are for a long time. If I wanted to see them, I could have done it a long time ago." His jaw was locked tightly, and his voice was so low he nearly hissed the words that he spoke.

Adrienne trembled at the glacial gaze he fixed on her. She was confused by his anger. "I . . . I don't know what to say . . . You used to love your family and I thought . . ."

"How dare you meddle in my private affairs!"

"I . . . I . . . I," Adrienne began to cry.

"Who the hell do you think you are?"

Adrienne's instincts told her not to respond.

His tirade was just beginning. He threw his wine glass at the wall, shattering the glass frame of one painting.

"Lloyd, take it easy," Adrienne began.

"No. I'm mad as hell, and I'll never forgive you for this. May I ask you a question?"

"What?"

"Why didn't you clean up your own backyard before you leaped the fence to fiddle around in someone else's garden?"

"My own backyard?"

"That's right. Don't you have serious issues in your own home? I mean, from what I saw at your brother's house, your marriage needs every ounce of energy you can muster up. Or have things changed dramatically? Tell me, Adrienne, are you and hubby soaking in a tub of marital bliss?"

"Lloyd, you're being mean, and if I thought you were going to act like this . . ."

"I don't have to read a list of phone numbers to know what is going on with my sisters. Did you talk to them?"

"I . . . uh . . . talked to Denise. I wanted to talk to Noney, but there was no listing for her on the search engine."

"That's how much you know about my family. Of course you couldn't find anyone named Noney. That's what I called her because when I was a little boy, I couldn't pronounce the word 'Noreen.'"

"Anyway, that's the only number that Denise doesn't have." She stood up. "May I have my coat, please?"

"No. Not until you understand what you've done. I suppose you told Denise everything about my new life?"

"No, I didn't. I simply told her that I was in touch with her long-lost brother and was going to surprise him with the information she gave me. She got very excited and can't wait to see you. She asked a lot of questions, but I figured it wasn't my place to answer them. She can't wait to see you."

"See me?" Lloyd laughed bitterly. "When I hired someone to find them a few years ago, he came back and told me that Denise has five fucking kids, no man, and runs the street all day. Pamela was a cable TV installer living in the Bronx with two kids and no husband. Annie was a drunk. No one knew where Noreen was. Brenda was the only one who graduated from college. The last I heard, she was headed for medical school. She was the only one who made something out of her goddamned life. Yeah, I'll just bet Denise wants to see me. She probably wants to know if I have any money to give her and that bunch of squalling brats."

Adrienne was disgusted. "Do you know how much it costs to go to medical school? Do you know how many loans and grants Brenda will have to get in order to make it? How much debt she'll be in when she completes her residency? How can you not want to contact her and do what you can to help?"

"Because she'll want to talk me into seeing the others, and it won't stop there. It'll be one thing after another until I'm dragged deep back into that world, and this time I'll never find my way out. Can't you see that?"

"No. I can't."

"Well, that's just too bad, Adrienne. If I get involved with those people again, they'll bring me down with them! God only knows how many kids, boyfriends, and bail bondsmen I'll have to pay for. I busted my ass so I wouldn't have to go through that again!"

"You hang out in five-star restaurants, ride around in a limo, and don't even know if your nieces and nephews have enough to eat. If success makes a person act like that, then maybe I was better off in the secretarial bull pen."

"You can go back there if you choose, but I worked hard to become a success, Adrienne, and I'm not letting anyone take it away from me."

Adrienne had heard enough. "You're not a success, LaMar Jenkins. Anyone who can turn their back on family like this is the worst kind of failure. I don't even see you as a man anymore. You're just a scared, sniveling, well-dressed coward. Now, I'm going to ask you one more time for my coat, and if you don't give it to me, I'm going to start screaming until someone calls upstairs to find out what is going on."

Adrienne snatched the coat from his hand, and when the elevator door opened, she left without saying good-bye.

Her heels clicked across the marble lobby floor, and she swept past the doorman and out onto Third Avenue. Although there were several cabs parked in front of Lloyd's building, Adrienne started to walk.

Charlene's words came and went as she made her way to the West Side. *Poor Mel, it was his loss, too, you know. . . . You shut Mel out when he needed you most . . . LaMar is gone, Adrienne . . . The man who came to dinner is nothing like the teenager you described.*

The more Adrienne remembered Charlene's observations, the more she realized that she had been running away from her problems for many years.

She had run away from her challenges in the music industry and buried her true self in a marriage to Mel. She ran away from Delilah's death by refusing to talk about it and hiding in darkness. She had been running from the reality of Mel's drinking problem for months by just ignoring all the signs. And Lillian! She had never stopped running from unpleasantness long enough to pin him down about that.

Adrienne paused at the corner to wait for the traffic light. Lloyd had just been a fancy place to run toward because her marriage was troubled.

No wonder Lloyd had achieved so much at such a young age. He was a coldhearted, selfish son of a bitch who thought only of his own needs. Mel had plenty of faults, but he always looked out for Debra. Mel believed in family. "I'm going to quit that job and make it without Lloyd's help," she told herself as tears of disappointment and rage stung the backs of her eyelids. "I don't need a knight on a white horse to ride in and save me from my pathetic life."

The light changed to green, and as Adrienne stepped into the intersection, she knew that neither Lloyd nor Mel was the source of her problems. It was time to stop running, turn around, and face her demons head-on.

Adrienne Montgomery Jordan was about to regain control of her life, and the place to start was in the unoccupied bedroom in their apartment, which held her stash of infant gear. Maybe someday she and Mel would be ready to have another baby, but they were a long way from that. The baby clothes were going to the Salvation Army first thing in the morning.

Adrienne allowed herself to feel the pain. By the time she got home and called Charlene, the events of the past hour already seemed part of the distant past. Much of her shock and anger had been replaced with sorrow for Lloyd. He was no longer a giant in her eyes. He was a punk.

*   *   *

After he finished his shift and parked his bus at the uptown depot on 125th, Mel found himself walking, and when he couldn't walk anymore, he ran. He ran down the inside of the streets and out in the middle of dark, dirty alleyways. He thought if he could just run fast enough, he could outrun his own desire, the need that seemed to be swelling up inside him until he couldn't hear anything but the longing and the blood. His body was calling for the cocaine, and the call was growing stronger with every minute. He would have called Debra, his wife, maybe even Lillian if he thought she'd give a damn, but he was too ashamed.

A man was supposed to be able to meet his needs, to know them and not be crushed by the weight of them.

Mel ran until his chest burned, and then he walked until his feet felt heavy and leaden, his hands trembling so, he could barely hold them in his pockets. No one met his eye as he stumbled past silent buildings and ramshackle storefronts, his MTA uniform not dark or formal enough to disguise the need in his walk. Back in another life, before a burning heartache sharp as a baby's cry in the middle of the night, he would have called his walk a junkie *stroll*. If he could have seen himself coming down the street as he was now, movements jerky, erratic, equilibrium off balance, lips all chapped, that would have been the first thought that crossed his mind. *There go one of them junkies, walk-running, skittering down the street.* When he was young and running the streets himself, he and his roughneck friends liked to shoot hoops and chunk rocks at the drug addicts, to watch them run, jaws slack, eyes vacant at first, then wide and frightened. They thought that shit was funny back then, but that was another life. Now Mel found himself doing his own version of the junkie stroll, and he couldn't stop himself to save his life.

Why bother? he thought as he turned a corner, searching for Little Jimmy or any other dealer with a pocketful of cocaine and an answer to quiet his hellish dreams. And it was the same dreams always. Delilah. Delilah dying. *I ain't worth saving,* he thought. *Couldn't even save my own child. What kind of fool would fall asleep with a lit cigarette?*

He couldn't tell Adrienne that he blamed himself. He didn't have to. She never pointed a finger at him, but he already knew she blamed him. It was in her face when she thought he wasn't looking, in her voice when she wasn't even saying anything, and in her heart when he held her close to his chest, and he still didn't feel any closer to her. But those weren't the kinds of things you said to your wife, not to a wife who's grieving, half out of her mind from grief. Mel carried those feelings down low, where nothing could touch them but the coke, where his need outweighed every thought, even Delilah. Even Adrienne . . .

* * *

At the same time, Adrienne was wandering around the apartment, wondering where Mel was. *If he is at Debra's house getting drunk, I'm going to tell him to come home, pack his shit, and go hang on to his sister's skirt tail for good.* She called Debra's house, but there was no answer. She made herself a stiff drink of vodka and orange juice, then rummaged around in the cabinet for some potato chips or crackers. There were none. Back in the bedroom, she put *Set It Off* in the VCR. Halfway through the movie and after her third drink, Adrienne was wishing that Queen Latifah or Jada Pinkett would lend her one of their weapons so she could blow Mel to kingdom come. *If he walks in here and says that he was at his sister's house, I'll know his ass is lying,* she thought. *After what happened at Dan's house, he probably thinks I'm so stupid that he can just tell me anything.*

The movie was over, and she was lying in bed thinking about the evening's shocking turn of events when she heard Mel's key turn in the lock. She looked up, and her nonchalant expression turned to alarm when Mel skipped into the bedroom. His face was dripping with sweat, and he was wearing a lime green windbreaker that barely covered his chest. Adrienne had never seen the garment before. As she swung her legs over the side of the bed, Mel spoke to her. His tongue was thick. His lips were twisted to the right. His eyes were even bigger and rounder than usual. "Hey, baby," Mel said. "I just came by to get something . . . can't stay . . . gotta go back out."

Adrienne stood up and reached out to touch him. *Why is Mel's mouth so contorted? Has he had a stroke? Can stroke victims have one and not know it? Do they move so fast?* Her thoughts came and went in a millisecond.

Mel jumped away from her and ricocheted to his bureau drawer. He spoke with his back to her as he riffled through his underwear, socks, and T-shirts. "I'm lookin' for my money . . . saved some last paycheck . . . be back later."

Adrienne's heart started beating erratically. "Mel, look at me!" she commanded. He did. His mouth smiled, but the eyes did not. He had some bills in one hand.

Adrienne reached toward the phone. "You're not going anywhere, Mel. I'm calling an ambulance and we're—"

Before she could lift the receiver, Mel sprinted around the bed, snatched the phone from the nightstand, and pulled it so hard that the line was wrenched from the wall jack. Fear and horror lodged in her chest. He ran from the apartment without a backward glance and left the door wide open.

Adrienne ran out into the hallway, calling his name as he thundered down the steps. She watched as Mel barreled out of the building. She ran back into the apartment with her eyes shut, fighting the reality forcing itself into her unwilling mind.

CHAPTER THIRTY-THREE

Mel had snorted over two hundred dollars' worth of cocaine that night. He had run out of money and gone home to get cash for more drugs. Now he dragged himself through the inky night. There were lots of people out on the street. Lovers walked hand in hand, kissing and laughing. Knots of teenage boys hung out on the corners enjoying the music that blasted from their big radios. The cafés on Columbus Avenue were crowded, and the people sitting at those tables were conversing; ice tinkled in their drinking glasses, and their knives and forks clinked against their plates.

Mel's thoughts were exploding in all directions, and he couldn't focus on any of them. Seeing Adrienne, and her yelling at him as if he were some child really set him off. *Lloyd Cooper and Adrienne's been gittin' it on,* he thought. *They gotta be crazy to think I don't see it. This is God payin' me back because if Delilah was still livin', none of this would have happened.*

He stumbled forward into traffic, hoping that a car would strike his body, send it soaring toward the top of the buildings and plummeting back to the pavement, where it would explode into a hot, red, sticky, gory mess. No, even that would not be enough to pay Delilah and Adrienne back for what he had done. Better that an eighteen-wheeler come barreling down the avenue and hit him, letting gasoline wash over his body; then a crackhead could saunter by at just that moment and idly toss away a cigarette. The fire at the end of the cigarette would come into contact with the gasoline, and he would go up in flames the way his daughter had.

He stood in the middle of the street, wondering where to turn as car horns blared around him. He walked west until he reached the Hudson River. As he looked down into the deceptively calm waters, a voice in his head told him to jump. Mel backed away from the river. He rushed back to Columbus Avenue and stood on Ninety-third Street feeling incredibly tired of the struggle that was his marriage, and even of life itself. Mel flagged down a gypsy cab. "Take me to a Hundred-and-sixteenth Street and Eighth Avenue. Make it quick. I'm in a hurry." He reached his destination in ten minutes flat.

The apartment was on the first floor, and Mel knew the neighborhood cops had to be on the payroll, because even a child could see that this was a drug den. There was more traffic going in and out of the rear apartment than there was at Grand Central Station. Mel waited until the hallway was empty for a moment, and then knocked. Two men guarded the door with their guns clearly visible while a young woman did the selling at a large kitchen table. The woman was high and trying not to show it. Mel stepped to her.

"Let me get a gram, sweet thing," he murmured.

"One hundred dollars," she mumbled without looking up.

Suddenly, there was a commotion. Some dude had made a purchase earlier and had come back to argue about the quality. Mel didn't turn around, but the angry man was talking fast and loud. Mel heard a click, which meant one of the guards had his piece at the guy's temple. The girl in front of Mel stood up and bumped against the table as she tried to look over his shoulder to see what was going on. Mel saw a chance to get some free merchandise. He scooped up two plastic bags and then shoved them into his pocket.

"Girl, let me get my shit and get outa here," he said nervously.

He threw five twenties on the table. She reached into a shoe box and put an envelope into Mel's outstretched palm. Mel nodded and pushed his way past the door dispute and walked quickly out of the building. He was barely halfway down the block when he heard shouting. A woman's voice yelled, "Hey! Somebody stop him!" Mel looked back and saw the girl who had sold him the coke, and one of the guards, running in his direction. Mel started running as fast as he could, hoping that the volley of bullets that he knew was coming would kill him quickly and not just leave him paralyzed.

The first bullet hit him in the left shoulder.

CHAPTER THIRTY-FOUR

A sobbing Adrienne called Dan as soon as Mel had disappeared.

"I'm coming over."

"No. If he comes back and finds you here, there will be trouble."

"If Mel is on drugs, he won't be back tonight," Dan said grimly.

Adrienne couldn't stop crying. "I don't want to take that chance."

But Dan insisted on being there for her. As she waited for him to arrive, Adrienne paced the floor and tried to pull herself together. Poor Mel. Her thoughts rambled in all directions. Had he been reaching out to her over the past few weeks? How had she ended up married to a cheating drug addict, anyway?

When Dan arrived, she was still alternating between loving and hating Mel. The only constant emotion she felt was worry. She was sitting on the sofa with her head buried in her hands. The faded T-shirt she wore was wrinkled and tearstained, and she could barely see his expression through her red, puffy eyes. Dan stood and massaged her back.

"Where is Charlene?"

"She has to get up at six. I decided not to wake her. Besides, I want you to come back home with me. We can talk all this out over there. Okay?"

"I'm going to have to find a rehab center. Mel needs help real bad."

"Charlene will help you with that. Right now, I just need you to get dressed and let's get out of here."

Adrienne wandered wearily into the bedroom and found a pair of sweatpants to drag on. She was looking for a matching shirt when the telephone rang. She listened to the voice on the other end, and a cry escaped her throat.

"What's the matter?" cried Dan as he rushed into the room.

Adrienne just kept getting dressed, unaware that tears were streaming down her face for the third time that day. Dan grabbed her by the wrist. It hurt, but she stopped moving.

"Tell me what has happened," he said sternly.

"Mel's been shot!"

Dan released her. "Oh, my God!"

They reached the street and in record time hailed a cab, one that that ended up stuck in an East Side traffic jam. "Can't you do something? I'm in a hurry!" Adrienne pounded the glass that separated her from the hapless driver, who started honking the horn in desperation.

Adrienne marched into the emergency room and up to the nurses' station with Dan trailing behind her. Several cops stood there. One of them stepped forward when she gave the nurse her name. "I'm Officer Delino, Mrs. Jordan." Adrienne stared at him without answering. She had mixed feelings about this whole sur-real experience. *Mel shot by a known drug dealer*, Officer Delino had said on the phone. The look on the face of the nurse at the desk scared the hell out of her. What if Mel was dead? Her knees trembled. *Please, God, let him be all right*, she prayed.

"Where is my husband?" she asked.

At that moment, a young doctor marched into the waiting room. He looked at all the scared and patient faces of the rela-tives seated on the hard chairs. "Are any of you related to Melvin Jordan?"

"I'm his wife," Adrienne said. There was something about the doctor's face that reminded her of the soot-covered fireman who had stopped her car on the day Delilah had died. Her heart began to race.

"Mrs. Jordan . . ." the doctor began as he fumbled with the stethoscope around his neck.

Adrienne couldn't stand to hear him say it. She started flailing her arms, pushing and shoving Dan and the nurses who stepped in to help. "I want to see him." Her voice was a breath of agonizing pain.

"Mrs. Jordan, please calm down." The doctor sounded surprised at her reaction. "I'll take you to him."

Their heels seemed to make a lot of racket as they started down a long hallway. Finally, one of the nurses stopped at room 503. She turned the knob and pushed the door in. The first bed was empty, and a curtain surrounded the other. Adrienne turned to face the doctor and nurses. "I want to be alone," she said. Everyone except the doctor moved back into the hallway. He didn't close the door. "Mrs. Jordan, your husband is heavily sedated. He won't be able to talk to you." Adrienne walked to the other side of the curtain. There was a form lying still in the bed with a sheet pulled up to its neck.

Adrienne yanked the sheet off. Mel lay on his side, his chocolate complexion now an ashy gray. His eyes were closed, and the lips were pursed tightly together as though still grimacing in pain. Tubes ran from his nose, and an IV needle was still stuck in one arm. Adrienne collapsed hysterically onto Mel. She cried for what seemed like hours. "Is he going to live?"

The doctor placed a warm hand on Adrienne's arm. "Yes, he will recover from his wounds."

Adrienne clung to Mel until she felt Dan's strong hands against her back. "Everything is going to be okay, Adrienne. Come on, let's go down to the cafeteria and wait until he wakes up. Come on, it's almost dawn now."

She wiped her eyes. "All right, but first I've got to call Debra," she said, her eyes tearing up again. She knew how much Debra loved her brother, and Mel would do anything for his sister. They were so close—for a long time had only had each other. Adrienne didn't know how she was going to break this terrible news to Debra, but she took a deep breath and mustered up the strength to punch the first few digits.

CHAPTER THIRTY-FIVE

The next day Mel lay in his hospital bed, staring out the window. One arm was hooked up to an IV. The other lay across his stomach. The bullet wounds were painful but not life-threatening, and for that he was grateful. That had been a suicide move. On some level he had wanted to die. He should have been a dead man, but once again his life had been spared. He needed help for his drug habit, and he knew it. Debra, who had gone downstairs to smoke, had called from the lobby to say that Adrienne was on her way up to see him. He felt that his marriage was over and now wished there were something he could do to save it. Mel was genuinely sorry about all the anguish he had caused Adrienne, and he wanted to beg for another chance, but that wouldn't be fair. It was time to come clean about everything and get out of her life.

She stood in the doorway. Mel closed his eyes, wishing she would say something to start the inevitable confrontation. She cleared her throat, but he did not turn toward her. His body did not move. She entered the room and tiptoed to his bed. "Are you awake, Mel?"

The question floated around the room. What should he say? *Yes, I'm awake and more alone than I've been since the day my mama died?* He could try pretending to be asleep and postpone the breakup until the next day. Mel sighed and opened his eyes. He was tired of playing stupid-ass-little-boy games. The only thing left to do was tell Adrienne how sorry he was and wish her better luck with the next man.

"How long have you been on drugs, Mel?" Her tone was weary, and when he turned over, her red eyes told a tale of lots of tears and no sleep.

"Things haven't been right with me since the fire. It was bad enough us being homeless and separated. But to make matters worse, I couldn't even hear your voice for a long time. You wouldn't come to the phone, and Dan always said you were out when I came to his door." He twisted his hands. "I know it's no excuse for all this, but I felt as down as a man can feel for a long time."

Adrienne sat down. "I want to hear everything you've done that I don't know about since the day of the fire, and I want the whole truth, Mel."

A long and painful conversation followed.

CHAPTER THIRTY-SIX

"Is Lloyd here?"

Sally's eyes did not meet hers. "Yes, Adrienne. He's been expecting you."

Adrienne squared her shoulders and walked into Lloyd's office with her head held high. He was standing with his back facing the door, staring out the window.

"I understand that you wanted to see me?" Her tone was crisp and professional.

"Sit down, Adrienne."

"I prefer to stand." Adrienne knew that she was probably about to be fired, and she didn't care. Lloyd Cooper sickened her, and it would be a relief not to see him around.

"I'm sorry about the way I behaved the other day."

"A lot has happened in my life since then. It doesn't matter anymore," she replied.

Lloyd turned around and sat down in his sleek executive chair. "We have a problem."

Adrienne met his gaze. "Go on."

"I think it would be best if we didn't work together anymore. However, you are my friend and I will not fire you."

"Then it sounds to me like *you* have the problem, LaMar."

He didn't smile. He didn't blink. He didn't wince. He pulled a folder toward him and continued his speech as though she hadn't said a word. "I think it would be best for all concerned if you were to resign."

"No. If I quit, then I don't get unemployment."

"Don't worry, PWE is prepared to give you a generous settlement, and I know a lot of people, Adrienne. I promise to help you find another job right away."

Adrienne searched his face and found genuine regret. "How much?"

"A year's salary."

"What about the loan?"

"I don't know what you're talking about."

"Sure you do. I still intend to pay you back with interest."

He stood up and went to stare out the window again. His back was facing her. "Forget the loan, Adrienne. There is a letter of resignation in the folder on my desk with a final PWE check attached to it in the amount of fifty thousand dollars. Please sign it before our friendship is totally ruined."

"I won't forget the loan. As soon as I get another job, I will pay it off. But not to you. Every payment will go to one of your sisters." Adrienne's chest was heaving with the injustice of the whole affair. "And you know what else?"

Dead silence.

"I'll put the money in a card and sign it 'In memory of your loving brother, LaMar.'"

He didn't turn around, but his shoulders hunched forward, and he shoved his hands deep in his pockets. The gesture didn't surprise Adrienne. LaMar always used to do that when he got upset.

"I'm scared, Adrienne."

Her heart softened. "So scared of poverty that you can't even call and let your family know that you're alive and well? So scared that you would force your oldest friend out of a job because she knows your weakness?"

Lloyd groaned. "Oh God, Adrienne. I'm sorry. You don't have to quit your job. Everything you've said about me is true."

"I'm scared, too, Lloyd."

He turned around. "Of what?"

She took a deep breath. "It turns out that you were right about Mel. He is on drugs. We still love each other and he has agreed to get help, but times will be tough for a while."

Lloyd seemed lost in thought for a moment and then massaged his temples. "So, Mel is going to face his demons. That makes him more of a man than I am. Will you please stay on at PWE?"

Adrienne patted him on the arm. "Yes and don't beat yourself up. It took Mel a long time to stand up. You'll get there, too. I'll help you."

He smiled gratefully. "I'm lucky to have a friend like you."

"Of course you are, Lloyd. I told you that seventeen years ago."

They laughed, and then Lloyd gave her a quick, friendly hug. "Yes, you did, and I'll never forget it again."

CHAPTER THIRTY-SEVEN

A week later, Debra stood outside the curtain that was closed around Mel's hospital bed, holding a pair of new jeans and a sweater for him to wear home. Inside, Mel submitted to the doctor's final examination.

"Let me see you move that shoulder." Mel raised his arm gingerly, wishing that they were sending him away with a painkiller that was stronger than Tylenol. Although the pain was no longer white-hot and throbbing, there was still a dull ache sometimes from the top of his left shoulder down to his fingertips. *I'll probably feel it on every rainy day for the rest of my life*, he thought. The doctor made some *tsk-tsk* sounds and wrote something on Mel's chart. "Turn over," he said.

Mel turned over on his stomach, lifted the white hospital gown, and submitted to the doctor's probing fingers, which inspected the wounds in his backside. "These are healing nicely," the doctor said. Mel didn't answer. Everyone at the bar and around the card table probably knew that he had been shot three times in the ass. It was undignified and embarrassing as hell. After checking his pulse once more, the doctor wished him luck and pulled the curtain back.

Mel had lost at least seven pounds from his already lanky frame, and when he stepped out of the bathroom after putting on the clothes Debra had bought for him, she told him, "You look like the devil done danced witchu."

"Yeah, I know."

His backside ached as he shuffled from the hospital room, clinging to his sister's arm. He leaned on Debra's shoulder as they made their way past the nurses' station, into the elevator, and out onto the street. Mel waited on the sidewalk while Debra stepped off the curb to hail a taxi. Suddenly, Mel knew that if he went back to Debra's house, it would be impossible to turn his life around. He waved his one good arm to get her attention just as a cab pulled up.

"I'm not going home with you," he announced firmly.

Her eyes widened. "Are you crazy? Adrienne's liable to meet you at the door with a baseball bat if you try to go back home right now." She opened the car door. "Stop this foolishness, Mel. Your wife done tole you she needs time to think all this out. You need to get off your feet and go lay down in the back room."

"I can't."

Debra slammed the door, and the taxi driver gave them both the finger before pulling away.

Debra looked worried and scared. No matter what, he was still her baby brother. "Mel, what's the matter witchu? It must be that medication got you acting like this."

Mel shook his head. "I'm going to Dan and Charlene's house. I need help, and Charlene will help me get it. She'll know what I should do next to get clean."

"Why you gonna do a fool thing like that? You can't just show up on your brother-in-law's doorstep without even calling first. Don't worry, I'll take care you." Her voice was tender. She stroked his face. "Just like I always have."

Mel took her hand and kissed the work-roughened palm. "Not this time, Debra."

CHAPTER THIRTY-EIGHT

Mel had paced outside Dan and Charlene's apartment building on West Fifty-second Street for what seemed like a hundred times, but he knew he'd only been standing outside the entrance for about twenty minutes. He watched the people come and go, mostly white, their faces open and curious, others closed and wary. They watched him as they passed, as if they knew he didn't belong there, a black man poorly dressed against the cold, shamefaced and weary on the busy street. Occasionally, a burst of laughter would drift down from an open window. Mel wondered when he'd be able to laugh like that again, deep and soulful without a trace of grief. He counted ten breaths, long, calming breaths; then he stamped his feet and pushed the buzzer to their apartment. Best to get on with it.

He buzzed again and waited for an answer. He hoped Charlene and Dan would cut him slack. It only took his nearly dying once to get the point. Life was too precious, no matter what was lost, what might not ever have been given. Mel thought about his mother, who had died unhappy, and his father, who had left Debra and him and never looked back. And he thought about Delilah and all the love he'd held for that child, his firstborn, his daughter, and for the woman he had loved, who loved him back. After Delilah died, he knew he had stopped living, but today he was going to try to put things back on track, at least in himself if nowhere else.

"It's me, Mel," he answered when Charlene buzzed him in. When he got upstairs, she and Dan were waiting for him, the door open, the inside of the apartment bright and warm.

"Glad to see you, brother. You worried us for a moment."

Mel didn't know what to say. He wanted to hang his head, but Charlene ushered him in and took his light jacket.

"You must be cold, Mel. Come on in here and let's see what we can do. I'll tell you like I told Adrienne: this house, our home is welcome to you if you need it."

"Yes," Dan said, heading for the kitchen. "You want something to drink?" Mel shook his head. He hadn't had much of an appetite since they released him, even though his stomach felt empty. "Well, you probably know Adrienne is going to need a little time. A little time to get herself together. Like Charlene said, you're welcome to stay here with us until she's ready to talk with you. In the meanwhile, why don't we eat something before we talk about this drug rehab program that Charlene recommends. It's a weekly. It's supposed to be very good, and later we'll catch the game."

CHAPTER THIRTY-NINE

Debra stared at Adrienne intently, lit a cigarette, and inhaled loudly. "I think Mel believes you in love wit' your boss."

"That's crazy," Adrienne said, "I didn't even really know him." Her hands fluttered helplessly. How could she make Debra understand? "He had money and a big-time job, plus I admired him. He was really poor when we were kids and . . ." Her voice trailed off because Debra was frowning.

"You shut my brother out when Delilah died. He was hurtin' as much as you. Then you take him back, only you wasn't really thinkin' 'bout him at all."

"I was thinking of us."

"No, you wasn't. You was thinkin' 'bout havin' another baby. But I ain't mad at you about that. I nevah had no kids, so I can't judge on what you did after Delilah passed away."

"Then what are you mad at me about?"

"I'm mad at you for comin' here today lookin' for trouble."

"Trouble? I'm not looking for trouble. I just want peace between us after all these years. Mel has a long, hard road ahead of him, and it would be easier for him if you and I were friends. That way he won't have to sneak up here to see you or be sad because you never visit us. If you and I stand strong together, he'll get well faster."

"I just want to get some money together to give him so he can get out of your brother's house and into a room somewhere. He gonna do better wit'out yo ass pullin' him down."

Adrienne took a deep breath and hoped the big woman did not hit her for what she was going to say next. "Debra, I'm sorry that Mel didn't marry your friend Rose, but you really need to get the fuck over it and help me save his life."

Debra took a few more drags on her cigarette and stubbed it out. "If your boss had done whatever it is you wanted him to do, me and you wouldn't be havin' this talk. You woulda run off wit' him and not looked back at Mel." She stood up and put her hands on her hips. "Now get outa my house." Debra walked to the front door, opened it, and stood aside. "Bye."

Adrienne shook her head and refused to move. She thought about Lloyd and how she had allowed herself to believe that a knight in shining armor had ridden into town to save her from her life. She thought about letting the music business beat her down and how that defeat had driven her into marriage with the first man who came along. At first, the marriage had been a place to hide out. A place to pretend she didn't care about her hopes and dreams of becoming a singer. Now it meant everything to her, and she didn't intend to lose it.

"I wasn't planning to run off and leave Mel for another man. I was just about to throw him out because he was drunk all the time, he gave you our rent money one month, and he went to bed with your man's cousin."

Debra gasped. "Mel told you 'bout that?"

Adrienne ignored the question. "Wouldn't you throw Big Boy out if he did all of that to you?"

Debra closed the door. "What do you want me to do?"

"Charlene told me that the program that he is in meets once a week in the evening. I'm going to surprise Mel by picking him up one night from one of the rehab meetings and taking him home with me. I'd like you to be at our house waiting with one of those nice, old-fashioned meals that he likes you to make so much. I want him to see you in my kitchen. That will tell him that the past is past and we're friends."

"If he don't drop dead of shock, first," Debra said dryly.

"Then you'll do it?"

Debra hesitated.

"It's not for me, Debra."

"All right. I'll be there."

They shook hands on it.

CHAPTER FORTY

Ready for Recovery met every Wednesday night on Seventy-second Street between Second and Third Avenues. Mel looked at the building number, which he had scrawled on a slip of paper. Several people smiled at him as they went inside. *I wonder what goes on in there,* he thought. *Are they going to ask me a whole bunch of questions?* He took a few steps back without even realizing it. *Maybe getting shot was enough. If I ever think about using drugs again, I'll come back,* he decided. Mel turned to cross the street and found himself face to face with a slim white man. His kind, gray eyes were filled with compassion. He placed a hand on Mel's arm. "Please stay," he said. "My name is Paul. Why don't you come inside, grab a cup of coffee, and just sit in the back of the room. I'm the group leader, and I give you my word that you don't have to speak."

Mel hesitated, not knowing how to respond. Paul smiled and removed his hand from Mel's arm. "Come on."

The room was set up like a classroom, with folding chairs in rows and a microphone on a stand in the front. Paul disappeared into a group of people who were talking on the far side of the room. There was another cluster of people standing closer to Mel, drinking coffee out of paper cups. A tall, slender black woman disengaged herself from the cluster and bounced toward him. She was smiling. "Welcome. I'm glad you made it. Would you like some coffee?" Mel nodded and followed her to the coffeemaker. She was wearing a green turtleneck sweater, jeans, and a pair of sneakers. He accepted the warm cup from her gratefully. She sipped hers. "I'm Nora." She beckoned to the cluster of people she had been standing with. They came over, and a man shook his hand. "Hello, I'm Steve. What's your drug of choice?"

Nora laughed. "You don't have to answer him."

Mel smiled. "Hi, everybody."

"Is this your first meeting?" asked a petite white woman with streaked gray hair.

Mel nodded, and to his surprise, he received a smile and a simple, loving hug in return.

Mel felt his fright and apprehension begin to melt. Paul appeared at the microphone and called the meeting to order. Everyone grabbed a coffee refill and took a seat. Mel made sure that his was in the last row near the door, in case he wanted to leave before the session was over.

Paul turned on the microphone. "Welcome to Ready for Recovery, the Seventy-second Street branch meeting of Narcotics Anonymous. Who wants to read the twelve steps tonight?"

Nora volunteered and Paul turned the microphone over to her. Mel listened intently as she recited them from memory. When Nora reached step number eight, Mel felt a weight fall from his shoulders. *"We made a list of all persons we had harmed, and became willing to make amends to them all."*

Forget steps one through seven, he thought. Here was the solution! To save his own life, all he had to do was find the courage to go to everyone he had hurt, scammed, or deceived, and confess.

Nora sat down to a round of applause, and Paul stood up once more. "We have a speaker coming to share with us tonight, but before that, has anyone here been clean for ninety days?" Several hands went up. Everyone applauded. "Six months?" More hands. More applause. "How about a year?" Nora stood up alone, and Mel found himself standing up with everyone else to give her a standing ovation.

"Do we have any new members?" Paul asked.

Mel scrunched down in his chair as a skinny white woman with pale skin and short blond hair stood up.

"Tell us your first name," Paul said gently.

She took a deep breath and her words rushed out. "Hello, everybody. My name is Lisa Johnson, and I am a prostitute and a crack addict."

"Glad you made it, Lisa," chanted the group. Lisa sat down.

Paul addressed her. "Welcome, Lisa. We only use first names here. We hope that Ready for Recovery will become your home group. However, you will receive a pamphlet at the end of this meeting that lists every center in the city along with their meeting days and times."

Paul's eyes swept over the group. "I am happy to say that yesterday was my third anniversary." The group cheered, but Paul silenced them with a raised hand. "Thank you, but every day is a struggle, and it always will be. Now I'll turn the discussion over to Mr. Archer Downs, who brings the message of recovery to us tonight."

Archer Downs was a six-foot string bean of a man. His bushy black hair was streaked with gray, as were his sideburns and mustache. His complexion was ruddy, which was unfortunate since his suit, which draped his gangly frame, was somewhere between red and cranberry. His voice seemed to come from a stout man. It boomed. There was no need for a microphone. He held his arms limply at his sides. He was a plain man who came with a plain message that he dived into without preamble. "I had a wife. I had four beautiful children and a thriving law practice. We owned a home in Montclair, New Jersey. We had a nice life until my dad drowned in a boating accident and I got on the pipe. I smoked crack once, twice, three times. After that, I couldn't find my way back to sobriety for five years. In those five years, I smoked away the house, our clothes, the children's toys, and their college funds. I embezzled money from the law firm and went to jail. By the time I got out, my wife had divorced me and moved away."

Archer told his story in a matter-of-fact manner, his voice devoid of emotion or self-pity. Mel understood that the man had somehow managed to make peace with the horror he had inflicted on his family. But how?

"I was on suicide watch in jail when a chaplain came to see me. He told me something which I found hard to believe." Archer paused and lowered his eyes. "The chaplain told me that God didn't want me to die. He wanted to embrace me. I laughed at that. I figured the chaplain wouldn't be spending time on me if he could see my crying wife, scared mother, and ragged children."

There was a muffled sob from somewhere in the room. Mel didn't know if it came from a man or a woman.

"The chaplain came by every day for a week. One day, I wasn't in the mood to hear what he'd come to say. I figured the best way to get rid of him for good would be to tell him every bad thing I had done to feed my habit."

Mel wondered what the chaplain would have said to a man who fell asleep with a lit cigarette in his hand, causing the death of his infant daughter.

"At the end of my recital," Archer continued, "the chaplain told me that God's love is mighty and strong enough to embrace every man. Even a man like me who forced his own retarded sister to sell her body one night so that he could get high. I got out of jail six years ago, and I've been sober ever since. That is my message to you. No matter what you've done, God's love is a mighty one and is strong enough to handle it. Thank you for listening."

After hearing that message, Mel decided to become a permanent member of the group. God had allowed him to survive the drug dealer's bullets because He wanted Mel to live. It was a sign from above that his debt was paid in full. He was looking forward to a drug-free existence. He left feeling empowered. It had been a long time since he had felt that way.

He decided to apologize to Big Boy first, so that he could start visiting Debra again without worrying about another fight, which would upset his sister. He called Debra's house the following evening.

"Hey, I'm glad I caught you."

"I ain't got nowhere else to go right now."

Mel cleared his throat. "Is Big Boy there?"

"Yeah." Her tone was cautious. "Why you wanna know?"

Mel told her about step eight. "Put Big Boy on the phone."

Debra whooped with laughter. "Can I listen on the extension?"

Mel felt foolish. "No. And this is not funny, Debra."

"So lemme understan' this. You gotta tell everybody you wronged how sorry you are. How far back you gotta go? It seems to me that just callin' up all them women at your old telephone company job would take a coupla years." Debra guffawed again.

Mel was puzzled. Did Ready for Recovery expect him to go that far? He had thrown away his little black book the day after he met Adrienne. How was he supposed to find all those women? Then a new thought occurred to him. *I don't have to call all those women, because I wasn't doing no drugs when I pissed them off. I also wasn't married to none of them, so I didn't commit any sin. Anyway, they should be over it by now.* "Just put Big Boy on the goddamn phone," he said.

Mel heard Debra tell Big Boy to pick up the phone. "Me and your brother ain't got nuthin' else to say to each other." Mel knew that Big Boy was shouting the words so that he could hear them. Then there was a long silence. Mel was about to hang up when Big Boy spoke into the receiver.

"What the fuck you want, Mel?"

Mel swallowed hard. "I'm sorry for what I did to Lillian."

"Say what?"

"You heard me, man."

"Tell her that, too. You hear me, Mel?"

"Yeah."

"I ain't playin'; you hurt her again and you gonna be real sorry."

Mel gritted his teeth in anger. "Don't threaten me, man." He hung up before Big Boy could say another word.

* * *

He lay on the sofa at Dan and Charlene's house and watched TV until it was dark outside. Then he got up and put on a sweat-suit and sneakers. *We made a list of all persons we had harmed, and became willing to make amends to them all.* It was time to go see Lillian.

* * *

He walked a block before he decided to call first. She might have company, and he didn't want to make matters worse between them by intruding on her privacy. He dropped a quarter in a phone booth and got her number from the directory assistance operator.

She picked up on the first ring.

"Lillian?"

"Yeah, this is me."

"Uh, Lillian. This is Melvin Jordan. I know you're mad at me, but . . ."

"Oh, Mel! How are you?" Her tone was cool.

"Fine."

"And Adrienne?" The voice was now glacial.

Damn. She wasn't going to make this easy. "Uh, she's fine, too."

"I'm glad to hear it," Lillian said briskly. And then there was silence. Mel gripped the receiver tightly, feeling like a fool. "Look, I'm sorry to bother you. Good-bye."

"Don't hang up so fast! At least tell me why you called."

Mel took a deep breath. "I owe you an explanation, Lillian. Can I come over?"

"See you when you get here," and then she hung up.

Lillian answered the door with two little girls staring out at him from behind her. She was dressed in jeans and a T-shirt. Her dark-brown hair was pulled back into a short ponytail. It made her look younger. She held the door wider, and her narrowed eyes never left him as he walked in and stood there awkwardly, not knowing what to say with the kids watching.

"Say hello to Mr. Jordan," she told them.

"Hello, Mr. Jordan," they answered in unison.

"How old are they?" Mel asked politely.

"Carol is six, and Betty is four."

Mel shifted from one foot to the other. "They visitin'?"

"My grandma had a stroke," Lillian said simply, "so my girls are living here with me now."

"I'm sorry," Mel said sincerely. So Lillian and her kids were living all cramped up in the tiny studio apartment. "When did it happen?"

"The same morning you left here," she said frankly.

No wonder she had broken down crying in Debra's kitchen. Mel felt like dirt.

She turned to the little girls. "Y'all go set the table. Dinner is almost ready."

They scampered away obediently.

Lillian beckoned to him. "Come sit down."

Mel followed her into the main room and perched on the edge of the sofa. Lillian sat next to him sideways, with one leg folded up under her so that she could look him in the face.

Mel turned slightly so that their eyes met. "Look, Lillian, when we went out that night, I knew me and Adrienne was gettin' back together the next morning. I lied to you and I'm real sorry about it."

She shook her head from side to side. "Not good enough."

Jesus! What did she mean it wasn't good enough? What the hell else did she expect him to say? He looked down at his hands.

Lillian gestured toward the kitchen, where her daughters were chattering happily and making a lot of noise with the dishes. "Only little kids like those in there have a right to think that the words 'I'm sorry' make everything all better. They do it all the time. They say 'I'm sorry' and believe that it washes their wrong away like an eraser on a chalkboard. You a grown man. Now I want to know why you did that to me."

If Lillian hadn't been a frequent guest at Debra's house, where he was bound to run into her again, Mel would have left the apartment that instant. Instead, he frantically searched his mind for the truth. When he found it, he decided to give it to her straight. "I wanted you and if I had tole you the truth, we wouldn't have spent the night together."

Her cheeks puffed up with anger, and her voice rose. "You don't know that. I'm a grown woman, I mighta done it anyway. I had a right to decide that for myself. But what you sayin' is that you wanted something and didn't give a flyin' fuck whether I got hurt or not? Ain't that the way it was, Mel?" Her eyes looked like dark-brown molten lava, and they nearly liquefied him.

He stood up. "That's the way it was. I better go."

As he fiddled with the locks on Lillian's door, she threw one last barb at him, and the tone of her voice was mocking and filled with contempt.

"You good at runnin', ain't you Mel?"

Mel knew that Lillian had the right to reject his apology, but at least he had done the right thing. He also knew that Lillian was right. He was very good at running, but he was sick and tired of the toll it had taken on his body and spirit. It was time to stand still and get well.

* * *

The following Wednesday night, Mel didn't hesitate when he reached the Ready for Recovery building. Many people recognized him and called out welcome greetings when he came in.

Nora was setting up the folding chairs. "Glad you made it back, Mel. Can you give me a hand?"

Mel nodded and took the rest of the chairs from against the wall and set them up. "How have you been?"

"I got a job," Nora said proudly.

"That's real nice. Congratulations."

"Thanks."

Before they could talk further, Steve clamped Mel on the back of the neck. "Good to see you, man. You're just in time to make the coffee."

"We don't give any breaks after the first meeting," Nora said with a smile. "From now on, when you come here, we put you to work."

Mel laughed. More people came in. After coffee and dough-nuts, Paul appeared at the microphone and called the meeting to order. This time Mel sat in the front row.

Paul turned on the microphone. "Welcome to Ready for Recovery, the Seventy-second Street branch meeting of Narcotics Anonymous. Who wants to read the twelve steps tonight?"

Mel volunteered and Paul turned the microphone over to him.

"Hello, everyone. My name is Melvin Jordan and I am a drug

addict." The words were barely out of his mouth when he realized that Adrienne was standing in the doorway. She had heard his admission and was smiling at him. He almost wept with relief. For the first time in a year, Mel really believed that he and Adrienne were going to make it.

We Need A Mighty Love

by Janine Yvette Gardner

Whether or not we want to admit it, everyone wants love. The feeling of being significant, needed, and cared for by another seems so crucial to human existence that we do just about anything to obtain it. How much harder is it then for African-American people to give and receive love from each other when our sense of self-worth has been shattered by a society that refuses to acknowledge we are deserving of love?

The black man struggles to gain respect as a man not only in society but to black women as well. Historically, black men were not allowed to take care of black women. The difficulty of never feeling like a man that can love and take care of his family is traumatic for many brothas. On the other hand, the black woman struggles to garner acceptance as a desirable female that deserves protection, support, love, and respect. Oftentimes black women carry the burden of being the mom, dad, and provider. As a result, many black women believe they will not find love from black men.

Impossible odds? Maybe, if we were not speaking of a culture of people that have persevered through slavery and institutionalized racism (and continue to persevere). Anita Diggs's debut novel, *A Mighty Love,* illustrates first that there is love between black men and women and, second, that the love between us can beat the most impossible odds. How do we obtain this love? By acknowledging that we as individuals have problems we need to resolve on our own and not expect a relationship with someone to make those problems disappear. When we learn that acceptance of who we are and how our troubles affect how we live, we can then reach out and grab hold of a love like no other. True love exists, black love is real, but *unconditional love* is mightier than any other feeling possible.

Janine Yvette Gardner is an editorial assistant for Black Expressions Book Club and an associate editor for *Black Issues Book Review.*

A Conversation with Anita Doreen Diggs

Janine Yvette Gardner: As African-American people, we all know too well the numerous relationship problems black men and women have. Mel and Adrienne are no exception. Why is it so difficult for them to have a successful relationship?

Anita Doreen Diggs: It is difficult for Mel and Adrienne to have a successful relationship with each other because of the tragedy that has occurred in their lives. They are unable to talk about the disaster, so their feelings about it come out in other, nonproductive ways.

Janine Yvette Gardner: I find it very interesting that you added the drug addiction element to Mel and Adrienne's marriage. Mel is an older man, not a teenager, who gets addicted to drugs. Why did you choose to incorporate this into the novel? How common of a problem is this within marriage.

Anita Doreen Diggs: Mel used drugs before he met Adrienne. When tragedy struck, he simply returned to his old habits in order to cope with his feelings of guilt. I don't think that it is at all common for a black man to turn to drugs when there are problems in his marriage. It was just a situation unique to this particular story.

Janine Yvette Gardner: Manhood is something black men struggle to prove they possess within society, but particularly to black women. How is this manifested in your character Mel?

Anita Doreen Diggs: Generally speaking, the manhood of the African American male is challenged every time he walks outside his front door but that is too big a subject for me to talk about here. At the beginning of *A Mighty Love*, Mel feels very much likes he's a man. He's holding down a job, he's being faithful, and he's making sure his wife and child have a nice place to stay. He's keeping food on the table. In fact, at that point Adrienne is on maternity leave, so he's actually paying **all** the bills. He's feeling more like a man than he ever did before. When the tragedy strikes he doesn't even really think about being a man. He feels so bad as a human being that notions of his manhood don't even occur to him until Lloyd Cooper appears on the scene. At that point, the whole manhood issue rears up. He feels that Lloyd has every-thing—money, education, style and his (worst of all) Adrienne's admiration. Mel feels that he is at the bottom of a mountain that is too high for him to climb.

Janine Yvette Gardner: Is Regina and Adrienne's relationship sym-bolic of tension between black and white women in the workplace?
Anita Doreen Diggs: No. Although there is a great deal of tension between black and white women in corporate America, I did not explore the issue in *A Mighty Love*. Regina is Adrienne's supervisor and she is jealous that Adrienne has a personal relationship with the new company president. Adrienne's relationship with Lloyd makes her more powerful than Regina and that is what causes the tension between them.

Janine Yvette Gardner: Discuss the differences between Mallory Guest and Adrienne.
Anita Doreen Diggs: Mallory is a black woman who will not hurt her own community while climbing the corporate ladder. She be-lieves that blacks in power have a tremendous responsibility and she takes this very seriously. Adrienne doesn't really have any thoughts of Black Nationalism. She's totally concerned with restor-ing order in her own little world. Mallory is a woman who sees the big picture. I really love Mallory and I may write about her again in the future.

Janine Yvette Gardner: Black people have the highest divorce rate of any ethnic group within America. Can the black family win? If so, how does *A Mighty Love* illustrate this?
Anita Doreen Diggs: First of all, I am suspicious of all statistics. So, I'm not convinced that we do indeed have the highest divorce rate of any ethnic group in America. Who compiled the numbers? What are their politics? Why did they undertake such a study? Do they plan to use the statistics to help or hurt those that were stud-

ied? In *A Mighty Love* we have two people who love each other even more than they realize. They are hit with death, substance abuse, massive debt and a rich man who wants the wife for himself. *A Mighty Love* reminds us that true love conquers all.

A MIGHTY LOVE

ANITA DOREEN DIGGS

ABOUT THIS GUIDE

The suggested questions are intended to enhance your group's reading of Anita Doreen Diggs's A MIGHTY LOVE. We hope this will increase your enjoyment of this book.

DISCUSSION QUESTIONS

1. What were some of the challenges within Mel and Adrienne's relationship before the devastating fire?

2. How does Adrienne's life contradict the stereotypes about light-skinned black women?

3. What are some of the ways Mel and Adrienne punish themselves for Delilah's death?

4. What is the significance of hair within this story? How does this tie into the importance of hair to African-American women and its value within the black community and society at large?

5. Discuss both Mel and Adrienne's addictions? How are they similar? Is one more fatal than the other?

6. Discuss the different ways Adrienne and Mel want to make their marriage work. Why do they conflict?

7. Lloyd Cooper and Mel both had very difficult childhoods. Discuss the differences in the two men's personalities and each man's reaction to their adversity.

8. What are the two special things that Adrienne sacrifices for both Mel and Lloyd? Why does she do this? What impact does this have on each relationship?

9. What are Lloyd's appealing qualities that attract Adrienne to him and away from Mel?

10. Discuss the striking contrast in Adrienne's relationship with both of her sisters-in-law. Why are they so different?

11. Lloyd comments to Adrienne "sometimes two people come to a fork in the road, and the only thing left to do is go in opposite directions." Is this true for Mel and Adrienne? Why or why not?